THE SOCIETIES BOOK 3

ASCENSION

SYDNEY REAMES

Ebook ISBN: 978-1-961057-16-6
Paperback ISBN: 978-1-961057-17-3
Cover Design by: Deranged Doctor Design

NIGHT LOCH
PUBLISHERS

Night Loch Publishers LLC

For Marvin

CHAPTER 1

The icy winds of Tundra whistled around us. I stared at the others scattered around the tent. We were crowded into the biggest one available, and it still barely held the leaders of each Society. The group gathered in front of me looked haggard and tired. Several displayed considerable injuries. We'd just retreated from Lone to this snowy planet. The unforgiving ice and cold were a far cry from the lush rivers and forests that once were home to the Societal Ancestors.

We were an alliance—of friendships, in many cases, though with a bit of antagonism in others—and despite our differences, we'd worked together. Even having managed that, we had lost to the Spear. At least that's how it felt. We had disabled several of their ships but hadn't been able to stop all of them. Their leadership had escaped unscathed, as had their mission to go after the rest of us. Soon enough, they'd take the forces they had left and go around to the seven Societal planets, intent on dominating each of them.

The resistance hadn't acted in time. The Coalition had been flawed, and I'd trusted all the wrong people.

Everyone had already given so much. And now I was about to ask them all to fight again.

"Listen." I stepped forward, fiddling with my hands as waves of opal light from my markings dimmed and brightened. "I've figured out Ama's journals. I think I know how to save us and stop the Spear."

My voice shook as I referenced the deceased Reader who had taught me everything I knew about interpreting Riftian marks, and projection. All Riftians possessed some level of the skill, but I was the first in recorded history to be able to use it to force the actions of others.

"I know no one wants to hear this," I plowed on, "but we need to go back to the Rift."

"Why *your* Society? What makes your home more important than ours?" Karo, a Crew captain, demanded. Residents of his seafaring Society were often brash and bold. I might have been given the nickname Queen of the Alliance, but they wouldn't let me dictate their response without a fight.

Grumbling and debate started up, and I faltered a bit. The confidence I'd gained since becoming a Riftian wasn't always consistent. I still had to work hard to not second-guess myself.

Fell, my Connected, stepped up and grabbed my hand. His twilight marks shone next to my opal ones. That he had supported me in my worst moments gave me the strength to press on.

"We need to go back to all seven Societies, actually," I declared. And with that, the noise in the tent grew louder.

Under different circumstances I'd have been more than happy to revisit the other Societies. Each had its own wondrous landscapes, and its residents their unique abilities. In normal times, I'd have enjoyed getting to know them all better.

As it stood, the Spear was forcing my hand.

Silas, another Earther turned Riftian, made his way to the center of the group. Several of the others turned to look at him as his crimson marks glowed.

"We've trusted Kena this far. And, I might add, we asked her to look into the journals because none of us could come up with a better plan. We had an opportunity to stop the Spear for good back on Lone. We didn't get the job done. If she's suggesting this, I'm sure she has a reason."

He stared down the other Societals, who quieted, one by one. As he backed out to the rim of the group, he shot me a smile.

Thank you, I mouthed at him.

"Fine. We're going to all seven. But I ask again, why yours first?" Karo glowered at me. The captain was covered in black and white tattoos, like all Crew. His form flickered in the light of the fire we had burning in the tent. They called it *shadowing* on their planet.

"Because our Society is where Assimilation comes from," Fell responded, his voice level as he came to my defense.

This time, I wasn't surprised when the conversations grew loud and heated. This news was a secret Ama had hidden away in her journals, even from herself.

When young people went through the Choosing, they had a choice of seven planets to Assimilate to, and through that process they attained all the unique physical characteristics and abilities boasted by their preferred Society. I'd taken for granted that the origin of this process was one of many Societal mysteries, but thanks to my mentor's journals, I had learned that the Rift is where it all started. So that was where *we* needed to start if we wanted to save everyone.

I waved my arms to draw attention back to myself.

"Listen. My Uncle Juliard was the leader of Earth's settlers lifetimes ago. He knew Ama was supposed to come down and conduct some ceremony. It's possible he knows or suspects something about the crystals already. Bayard could just as easily have figured out something for himself in all the lifetimes he's been in the Rift. If we want to have a chance of beating them, we need to get to those crystals before they do. And that means going to the Rift. Bayard is Riftian, and that's where he'll go first. That place means more to him than anywhere else, except perhaps Lone."

The aim of the original Spear had been simply to return to the Ancestors' planet. Bayard hadn't been satisfied with that. He'd aligned himself with the Earthers and let them spread lies about us. They had their eyes set on new worlds—and domination of those already in existence. If he could control Assimilation—wield the crystals that controlled it like currency, and withhold the resource from those who needed it—he would be able to lead all the Societies without killing another soul.

"Just what did these journals say, Alliance Queen?" Sarah asked, her swift viper nearly concealed by her orange hair. The other Rovers looked up and listened. They respected the Serpentina as much as they respected their official leader. If she agreed to my plan, I'd have all of them on board.

I relayed the rest of my findings to the group. How the Ancestors had left Lone and gone to the three original Societies of Canopy, Dagan, and Rift. How only the Riftians had success on their planet, thanks to Assimilation. How they'd figured out that glowing crystals in their cave systems were responsible, and how they'd determined a process to plant those same crystals on all the Societies and save the others.

"That detail is likely to bring us one of our biggest problems. With the crystals being planted, just like anything else that grows, they can be killed. My solution is to use projection to force them to become part of each Societies' permanent structure," I explained.

"And that's a skill you have already?" Acaius, a dragon-winged Kite, looked genuinely curious. His wings flexed as much as the cramped tent space would allow, head tilted like a bird's as he waited for my answer.

As I responded, I struggled to keep my marks from flaring, as they often did when I was feeling strong emotions, well aware how foolish it might make me seem.

"Not exactly. I *think* I can use my ability that way, and I hope to be able to instruct many of the other Riftians to do the same. That's what Ama did when she planted the crystals originally."

"That's just great. We *think*, we *hope*, we *wish*," grumbled Everleigh, another heavily tattooed Crew captain.

I went right on, pretending she hadn't spoken. If I let every comment sidetrack me, we'd never get through what I had to say.

"The second problem is that we have no way to know exactly how much of this information Bayard does and doesn't have. It's safe to assume some, but I can't say if it's enough to bet his strategy on. He might skip the crystals entirely and go straight for terrorizing the people in each Society. Perhaps even worse, in the long term, he might not know the crystals can be killed and he'll destroy them trying to remove them. We are gambling."

If I turned out to be right, the plan was to go through each Society and ensure Assimilation was protected. That would undermine his ability to control it and strengthen our resistance against him. If I was wrong, or we went to the wrong place first, he'd wipe other Societies out while I was busy messing around with crystals.

When the Spear first showed themselves, they had trapped many of us on our own planets. Our group had used secret Doorways to get back to the central space station, the Hub, where they had holed up. Once there, we'd managed to rescue many of our fellow resistance members and Societal delegates. But the Spear had destroyed the Hub and we ended up stuck on Lone. It was only thanks to my mentor, Ama, sacrificing herself that we had made it back to Tundra. If we had the Doorways, and all he had was ships, we had another advantage. It would take him far longer to travel between Societies. Still, I felt compelled to mention a final obstacle.

"Juliard left to go to his son. His note indicates that he wants to try to right a wrong. Maybe he's going to try to convert Bayard back to the side of good—"

"Fat chance," Hale interjected. My best friend snickered into his hand. I scowled at him and he shot me a repentant look. "Right. Sorry. Carry on."

"Juliard knows we have Ama's Doorway, and the ones here on Tundra. If I'm wrong about his motives, and he's actually left to help the Spear—"

"He could tell Bayard about the Doorways and show up on Tundra in our absence. He'd wipe out the menders, the children, potentially every person we've saved," Dex finished for me. Unlike Hale, I didn't scowl at the horned and furry-legged former Earther. He and Silas both had plenty of battle experience, and he wasn't wrong.

"There are risks. Significant ones," I agreed, "but we've come this far. We found our way to Tundra together and rescued prisoners and children from the Hub together. It was only because we worked as a team that we were able to disable several of the Spear's ships on Lone. We know it hasn't always been pretty. We've had our disagreements, but this is one of those times where we need to choose as one."

We'd done things diplomatically, but I couldn't afford to let them vote me down this time. I had no backup plan if they said no.

"You don't have to like it. You don't even have to believe me. *I* am going back to the Rift. If no one else follows me, that won't change my mind. But, I have to be honest, I can't think of any scenario where we win if we don't do this together. I need help. Please."

If they refused to assist me I'd still go alone, but I had no hope of finding and protecting the crystals of the other Societies without their cooperation.

The whispers and grumbling resumed, and I began to worry I'd put too much stock in our alliance.

"Hey! You heard Queen Kena. Any of you have any better ideas?" Sarah shouted over the rest of them. She'd been spoiled and timid on Earth but had found herself on the desert planet of Rover. As Serpentina, both she and the serpent she carried had a deadly venom they were able to use on their enemies. She was the one who'd nicknamed me Queen of the Alliance, and the name had been sticking, much to my embarrassment.

"It's either her plan, or we sit here and freeze. I, for one, would like to get back to my ship and my home," Nix sounded off. When Hale had first introduced me to his new girlfriend, I'd found her grating. Recently, though, she'd been growing on me.

"You already know you have our support," Vanya volunteered. The rest of the Riftian weapons instructors nodded alongside her.

"Anyone from Clan want to disagree?" Dex stared the mining Society down. He was well over six feet tall and had possessed massive muscles even before he'd Assimilated. Now that he sported horns that he frequently wrapped in spikes, and hefty furred legs ending in hooves that could kick down a barn door, no one argued. The Clan had the most members involved with the Spear, so there weren't very many individuals available to disagree with him anyway.

One by one the others gave in, until I had reached unanimous, if begrudging, support.

CHAPTER 2

T ime was of the essence, but I knew better than to think we'd get things settled in one sitting. Fell and I made our way back to our tent. It was too small for us to stand upright in, and with the howling winds outside it didn't really qualify as cozy. The biggest benefit was that it gave us a place to speak privately.

"You did great. Everyone's on board," Fell praised me as he sat on the floor of the tent. The bluish-purple of his twilight markings cast a glow over the walls of our temporary home. I squeezed in next to him, leaning on his shoulder as he pulled a blanket around the two of us.

"They don't all *want* to be on board," I countered as I glanced up at him. "Even if we win this thing, there's still so much to fix."

Fell sighed. He was aware. We'd spoken before of the problems with the Societies. One thing the Spear had done was expose how divided they each were within. Their previous governing system was a Coalition made up of representatives from each Society and a head delegate, but all this system had really done was put a civilized mask over the deep resentments that ran between certain groups.

"One thing at a time. We save everyone's lives, we make sure Bayard can't destroy Assimilation, and *then* we build a new government. Perhaps even a new Hub, if we're feeling particularly ambitious." He grinned at the last bit, well aware that neither he nor I had any idea how to construct a new station.

"Thank goodness it's an easy list." I managed a laugh. Fell didn't share his sense of humor with most people, and I was glad to be one of the few.

"How about we focus on the next step? They've agreed to go. As soon as the leader of each Society can get their respective groups prepared, we'll be headed back to the Rift. What's our first move going to be once we get there?"

I thought through my answer, comforted by the sound of his steady heartbeat in my ear.

"The Doorway will let us out at the Mists. Maybe we should check with the Whispers and see if they have any information of value."

"Hmm," he remarked noncommittally, the sound rumbling in his chest.

The Whispers were Riftians, but they kept to themselves in a secluded forest. Their eyes swirled like the mists and fog surrounding their home, and they received involuntary visions that tended to drive them mad. Most of us projected onto others; with Whispers, it was as if bits of the future, or insight, were forcefully projected onto them, internally.

I'd never witnessed it, but Ama had used their advice when counseling me. My Hub instructor, Nien, had relied on it when he altered my Choice and sent me to Rift in the first place.

"We'll have to be very careful with how we interpret anything they say, but it could help. Then we make our way to the Lake of Death. That's where Ama's journals said the crystals were."

My voice broke as I mentioned my mentor. Without her, we'd never have gathered the information necessary to defeat the Spear. But then, without her, we might not have had to. She'd known the information all along but, by using projection, had tried to protect the crystals by wiping them from peoples' memories. Unfortunately she'd cleared her own memories of them in the process.

Only a handful of Riftians had projection that powerful: Ama, myself, Bayard, Juliard, and probably my father before he died. Juliard had concealed his markings and origins. Bayard had hidden his true identity and motives. Ama gleaned thoughts from people and influenced their thoughts and memories in turn.

My own ability frightened me all the more because of the fate that had befallen each of them. A mentor who had sacrificed herself; a father I hadn't really known, who had been both a loving parent and a killer; an uncle who left me for Bayard; and Bayard himself—a man intent on wiping out scores of people in the lust for power.

If I continued down this path, I would undoubtedly have to keep using projection. I'd already said I would, if saving those close to me required it. But I wasn't sure who I would become in the end.

"You wield projection like some of us wield a weapon," Fell said, noting something that was both a matter of pride and one of my greatest fears. "All Riftians have to master at least one weapon, but you know how rare it is for us to wield a second. And here you are with three."

A laugh made its way up my throat and escaped before I could stop it. I had my ax, and a set of twin daggers Vanya had taught me to use. I hadn't considered projection a third option, but I supposed it was.

"I meant it as a compliment," he assured me.

I waved my hand.

"I know. It's just, nicknames. *Conspiracy Group Princess, Queen of the Alliance.* Don't let Sarah get wind of your opinion. If you do, I'll be labeled Triple Threat or something equally ridiculous."

"Then we'll keep it between us," he promised. "Kena, we

need to rest up for this trip, but before we do—"

I took a sharp breath in, my heartbeat picking up speed, thinking he might have a more intimate activity in mind.

"—will you work with me on projection? Try to explain to me how you do what you do? I'd like to have some knowledge beforehand. Maybe I can help explain it to the others once we get to the crystals."

My marks flared to life with my embarrassment.

"Oh, that. Yes, of course."

I twisted out of his lap and sat across from him in the confined space.

He gave a sly half-smile as his eyes focused on the mark I had that he shared. The one that said *soul*.

"But before all that."

He closed the distance between us, his lips meeting mine.

Despite distractions, and trying to explain to Fell how my control over projection worked, I actually managed a decent night's sleep. That had become more and more rare since conflict with the Spear began.

As Fell and I made our way to the Doorway, Hale raced up to me, shoving a warm cup of what in the Societies passed for coffee into my hands. Another rarity I was thankful for.

The fact that Bayard, along with his Spear and Earther army, hadn't come bursting through the Doorway to Tundra overnight had bolstered my mood further. Maybe Juliard wasn't going to betray us completely.

Hok stood in front of the Doorway, organizing the trip. Each of these portals, with the exception of Ama's, was housed in a constructed tunnel of sorts. The ones on Tundra had ice frozen over the metal. One downside of Doorways was that only one individual could go through at a time. Being tall and intimidating helped at times like this. Hok had the top half of his black hair tied back from his face and a hand up to his mouth as he shouted orders at everyone. Sarah stood at his side, much smaller but equally frightening as she and her serpent glared at anyone who didn't move quickly.

As the weapons instructor waved us to the front of the line, I reached out and grabbed his free hand, squeezing it.

"Thanks for having our backs."

"Anything for the queen." Hok winked at me.

With one last deep breath, I strode through the Doorway.

Fell was behind me before I'd taken three steps into the forest, his head swiveling to take in our surroundings. He wielded the twin daggers he'd mastered, sheathing them only after he'd run a watchful circuit around the perimeter of the clearing.

"All right. We should be safe for now."

By that time, another dozen or so resistance members had joined us.

While I'd been a Societal less than a year, the Rift felt like home. The shade of tall trees that blocked out the sky and the light filtering through the leaves welcomed me back. But returning without defeating Bayard, and after my uncle left to join him, felt like a failure. Returning without Ama, on top of everything else, was almost unbearable.

Fell put a hand on my shoulder, saying nothing, but just the gesture steadied me.

The Doorway to the Rift was in a place even most Riftians didn't venture often. The Mists were as quiet as ever as the last of our group joined us and we made our way through the eerie wall of fog into their clearing. The woods where the Whispers resided was isolated from the other hidden forests of the Rift. Grey, swirling fog lingered in the trees, and the Whispers themselves appeared to float across it, with their smoky marks.

My fingers interlaced with Fell's as I savored the earthy scent of the trees.

"I don't know how I'm going to stand leaving this place behind again," I confessed, staring deep into his glowing purple-blue eyes. Maybe starting here wasn't such a good idea. How was I going to abandon my home again, with no idea when or even if I'd ever return?

"I feel the same. But we have a job to get done. The sooner we make it through the other Societies, the sooner we get to come home."

Vanya, one of my favorite Riftians and a talented weapons instructor, nudged me with her elbow and looked pointedly across the clearing. She had her own double daggers sheathed at her side and a bow slung over her back.

"Look alive. Mom only glows like that when she's got a vision." Vanya was tall and muscled, and her Riftian markings were a leafy green that shone against her light brown skin. She pointed at an older woman making her way over to us.

Vanya's mother, a Whisper, had the same markings as all the other inhabitants of the Mists: a swirling grey that appeared to rise from her skin like smoke. At the moment, her mother's eyes were lit from behind with a white glow. As the Whisper approached us, she reached out a hand and grabbed my arm.

My own opal marks flared to life, and Vanya and Fell squinted beside me.

Vanya's mother locked her misty gaze on my face as she spoke.

"The Reader is gone. The Reader is here. Do not be so quick to trust him. Do not be so quick to mistrust him. There is the appearance of death, and then there is death itself. More than a Reader must ascend to save us all. Seven worlds. Seven chances. If you will it, you can join them. The source, and the people. Embrace your will. Project it. There will be destruction before the end, but after that, a new beginning. What is the weight of what is lost, compared to what is gained? No victory without cost. No gain without loss. You must be willing to let go. Risk yourself, or risk everyone else. The *Choice* is yours."

The Whisper released me and stumbled back. Vanya caught her under one arm and Fell under the other. Without his presence to steady me, I felt ready to fall over as well. Vanya's mother had started to hum, and her eyes were no longer glowing.

"I'll take her somewhere to rest," Vanya muttered, leading her mother back toward the huts where the Whispers resided. Fell let them go, staring after the two of them.

"Are you okay?" He turned back to me and his gaze softened.

"It's not as if she said anything we didn't already know. At least not the parts I understood. Ama is gone, and I'm the next Reader. I'm guessing I wasn't supposed to trust Juliard and Bayard, but that ship has sailed. I'm not sure who I'm supposed to stop distrusting. We've already seen death, and Ama ascended to save us and get us back here. Now I have to take everyone to make sure the crystals are beyond Bayard's reach, and we know that's risky. Can Whisper predictions be about the past?"

I tacked on the last question as an afterthought. I'd assumed part of the vision pertained to Ama and what had already transpired, but if it meant me …

Fell shook his head.

"I don't know enough about them to say with any certainty. I don't even know if *they* could say. The visions aren't voluntary, and they can't make much more sense of them than we can. It does put me on edge, though. We need to be careful. I'll go with you every step of the way, but I'm not sacrificing you for this mission."

Fell was normally more practical.

"If it were anyone else, would you be willing to trade one person for the rest of us?" I challenged him.

"I wouldn't put anyone in harm's way, but I wouldn't stop them like I'd try to stop you."

He didn't say anything else, but I guessed he was feeling the same regret about Ama that I was. We'd had no other way to escape the Spear, but I still felt that we should have stepped in.

My concentration was broken as Hok approached us. His silver markings were too bright to be mistaken for a Whisper, and he held hands with Sarah as he walked over. Her smaller, leather-skinned hand nearly disappeared into his larger, tan one.

"When does this show get on the road?" she yelled in our direction.

"Everyone is ready. I saw Vanya's mother speaking to you. Anything we need to know?" Hok asked.

"No," I responded before Fell could say anything. "We're ready."

"If we travel quickly, we can reach the cavern and the lake the day after tomorrow," Fell added as the four of us walked back into the center of the clearing.

Traveling through the Rift without stopping at my home felt wrong, but we weren't here to reminisce. We were here to look ahead. The journey from the main grove of the Rift to the Mists would take more than a day. The Lake of Death would be even farther. Even if Bayard was limited to using ships to travel, we needed to hurry.

"You could reach it by tonight." Another Whisper floated at our side, eyes swirling.

At first I thought we were about to hear another vision, but his eyes weren't lit.

"How?" Fell inquired of the Whisper, who chuckled in response.

"How do you think we are present for last rites at the Lake of the Dead, without being seen in the other groves by our fellow Riftians? There is a back way. If you move south from this clearing, you will find the entrance to the same cave system that houses the lake. Follow the light, and you'll find the crystals you seek."

Whether it was good sense or a vision didn't matter much. We needed whatever head start we could get with the Spear on our tail.

CHAPTER 3

Darkness overtook our group as we moved through the caverns. The entrance was just where the Whisper had indicated. What he hadn't mentioned were the boats. The cave system had very little space to walk, most of it being taken up by waterways. There were small canoes tied off at the entrance, and we had crowded into them, with the Crew, more at ease on the water than the rest of us, taking the lead. Some of the Dagan swam in the shallow water alongside the vessels. The oily coating covering them made them hard to spot under the water. Only the vibrant neon patterns that decorated their skin were visible.

The sound of dripping stalactites, boats bobbing in the water, and even our breathing echoed back from the walls. We moved slowly, but we were able to steer to follow the growing light ahead. I wished there was a way to hasten the journey. Who knew what Bayard had figured out, or what Uncle Juliard had already revealed to him? The idea of what he might do to the crystals here, and how that would affect the abilities the rest of us had Assimilated, ate at me.

"There's something up ahead!" Hale's whisper reached me from the boat next to ours, followed by the splash of a plunging stalactite as it hit the water. It landed so close that a few droplets hit my arm, obscuring one of my opal marks.

Hale was right. There was a glint of blinding light ahead, and as our boats drew nearer I was able to make out a bend in the waterway. Our boats followed the curve, and I had to slam my eyes shut against the onslaught of glittering light as we emerged into the back of a tall cavern. It was larger by several times over than the cavern at the entrance of the Rift.

Beneath the water's surface, emerging at the shoreline and then winding their way up the walls, were crystals. There were even some overhead, interspersed with the stalactites. I gasped, grabbing Fell's arm as I pointed toward one glowing cluster.

"Just like your marks!" I exclaimed. The crystals in that bunch had the same twilight, bluish-purple glow. The color I'd only seen in the night sky of the Twilight Grove, and on my Connected.

"And yours," he stated, pointing into the water as we sailed over a twisting row of opal crystals.

Silas waved everyone toward a shelf of rock just a bit wider than the rest, with stalagmites rising from the floor, large enough to tie the boats to. We roped our canoe off next to a midnight blue crystal, while Hale tied his beside a summer-grass green one. So many colors surrounded us. Some I'd never seen. My throat tightened as I noted gleaming bronze and gold crystals, just like the marks my father and Juliard wore.

We stood, clustered together on a narrow, rocky beach in the cavern. We had to be careful not to jar any of the crystals around us.

"All right, then." Silas clapped his hands together as he surveyed the cavern, at ease as long as he had a mission to work toward.

Beside him, Dex assessed our surroundings.

"Kena, what do you need us to do?"

"Well." I tapped my chin. I'd thought of it over and over since reading what Ama had left for me.

Most Riftians unconsciously utilized projection. I needed to teach them how to control it.

"I think it's going to be trial and error more than anything," I confessed to the group, thankful that several individuals who might have scoffed were shushed by my allies. "Ama willed the crystals to take root and grow in the other planets. I'd assume I should do something similar and will them to fuse with the cavern, instead. Meld themselves to the cave in a way that cannot be rooted or mined out."

Fell stepped past me, holding one hand up and running it along a stripe of crystal on the cave wall. He turned toward me.

"Maybe you can try it with one of the smaller crystals first," he suggested.

It was worth an attempt. Better for me to exhaust myself than have everyone do it before I'd figured it out. I pushed a stray blond hair out of my eyes as I moved toward the wall. Arms outstretched, I reached my flat palms toward the wall until they nearly touched. I'd realized I didn't need to hold them out to make my projection work on people, but it's how I had started, and it helped.

Giving the task my full focus, I willed the crystals to knit together with the cave itself.

I strained, muscles tensed.

"Um, Kena, nothing's happening." Hale interrupted my concentration, tapping me on one shoulder.

"Yes," I responded through gritted teeth, "I'm well aware." My brief flash of annoyance soon faded. Hale and I were getting back to how we used to be as friends before we'd joined different Societies and everything had changed. I dropped my arms, frowning at the wall, and pacing a circle before going back to try again.

. . .

Hours later, I let my arms drop with a huff, exhausted. Fell gripped my shoulder, steering me to where the others sat on the narrow, rocky beach. Nix was whittling a piece of wood. Ryshal, Acaius, and Cassius were stretching their wings. Vanya leaned against Silas, napping, as he spoke with Dex.

"Nothing is happening," grumbled Saf. The Rover resident had her vibrant blue snake draped over her shoulders. Saf scratched at her scaly skin.

"She'll get there. Just give her some time," Veronica urged at her side. The former Earther had gone to Dagan and was covered in gelatinous, inky slime, but also stark blue patterns that matched her eyes. It wasn't lost on me that the group's alliance was tenuous at best, and it was only because of my staunch supporters in each Society that the others kept up their confidence.

That, and a lack of any other options.

I was it. If this didn't work, our only choice was to wait for Bayard and the Spear to attack each Society one by one, until everything was destroyed or brought under his control.

The very idea made me furious, and my marks glowed as bright as the crystals around me. It couldn't happen. It was a reality that couldn't be allowed.

Then it struck me.

I'd been trying to get the crystals to tie themselves deeper into the cave, but that wasn't what we needed. What we *needed* was for them to be something else entirely. Not something that grew and died like plants, but something that was a part of the planet.

I threw one hand out toward the wall, determined that if this attempt didn't work I would rest.

"Exist," I commanded a glowing portion of orange crystal, willing it to be what I needed, instead of what it was. I squashed down the part of me that felt utterly ridiculous speaking to an inanimate object. The crystal started to glow, brighter than it had been. Light flashed, and I snapped my eyes shut. Something pulsed through me, taking my breath away.

"You did it," Fell whispered behind me in awe. I opened my eyes and stared at the rocky wall. Instead of a piece of glowing crystal, part of the rock wall itself had a vein of sunset orange running through it, the surface smooth. I ran my hand over it, and the glowing portion felt like a stone washed smooth by repeated ocean waves. My fingers slid over the surface like it was glass. Giddiness bubbled up in me, but I was determined not to give in to the joy until it was confirmed.

"Dex!"

He lumbered over.

"Try to break it."

He smirked at me, one corner of his mouth turning up.

"With pleasure."

I expected him to grab one of the many weapons we'd hauled along with us. Instead he backed up as far as the thin stretch of rocky beach would allow and ran at the wall. His horns smashed into it with a force that echoed through the cavern, and in the darkness beyond I heard the splash of more stalactites falling.

Dex shook his head as he stepped back from the smooth wall. There wasn't even a scratch. The light shone defiantly back at him.

"I did it." My voice was barely a whisper, and the tenuous hope I hadn't wanted to let loose spilled free.

It took twice as long as my first successful attempt to organize the Riftians into helping. They were willing, but none of them had tried exerting conscious control over their projection before. Throughout the afternoon, or evening—it was impossible to tell within the dark cave—we worked on the skill. No one was able to manage it without holding onto me, or me to them, but with the help it was possible.

I had a line of Riftians standing on the narrow beach next to me. We'd linked our arms to form a chain. I wasn't sure whether they were all exerting their own control, or if I was somehow channeling their projection through myself. Either way, I would never be able to thank each of them enough for their willingness to try. I interlaced Fell's left hand with my right, throwing the other hand toward a cluster of crystals.

The other Riftians mimicked me, some silent and some yelling as they put vocal force behind their will. As we tackled the largest cluster of crystals yet, I felt the same surge as before when I'd tried alone, but magnified tenfold. If Fell hadn't held me on one side, with Hok supporting me on the other, I would have fallen backward.

After several seconds everyone dropped their arms, huffing and out of breath. The effort had been immense, but the results were worth it. A good stretch of the cavern wall was now shining and solidified under the rock. Crystal veins that were the lifeblood of Assimilation. Safe from Bayard and the Spear.

We continued on and on, directing our projection—the walls, the ceiling, even beneath the waters. One by one, the Riftians began dropping out, forced to rest from the immense strain of the attempt. By the time we came to the last section of the cavern, only Vanya, Hok, Silas, Fell, and a few others stood beside me. A sheen of sweat covered Fell's fair skin, and a stray lock fell over his forehead. Hok was panting, open-mouthed, and Silas grimaced as he dropped his arm after our latest effort.

"Only one or two more sections to go," Silas encouraged everyone, stretching his arms over his head and then wheeling them in a circle before linking back with Vanya.

I didn't say what the rest of them must have been thinking. We still wouldn't be done. We'd have to go through each Society and do this. At least, here we'd known where to look and had been able to get to the location. According to Ama's journals, the other areas where the Societals had chosen to hide the crystals on their own planets were treacherous and difficult to reach. We didn't even know where they all were. Her records hadn't indicated. We'd have to deal with all that and do so with the Spear on our heels.

The idea of Bayard arriving to find I'd beaten him to the Rift brought a smile to my face, but it also struck fear in my heart. My once-controlled cousin was unraveling. What would he do when he found out he'd been beaten, even on this scale?

"We have a few more stops to make before we can leave the Rift," I told the others after we finished our last section.

Hok groaned, sitting back against a wall. Silas looked out of breath as well, but he nodded.

The other Societies had thought of the Riftians as haughty and delicate before the Spear had forced us to expose our real natures to everyone else. Even before that, I'd known the truth.

We were strong. We wouldn't let Bayard break us.

CHAPTER 4

t wasn't an easy detour, and it would take us another couple of days, but we couldn't leave the remaining Riftians to fend for themselves. Especially not without a warning.

Vanya, Hok, and Silas peeled off, along with most of our group, to go warn the other Riftians of what was probably coming. We didn't know *all* of Bayard's plans, but the other Riftians knew next to nothing. The weapons instructors promised to warn everyone to make themselves scarce in less populated areas of the forests, assuming Bayard would check the main grove first.

Fell and I, along with Hale and Nix, planned to stop by Ama's home. She had told me that the tree was being left to me, and I wanted to find out what she had left for the others. Once we had finished up at the Reader's, we'd meet the rest of the group on their way to Twilight Grove. It was the one other place where Ama's journals indicated there were crystals in the Rift. She had planted those herself when she was experimenting with how to use them to save the other Societies.

Most Riftians only visited Twilight Grove once in their lives, when they received specially branded items made of Ocala, a rare and near-unbreakable material. The markings branded into the materials were chosen by Ama herself. Only the makers who crafted the items resided in the grove full time.

My body begged for rest, but I couldn't give it any. We had to make it to Ama's and then the grove to finish what we'd started in the cavern. If Bayard was left with one stray crystal, one means of building his new worlds and controlling the resources, he'd take it. I was as certain of that as I had once been about his innocence.

As we got close to Ama's home I heard the wind chimes that hung from her willow's many branches. They played the music of emotions, and I recognized this song as loss. My breath hitched in my throat, but I swallowed down any tears. I didn't think it was wrong to cry over her, or Pim, or anyone we'd lost, but we weren't here to mourn.

"I'd almost expected them to be silent." Fell moved through the branches, examining each windchime.

"Wow." Nix stared, wide-eyed, at the former Reader's home. "I know you told us about the chimes, but still."

I was just glad she hadn't come up with anything snarky to say. She and Hale had carved a chime to leave for Ama back on Lone, and since then she'd demonstrated more of a respect for some of the Riftian habits.

"I see what you meant. This place is special," Hale concurred.

Under the branches, several birds flitted about. My own experience with Riftian wildlife had been a saber-toothed ixtor and a puffy bird with rows of sharp teeth, called a pentall. Both were fierce predators. The birds surrounding Ama's house appeared much more docile. A bird the same blue as a morning sky on Earth hopped over to us and flew up to perch on my shoulder before pecking at my hands. A few taupe birds circled Nix and Hale, twittering at them.

Fell let out a sigh.

"I told her over and over that she'd regret feeding them. Now they don't know what to do without her."

Before we entered the tree itself, I wandered around the

outside. Ama had said the arborists provided her food for the birds, even though they weren't supposed to. Sure enough, there was a large wooden container with a latch on the lid around the back side of her home. When I opened it I found a feed mix of various seeds, dried petals and dried fruits. I scooped some out, scattering it on the ground, and the birds descended from every direction.

"Do you think we should just dump it all? Who knows when we'll make it back here?" I looked at Fell, who had followed me, afraid to voice my real fear that once gone we might not make it back here at all.

"We'll see if there's anyone who chooses to stay who might be able to take care of it. But yes, for now I'd throw out what we can."

My first task from Ama, and already I was uncertain what to do. In the end I scooped the bin until it was down near the bottom but left some of the feed so that anyone who took over the duty would be able to ascertain what items the birds were meant to eat.

Once done, we walked back around the front of the tree where Nix and Hale were waiting.

The door swung open easily, and I was overcome by the familiar scents of the Reader's abode. The contents were still in a state of orderly disorder. Tipping piles of books alongside odds and ends that had made sense only to Ama. A kitchen area with wooden shelves that held the lingering scents of sweet baked goods. Containers of her favorite whirlpool whiskey.

On the table where she had spent hours with me looking through old books and teaching me to interpret Riftian markings sat a series of labeled, folded papers with wax circles depicting the Riftian seal: a blackened tree encircled by a blue ring on a slate background.

I read the names on the folded papers aloud.

"Kena, Fell, Silas, Bayard, Hale."

"What in all the worlds?" Hale snatched his own envelope from me, and I just as quickly snatched it back.

"Hey! That's for me!" He tried to grab my arm to retrieve it.

"Yes, and *I* am the one who's meant to distribute these."

I stared at the envelopes in my hands. In the end, I played favorites, just as Ama would have.

"Fell. You go first." I handed over the envelope with his name on it.

With a somber expression, he took it, careful not to tear the paper as he sliced through the seal and opened the note. He held it up as he read it to us.

"Forest Walker. It has been an honor and a privilege to have your friendship all these years. I'd like to think of it as mentorship, although you perhaps thought of my actions as a bit of mothering. In fairness, if I could have chosen a son, I couldn't have picked a better one. I'm proud of who you've become. I've left you a gift in the wooden chest by my books. I'm basing this on a hunch, but since we both know I'm almost never wrong, I think it's a safe bet. With Love. Ama."

Fell's fingers were tight on the paper, his eyes watery as he stared at the page.

Ama had piles of books and knickknacks scattered around, but there was only one chest in the room. Fell went to it and flipped open the wooden lid.

"What is it?" Nix demanded, her view obscured by the forest walker's back.

"Ocala," Fell answered. He pulled the items out, and I gasped as he unrolled the clothing.

Each Society had their own style of dress. Riftians favored long, hooded cloaks. We hadn't shown our markings to anyone until the Spear led an attack at the Coalition Meeting. Beneath the cloaks we often wore earth-toned pants with boots over them, and soft tunics. On the Hub, everyone wore grey jumpsuits.

This didn't look like either of those fashions. In fact, it looked eerily similar to the ocala bodysuit Ama had made for me, which I wore at all times.

"I'll be right back," Fell murmured, stepping back out into the woods.

When he returned I saw that his new clothing had been constructed by the makers in two parts. The black pants were form-fitting, with some pockets and holsters up the sides, built into the ocala. The top was also fitted to the forest walker's lithe muscles, with sleeves that ran nearly to his elbows. My bodysuit showed many of my markings. Fell's covered many of his, but over his heart was stamped the symbol we each bore on our skin. The one that read *soul* and marked us as Connected.

Fell looked down and smiled at the marking.

"She's right. She would have had it created before the marking appeared, but she knew what she was talking about."

"Mine next?" Hale asked, reaching out for his letter before I'd even answered. I rolled my eyes as I handed it over, but in truth I was just as curious.

Unlike Fell's careful handling of the letter, Hale ripped the seal off his, with the back of the paper tearing a bit.

"Oops," he commented, undeterred, as he opened his letter. His eyes scanned the page without reading anything aloud.

"Woah," he exclaimed at one point. A few moments later, his expression twisted into confusion as he chewed his lip, then split into a grin.

"Well!" I demanded when I could no longer take the anticipation, "Are you going to share what she said or not?"

He looked in my direction with a mischievous grin.

"Only if you're nice to me, Kena."

I sputtered, hands on my hips, as I marched over to him. He raised the letter to put it out of my reach, which would have worked far better if I weren't slightly taller.

"I'm just messing with you. I finished reading it almost immediately; there's almost nothing to it. I just wanted to get a rise out of you," he admitted as he handed the letter over. I snatched it, eyes taking in the words greedily as Hale darted out the front door.

I read the short missive aloud.

"You will find your gift within the emerald elm just west of here. We all need friends, and the Societals would do well to remember that where you end up after the Choosing doesn't dictate loyalties. Friendships change, but they don't have to end. She will need you."

I screwed up my facing looking at it. Fell had already anticipated my thoughts and held the door open for me as I barreled into the woods after my best friend.

Hale was just outside, in front of Ama's willow branches, staring around at the grove.

I rolled my eyes again.

"You have no idea what an emerald elm is, do you?" He jumped before turning around, a sheepish grin on his face.

"I do not."

I gave a fake sigh of exasperation, grabbing him by the crook of his elbow and dragging him to a tree well within eyesight of Ama's place. The tree was aptly named, with emerald leaves that held some gloss, reflecting whatever light source perforated the obscuring branches of the Riftian forests. There was a door to the tree, but many Riftian trees were like that; readied for eventual residents without actually having anyone inside.

Hale hesitated for just a moment as his hand reached for the door, before pulling it wide.

The interior was empty, without even the basic wooden furniture a lot of not-yet-occupied Riftian homes had. Lying in the center of the small front room was a dagger similar to the one he always wore. This one had a black ocala handle, and the blade was black as well.

Hale lunged for it, grabbed it and held it up to the light. The blade glinted, and I spotted a symbol stamped onto the handle.

"Friend," I informed him when he looked from the blade to me. He reached down and moved his own blade from its holster, sliding it into his belt instead as he gave the ocala dagger the more secure spot.

We went back to Ama's, and with none of the other recipients present to delay me further, I opened my own letter. The wax seal popped open with ease, and the note was brief.

The words were for me, but I read what the note contained so the others could hear.

"For my brave protégé. I have taught you everything I could with the time that we had. It has been a privilege to witness Earth coming back into the folds of the Societies once more. Do not think things have to remain as they are, just because that's how they've been. Everything will change, and that is good and bad. If you want to help, my advice is this: be willing to give everything to fight for who and what you love, but *don't* make the mistake of thinking that you are not also worth fighting for."

I reached a hand up and wiped the edge of my cheek, almost expecting a tear, but my face was dry. My marks hummed opal light around the room. The letter appeared vague, but I knew what Ama meant. The Coalition hadn't been perfect, and the change of having us up there was good, but that didn't mean Earther inclusion as a whole was. Kaiser and his armed militants proved that point well enough. If we ever got through the Spear, we had an entire planet convinced that Societals were evil beings intent on wiping them out. The damage would be hard to undo, on top of everything else we were facing.

"What about the other letters?" Nix questioned, reaching toward them on the table. I scooped them up.

"We'll let Silas open his own." If whatever Ama had given him was at her home, that would mean a detour for him as well, but I didn't feel right snooping when it came to my friend.

"And Bayard's?" Fell posed the question as he did most of his statements, his tone even and relaxed. I never felt like he was judging me.

"We open it with the others. Everyone has a right to know

what Ama had to say to my cousin. I don't want any more secrets where he's concerned."

"Then it's settled." Fell scooped up his old clothes and moved toward the door. "We'll take the letters with us."

He opened the door. Nix and Hale followed him out. I stepped after them, turning and placing a hand on a tree that I wasn't sure I'd ever see again.

"Goodbye. Thank you for everything."

We made our way back into the woods, headed toward Twilight Grove.

CHAPTER 5

The journey took us another full day, but we stopped to rest only once.

When we got to the large wall of trees that marked the entrance to Twilight Grove, Marx stepped out.

"Glad you could make it," Fell's maker friend smiled at us, guiding us back through the trees.

We emerged into the grove, and Marx's emerald markings glittered under the light.

"What in the worlds!" Nix exclaimed, staring up. Inside the Twilight Grove it was near-night all the time. The sky above was purple and blue, deepening to black and riddled with stars. It was the only place in all of the Rift where you could see the sky.

"We got everyone warned in the main grove," Silas informed me as he approached us.

"And we've got something for you," I responded, handing over the letter Ama had left for him.

He tucked it into a pocket.

"I'd open it before we leave the Rift. She'll have left you something here," I warned him.

"As soon as we finish with the crystals," he promised.

Vanya and Hok joined the group. Both weapons instructors

were well-equipped for a fight. Vanya had her bow slung over her shoulder and daggers at her side. Hok's sickle swords were holstered on his back, and he carried a fighting staff at all times.

Hok gestured to the crowd of resistance members in the grove, which appeared to have grown significantly since our time at the lake.

"We've also picked up quite a few more Riftians who want to join our resistance efforts. They were none too pleased to hear that their ruler had been the face of the Spear and their head delegate was its actual leader."

Vanya scowled at his side. I imagined it was a great shame for a Society that valued its good judgment to have been so fooled.

"What exactly did you tell them?" Whether they sided with us or not, hearing that I'd forced their former king to throw himself into the flaming wreckage of the Hub while we escaped might not go over well with everyone.

"We told them that Kidan is dead, destroyed through his own hubris in thinking he could take out the Hub without consequences," Hok answered.

I breathed a sigh of relief. I'd used my projection to force the king and his lackeys to run directly into the flames of the collapsing station. They'd been the ones to destroy it in the first place, and the ship we escaped on wouldn't have held us all. They'd have killed us if I hadn't stopped them. Even so, it was murder, and I wasn't ready to face the consequences if the other Riftians didn't forgive or understand.

"And my cousin?"

Silas gave a half-smile.

"I don't see why your family relations should be anyone else's business."

The others nodded, forming a half-circle around me. Protecting me. I owed them so much. If we lived through this, I'd have to find a way to repay them.

"Oh!" I pulled the last letter from the pocket on my ocala

bodysuit, tucked behind the moon quartz I'd been given on Clan, which I still had to find a use for.

"A letter from Ama, for Bayard. We waited to open it until we were all together."

The others stared at it. I noticed Vanya's fingers twitching at her sides, and I imagined she was eager to see what words the Reader had left for the traitor.

"We'll open it along with mine, as soon as we fish in the grove?" Silas offered. Vanya and Hok nodded their agreement.

"Then it's settled. Let's get Kena introduced to everyone so we can get to work." Vanya grabbed the ocala bracer that covered my wrist and hauled me over to a group of newcomers.

The sheer number of new Riftians bolstered my confidence.

"They're all here to help?" I confirmed with the weapons instructors.

"Yes. All the other Rift residents have been instructed to find some of the more isolated areas of the forests to seek shelter for now, or even to go to the Mists or to Tundra."

So many new people. It would help speed things along, but it required that I give the same speech I had before the Lake of Death all over again.

When I'd finished, the Riftians had a few questions. How they had to stand, how my ability worked, if it was possible any of them would be able to do the same. I answered them as best I could before we formed a line and got to work.

The crystals here were easy to spot: twilight purples and blues behind the first circle of trees.

"We've always known they were here. I just had no idea they served a purpose like this," Marx explained as he led our group to them.

With all our new help and a familiarity with the process, along with the area around the grove being smaller, we moved faster than we had at the lake.

When we reached a halfway point, everyone took a much-needed break. Fell was underneath one of the ocala trees, his back leaning against it and me in his arms, with my head on his chest. I was somewhere between waking and sleeping when the ground shuddered and shook beneath our feet.

Thundering booms echoed around us, and I leapt to my feet, grabbing for my ax. Fell had his daggers out and was positioned in front of me with my back protected against the tree before I'd even noticed him move.

"Spear!" Vanya yelled across the clearing, nocking an arrow and letting it fly into the shadows at the edge of the grove. A grunt signaled that it hit its mark. A second and third arrow followed before I even spotted a clear silhouette of anyone approaching.

Fell hauled me against him and spun us around, using his daggers to knock aside an incoming throwing knife. Several more throwing knives followed the first, and Fell twisted himself around me each time, throwing the projectiles off their target—me. The final one was so close it glanced across his cheek, opening a shallow wound. Fell didn't so much as flinch, instead grabbing me and hauling me along as he made for the cover offered by one of the ocala trees.

"Bayard carries those," I reminded Fell. "He's got to be he–"

"Bring me the crystals, and bring me my cousin! I'd say it's more than time for a family reunion. Kena, I'd just love to hear how you managed the lake." Bayard strode into the clearing, arms raised and waving as he directed the Spear members in their attacks.

Fell's cheeks drained of color.

"He will not get to you." For a moment I thought he'd ask me to hide, but perhaps he knew I wouldn't have listened.

"Do what you need to do. I'll cover you," was all he said before sprinting past me and engaging the Spear members that were closest to uncovering our spot behind the treeline.

I moved on my hands and knees, scrabbling in the brush

under the trees and stopping at the roots to work on the crystals. I knew we needed to hurry, but without the others I moved slower than before.

Over the yells and screams, I saw commotion on one side of the grove. Several of the Clan members Bayard had brought along had taken out pick-axes and were demolishing the root systems of the ocala trees. They hacked away at some clusters of crystals we hadn't gotten to, pulling them up from the ground.

"No! Don't do that!" I screamed, rushing toward the nearest bovine-nosed and horned Spear member. "You'll destroy them!"

The individual I'd spoken to froze, dropping the broken crystal into the dirt. The light within it shuddered and died. Bayard had gone truly mad if he was willing to destroy them all. Or maybe he hadn't realized that removing them this way would damage them.

I swung my ax at the Clan resident. What normally felt like an extension of my own arm weighed heavy in my hand. I barely managed to block his first blow, my arms trembling under the weight as I pushed his sword away from me. All my work with the crystals had drained me.

With a yell, Hale landed on the Clan resident's back, hacking away with the dagger Ama had given him. Nix and Digit ran to his aid and made quick work of my would-be attacker. Digit may have been permanently injured by the Spear, but she hadn't let them take her fighting spirit. The techie grinned, the scar on her face highlighted as she took down another one of our assailants.

"There she is!" one of the Spear shouted, a Dagan pointing an oily finger in our direction. For a moment, fear boiled a hot trail down my throat and into my belly. They were coming for *me*.

"She's the one who wrecked the other ships! She's the one who tried to trap us on Lone."

It took me a few moments to connect the accusatory words with the petite techie who had gone wide-eyed at my side.

Digit's expression transformed back into a maniacal grin as she gestured at the Dagan with a come-hither hand motion.

She might be tougher than she looked, but I still didn't want her in the line of fire.

A row of Spear broke away from the main group and charged at us. I counted two Dagan, two Clan residents, a Kite with rose-gold wings, and a Canopy woman who had golden fur on her face and curved talons springing from the ends of her fingers.

Hale bent at the knees a bit, lifting his arms and flicking a second dagger out.

"Ready?" He glanced at Nix. She grinned, Kaos sliding up her arms with a soft hiss. The snake had belonged to her uncle and the former Magistrate. According to his notes, it was more suited for sneaking than attacking, but it flashed its fangs just the same.

Nix bellowed, and she and Hale charged the line. They took down the two Clan together. I threw myself on Digit and shoved us both into the dirt as Dagan puffer darts thudded into the ground next to us.

"Roll!" I yelled as they burst into clouds of colorful poison. We escaped them, but Nix and Hale used the opportunity to shove one of the Clan into the colorful clouds. Soon he was screaming.

I screeched as something yanked on my arms. Looking up, I saw rose-gold wings flapping and trying to haul me away.

"Kena!" Digit yelled as she lost her grip on me.

"Behind you!" I screamed back. She turned in time to raise her cutlass against the two Dagan. I was relieved when I saw Dex join her. My toes were dragging the ground as I swiped with my ax. I was off-balance and couldn't make contact with the Kite hauling me up. Not unless I wanted to risk slicing off a chunk of my own arm.

A blur slammed into the Kite, and I was thrown to the ground, sent tumbling as we made a crash landing. When I rose,

I held my ax in one hand, spitting dirt and looking for any new threats. Fell stepped over a pile of ruined rose-gold feathers.

"Thank you," I managed. He wrapped an arm around me, holding me close. I thought for a moment he might kiss me, raging battle and all. Then he spun us and threw one of his daggers at the charging golden-furred Canopy Spear. The dagger was aimed well, and as the Canopy resident went down, Fell let go of me and ran over to retrieve the dagger.

I scanned the crowd for Bayard. He'd called for me and then disappeared. And where was my uncle?

"Kena, get down!" a voice shouted just before a body collided with mine. I was thrown to the ground, shocked to find Captain Karo, of all people, on top of me. The Crew leader and I rarely saw eye to eye. I looked over his shoulder to see a crater where I'd been standing.

"Karo, thank you, I—"

He coughed, red staining his face.

"Can't win if we don't work together, right?" he asked, voice raspy as he continued to hack and cough.

I slid my legs out from under him, moving so I could cradle his head.

Oh no. Oh no.

I placed one hand on his chest, and it came away sticky and crimson.

"Karo!" Captain Everleigh ran over and dropped to her knees next to us. "What happened?" she demanded, glaring at me as if I'd injured him myself. In a way I supposed I had.

"He was trying to help me. He saved me," I managed to get out.

Karo put his hand over hers.

"'S all right, Ev. You show 'em … how we can fight," he rasped.

She pulled at his shirt, but before she could even get a look at his wounds he let out a shaky breath and went still.

CHAPTER 6

Captain Everleigh slammed her fists into the grass.
"Blast it!"

I reached for her, wanting to apologize even though there was nothing I could have done. Everleigh pushed herself up off the grass. She yelled as she sprinted toward the nearest Spear member, cutlass raised.

It felt wrong to leave Karo, but I knew if I didn't get moving I was going to get myself killed. That would have made his sacrifice worthless. I stood as well, staggering a few steps. A Clan member bellowed in my face, horns pointing off the side of his head, like an enraged bull.

The sound was jarring. It made me want to yell back, to vent all my frustration and the pain of all the loss we'd suffered. I'd been using my ax, worried that my projection wouldn't be effective with how tired I was.

But the turbulent emotions I was feeling fueled the ability.

"Stand down," I commanded the Clan resident. My fury gave way to satisfaction when he clamped his mouth shut and cringed away from me. Ama had instructed me both to use my ability and to be wary of it. I knew well enough what could happen if I let it get out of control.

"Run into the forest. Harm no one," I insisted, and the Spear member turned and barreled into the trees. I had no idea what would become of him. The Rift has all sorts of creatures hidden within the forest. He'd either find his way out or he wouldn't.

I looked across the grove, eyes searching. Fell spun and ducked under attacks as he kept the area around me largely clear. In spite of what had happened, I was facing better odds than the others. Dex and Hok swung away at several attacking Kites as they shielded Digit between them. The petite Crew resident had her cutlass drawn, stabbing through the holes the larger fighters' movements created.

Vanya threw her bow over her shoulder and transitioned to her daggers. Fell had taught her how to use them, and I had confidence she'd be fine. Hale and Nix had teamed up with the twins. Cassius spun and sliced with the edges of his white and golden-flecked wings, his deep brown skin slick with sweat. His sister tore and ripped with her sabertooth-like teeth.

My relief at being able to account for all my friends was short-lived. Just because those closest to me had escaped unscathed didn't mean everyone had. I spotted a few others lying in the grove who weren't Spear. We were losing more people because of my decision to bring us here.

My eyes landed on Bayard when I spotted his sapphire markings lit up under the trees. His smile was cold as he surveyed the damage he'd wrought. His eyes were open, the color frozen somewhere between translucent ice and the blue they'd once held. The scars around his eyes had faded to a dull but garish red. He turned to me, pointing an accusatory finger as he shouted.

"Well, cousin? What will it be? You can work with me, or you can watch the Societies fall. It doesn't matter to me. I can always rebuild from the rubble."

I bit my lip, tempted to argue against him, but what good would it do? He didn't trust me. He had no reason to.

"Not so bold now, are you? Now that my father's proved

himself more useful than I would have thought, and given me the final puzzle piece to my plan. The crystals. That's all I need to control Assimilation for *all* the Societies. There is no greater power."

I gasped.

Juliard *had* betrayed us, then. It was his fault Bayard knew what to look for, and where to find it. At least the way his army had been digging at the crystals told me he didn't know how to keep them alive. That was good, if we wanted to prevent him from gaining control of their entire supply. It was bad if we wanted to avoid seeing him destroy them and leave Assimilation a thing of memory.

My uncle stood in Bayard's shadow, a frown on his face. He flicked his hickory hair back from his head, a telltale sign of agitation, but he did and said nothing. He was tall, wielded a golden scythe, and bore bronze marks. I had to admit, he looked formidable. The two made quite a pair, and I'd never been more ashamed of my family.

"Uncle! Don't do this," I yelled at him, ignoring my cousin entirely. Bayard knew where I stood. No matter what he said, he was just posturing. He was well aware I wouldn't help him unless forced to do so.

The words weren't a command; just a plea. Juliard had been against my using projection against people.

My uncle took a step forward, but Bayard threw an arm out and Juliard stopped.

"You don't tell him what to do. Not anymore."

As if I'd ever had control over my uncle.

"He answers to me now. He knows where his loyalties lie. Your resistance *bores* me. I've got better things to do than squabble with you over some tiny spot of forest. Pick up the scraps here, if they mean so much to you. I've got bigger concerns."

What did he mean? The other Societies?

"Destroy it." Bayard snapped his long and graceful fingers,

and the Spear members ceased fighting the resistance and turned their ire back to the trees themselves.

"No!" Yells sounded from across the grove. I heard Fell's and Hok's over the others, but I was certain more Riftians joined them. This wasn't just a spot with crystals; it was a sacred place. It was the only area where the rare bark of the ocala trees could be found in abundance.

Resistance members threw themselves on those destroying the Twilight Grove, but Bayard swept through the group, and blows that should have landed didn't. I knew his ability with projection was similar to Ama's—distract, deter, push people's interests away—but I had my own power. I didn't waste it on Bayard, knowing he was more resistant to it than anyone else. Instead, I targeted the Earthers and Spear members under his command.

"Drop your weapons! Stop! Leave this place!" I ran through the trees, throwing my directives at every enemy I could.

I still had Juliard and Bayard in my sights as they retreated to the edge of the grove. From their direction, a shot rang out, blowing a hole in the ground near my feet.

When I looked toward the source, I saw Kaiser holding a gun.

The head of the Earther militants was little better than a hired killer. He didn't even like the Societals, but for the right amount of money he'd been more than happy to join the Spear. Juliard's hand was on the top of the weapon, and unless I was mistaken he'd ruined Kaiser's shot.

"You know we want her alive," Juliard snapped.

So Bayard could try to use me. He was desperately jealous of what I could do with projection, and he'd wanted me to show him. I doubted that desire had changed.

"You're defending that puppet master? She's a killer! It's unnatural how she makes our forces move—she makes them drop their guns in the dirt."

He started to raise the weapon again, but Juliard whipped out his scythe and sliced the gun clean in half.

"Why, you!"

Bayard put a hand on Kaiser.

"Priorities, gentlemen. We have places to be."

Juliard and Kaiser scowled at one another but followed Bayard out of the grove. I lost sight of them in the trees.

Someone had set a fire, and flames roared around us. Members of the Spear threw torches against the bases of the ocala trees.

"Put it out!" Vanya screamed. Samell, a Riftian arborist, led a group of the others away from the trees. Surely there was a water source nearby.

The Spear, those able to move, anyway, followed my uncle and Bayard out of the clearing, leaving us in the burning woods. I steeled myself against my uncle's betrayal. I was determined that I would make him mean nothing to me, if it took every ounce of effort I had.

The last Spear member had disappeared by the time Samell and the others returned.

"There is a creek not far from here. We can form a chain."

We spread out, each resistance member further and further from the flames until the individuals at the end of the line reached the creek. We passed water in shirts tied together as makeshift buckets, packs that had held their supplies, and anything else available.

In the end it took us longer to fight the fire than it had to work on the crystals, which we still finished after the blaze had died down. Once done, we stood in the smoldering grove. We'd lost maybe half the trees.

"We will care for them, and they will grow back," Samell assured me.

"We will make sure that they do." Marx stepped forward, other grove makers at his side. "Well, the others will. I intend to keep helping you until the Spear has been taken care of." He glanced over my shoulder, and I looked back to see Thea, a former Earther assimilated to Dagan, who grinned at him with spiny teeth.

The grove was safe, but Bayard was long gone.

"What about Ama's letters?" Fell reminded me.

"That's right! Silas, do you want to open yours?"

He pulled it out and pried the seal off, scanning the page.

"I'll need to make a detour to the training grounds," he informed us.

"We'll catch up to you," Vanya said, grabbing hold of Silas's hand.

"And Bayard's letter?" Hok asked.

I pulled it out, aware before I read it that nothing it contained was likely to fix things. Ama hadn't known when she wrote it that Bayard had betrayed us. Even she couldn't predict everything.

When I unfolded the paper, a small black ring fell out. Fell kneeled to catch it before it hit the ground. He handed it to me, and I saw that it was made of woven ocala. The symbol on it was minuscule, and I held it up to my face to interpret it.

"The right path."

I handed the page to Fell while I examined the ring further.

That was what it said on the surface, anyway. Based on what Ama had taught me, it was more accurately interpreted as making a conscious decision to do the right thing, with the symbols for 'right' being something along the lines of 'greater good.'

I looked up to see Fell frowning at the page.

"What?"

He cleared his throat.

"It starts with his name, then states, 'I know you and I have never been close, but you've represented the Rift's interests at the Coalition for as long as I can recall.'"

He had used his projection to beat Ama at her own game.

"She tells him that he will need to act on behalf of the greater good, then mentions a set of brothers she once knew with similar potential."

He handed the remainder of the page to me to read.

This ring belonged to Tiberius, one of the brothers. When he left the Rift, the ring was left behind. He abandoned the greater good. It is my hope you will help us uphold it.

"Kena."

I started at the sound of Fell's voice and looked down to see I'd squashed the paper into a small, wrinkled ball.

"Right, sorry."

She'd given him my father's ring. Bayard had killed my father. Sitting in my hand was the only family heirloom tying my father to the Rift, and it had been left to Bayard instead of me.

"He doesn't have any right to that. You should wear it," Silas insisted.

I took the ring, glaring down at it before pocketing it.

"No. I don't want anything from Bayard and my father. But I don't want him to have it, either," I admitted.

Keeping it close would be a compromise.

The journey back to the Doorway in the Mists was trying. When we arrived, it was a relief to see that the Spear hadn't been through there. The Whispers stated they hadn't seen anyone but us wandering through their woods.

"Do we think that means Bayard has his own Doorways, or he used some of his remaining ships?" Silas asked the group.

It didn't matter to me how he traveled, only that we beat him to wherever he was going next.

CHAPTER 7

The first thing we took care of on our return to Tundra was prisoners. On Lone, we'd just left the Spear with their ruined ships. In this instance, though? No one wanted to leave the Riftians with the added responsibility of injured and potentially dangerous Spear members and Earthers.

To my great relief, some of the others with far more knowledge in the area than I had took over.

Silas and Dex were in a conversation with the Rover leader, Sorvay. The scaly-skinned Societal still walked with a cane, courtesy of his Spear-given injuries, and he glared at the prisoners. Everleigh joined them to give her input as well.

I had no say in any of it, and I didn't want any, but Sorvay still came over with Sarah to let me know what had been decided.

"We're going to fall back on a Rover classic—let the environment decide whether they live or die," he informed me.

I glanced between him and the Serpentina.

"And just what does that mean?"

Sarah stepped forward, holding her arm out so Charles slithered to the end of it.

"Rover is full of treacherous terrain. My serpent Charles

found me when I'd been shoved into a swift viper pit. It should have been a death sentence. Living meant avoiding the deadly snakes and climbing up the shifting sands. We'll employ a similar tactic here, but without the sand, and the snakes."

I blinked at her, still confused.

"We don't have the *same* terrain, but we have equally dangerous terrain," Sorvay clarified. "We drop them in an ice pit, once they've been seen by the menders. There's a steep valley surrounded by ice not far from here, and the rim is frequented by polar beasts. That, combined with the harsh snows, would make it inadvisable for anyone to attempt an escape."

Sarah nodded along.

"If they stay here, they get fed and are provided with tents and warm clothes. If they make a run for it, that's on their own heads."

It was as good a solution as any. Remembering what had been done to Twilight Grove and Karo kept the guilt at bay.

"That works. Can you get it set up?"

The two Rovers ran off, taking Dex, Silas, Hok, and Everleigh with them. When Silas returned from the Rift with Vanya, he'd carried a package with him. I was well beyond curious, but he'd tell me when he was comfortable.

I went over to where Fell was with the other Riftians, including Vanya's younger sister, Ariadna. The purple-eyed Societal had four red scars along her face. At her side stood a massive, six-legged creature with shaggy fur. It reminded me of a polar bear, but with a longer snout. Her very own polar beast.

I cleared my throat.

"I know we discussed fusing all the crystals, so I hope you won't all be too mad. I don't want to risk Bayard getting his hands on any, but it occurred to me that we might need some of our own."

I emptied the various pockets on my bodysuit.

"While we worked, I found a few small clusters of crystals that I was able to uproot without harming them. There aren't many, but we could try to harvest some in each Society we go to. That way, we have something for Tundra."

And Lone, if we ever decided to go back.

"Exceptional," Fell said, exhaling. He ignored the crystals, striding past them and reaching out to place his hands on my cheeks and pull my lips toward his.

"It was just a thought," I murmured when the kiss ended.

"A good one. The Societies are lucky to have you. At the very least, we can evacuate people here if need be, and these will allow everyone to be more comfortable."

That had been my main motivation in taking them. Some Societals, such as the furrier citizens of Canopy or the bulky Clan members, acclimated to the climate relatively well. Others, like the cold-blooded Rovers and oily-coated Dagan, struggled in the frigid environment. Technically, none of the current refugees would be likely to Assimilate to Tundra. My previous Societal educator Nien's Riftian mark was the only instance I knew of such a thing happening to even the smallest degree—dual Assimilation. Still, it was possible.

One thing I'd kept to myself was the fear and hope I felt simultaneously that, as the crystals changed, so would the Assimilation process. Whether it worked that way or not, my actions would affect thousands. No small weight to carry.

"Now we just have to figure out a safe spot to put them. I vote against right here, by the Doorway and in the middle of camp," Vanya stated, fixing a braid on the unshorn side of her head as she spoke.

"I think I can help with that. I've been hoping to show you what we found, anyway," Ariadna offered, from astride the polar beast. I was still desperately curious as to how she'd ended up with the creature.

After a moment of hesitation, I accepted her arm and Fell's assistance to clamber onto the polar beast's back. It grumbled beneath me, and my hands tensed in its fur.

"Don't worry. We're only here because he allows it. If Artox decided he didn't want a rider, we'd be in the snow. I can promise you that."

"You named him?" I couldn't help asking. As a general rule, Societals didn't have pets.

She blushed.

"You know how some of the Canopy have a certain affinity for animals? They helped me figure it out."

I was aware. Nien had insisted that the citizens couldn't exactly talk to animals the way Societals held conversations with one another, but they could communicate. It made little sense to me, but I was reassured that Ariadna had such a connection to the giant creature underneath me.

The others walked beside us.

The polar beast lumbered out of camp and across the flat snows. We came to a narrow path between two massive walls of ice, and I had to crane my neck to the sky and still couldn't see where they ended. If they collapsed for any reason, or some avalanche from the snows above came tumbling into the crevice, we'd be buried.

The whole planet was blinding with light reflecting off the snow, but the light took on a warmer glow when Ariadna informed me that we were nearing our destination.

"Almost there! I'm really excited to show you this spot, Kena. It's so amazing; you'll see. And it's the perfect place for what you're trying to do."

The creature underneath us roared, and I couldn't help flinching as a few bits of ice tumbled down the walls of the crevice. My fear was forgotten when we emerged from the narrow path and onto a field of wildflowers. Soft buttery yellows, blushing pinks, and calico blues. It wasn't the first time the truth of a seemingly harsh Society had stunned me, and if we ever won against the Spear I was sure it wouldn't be the last.

"I think you should put the crystals here." Ariadna gestured at the many plants. "We don't know what Assimilations this planet will produce, but I think it'd be nice if they were tied to the fields here. They provide beauty, ingredients for the menders, and food."

There were trees lining the field that had long vines trailing to the ground. The vines each held vibrantly colored fruits.

"How did you decide they were safe to eat?" Hale held one on his palm, staring at it as though it might poison him.

Ariadna shrugged.

"Trust, and menders at the ready. So far, though, nothing here has been harmful except the cold temperatures."

He raised an eyebrow. Ariadna touched her scarred cheek.

"Well, and some of the wildlife. But that was entirely a misunderstanding," she promised, patting Artox's side.

"Uh-huh." Hale sounded unconvinced, but he plucked the dark blue fruit off the vine all the same and sank his teeth into it.

I was interested in trying some of the food myself, but it would have to wait. With only a few, small crystals, our limited numbers made quick work of fusing them into the grounds under the wildflowers.

That evening, I snacked on one of the field fruits while we sat around a fire to determine our next move. Small groups had broken off, debating which of the remaining six Societies ought to be our next visit.

I watched the smoke as it spiraled upward and out the hole in the top of the tent, the color reminding me of Pim's wings. Lost in thought, I hardly noticed when Sarah nudged me.

"Going to have to scooch over, Queen of the Alliance. Make room for the rest of your lowly army." She grinned as she pushed at me with her leathery, dirt-red, lizard-skinned arms. Charles gave a soft hiss and slid from her shoulder to mine. He circled from one side to the other before sliding back onto her arm.

"I think, that *he* thinks, that you're overwhelmed," Sarah informed me knowingly.

Who was I to argue with the wisdom of serpents?

"I *am* overwhelmed. This whole thing is complicated."

She shrugged. "I don't see what's so complicated. We go to the planets one by one. We save the crystals. If we see any Spear, we decimate them. Once they're all gone, we take back the Societies. The only tricky bit is rebuilding the Hub, but I'm more than happy to leave that to people like Digit who excel at that sort of thing."

When she said it that way, it sounded easy enough. And not at all like the weeping, bratty, timid Earther she had been when she'd arrived at the Hub in the first place. I wasn't the only one with problems. Sarah's father was a wealthy businessman on Earth's task force, and he'd sent people to Lone to try to take her back against her will. It was awful, but it reminded me I wasn't alone. Everyone was dealing with something.

Ariadna and Ryshal passed around bowls of fruit from the wildflower fields. The bat-winged Kite had to watch his arms where they connected to his wings, to prevent knocking over anyone's plates. Once everyone had food, Veronica and Cassia moved to the center near the fire, along with Nien and a few others from Canopy and Dagan. They were the two planets nearest Rift, and that made them the only other Societies in the same system as Lone.

"Rift was the obvious first choice," Nien began. I scowled as he mentioned the word *choice*. That he had forced me into the Rift behind my back still rubbed me the wrong way. "But now we must determine our next steps. Twilight Grove is proof that Bayard will be after us, and if we are to win we must beat him to these Societies."

"We need to determine what his strategy will be and adjust ours accordingly," Veronica insisted, the vibrant blue shapes on her inky skin casting shadows in the firelight.

"This is a matter of strategy. We have to assume Bayard is relying on ships. If he is, he'll go to Canopy or Dagan next. One of those two Societies needs to be our next destination. The other one needs to be our last," Nien insisted.

"Why last?" Dex questioned, grabbing a huge handful of grape-sized fruits and popping them one by one into his mouth.

"If we secure Dagan first, Canopy could be lost. The same holds true for the reverse decision. Whatever we pick, if Bayard goes to the other Society first, he'll have the advantage. Even with the Doorways, we can't beat him to both," Nien explained.

"I triple-checked, Kena. We might save one, but it would mean walking into an ambush on the second." Digit held up her tablet, showing schematics that made no sense to me. The blue circuitry tattoos she'd had on Earth contrasted with the bold black and white one on her scarred cheek.

"That could mean condemning one Society. Sacrificing one."

It was unacceptable.

"It might," Silas concurred from his spot in the group. "It's not realistic to think we won't have losses. In the end, this decision has to come down to common sense. What will save the most people, and what helps us in the long run?"

Veronica spoke again, drawing my attention back to her.

"We know Bayard has more support from Dagan and Clan than from anywhere else, just based on numbers. Most Dagan aren't what I'd call team players. They like to keep their own business their own business, but if they're forced to choose, they'll side with whoever they see as the likely victor. That gives us an advantage if we go there first."

Cassia stood next to her. The base of her torn ear twitched.

"Canopy residents are different. They are independent but have no issues working for the collective good. Bayard has had few Canopy members in the Spear. They're also equipped with all sorts of skills, like camouflage, that can help them stay out of his path if he descends on the Society." Cassia flickered and went invisible as she spoke, proving her assertion. Not all those on Canopy could execute camouflage with quite that level of skill, but I took her point.

Nien stood beside Cassia as she flickered back and became visible again.

"Canopy citizens are fierce," he concurred, "and if they weren't won over by Bayard before, they certainly won't be now. As a whole, they appreciated the balanced method of running things through the Coalition. They won't appreciate the violent methods Bayard used to take away those options. They'll resist him down to the last individual if necessary."

"Kena?" Cassia looked over to me.

"We know where the crystals are on both planets. Ama mentioned them in her journals. Our choices are the Deep of Dagan, or the Wilds of Canopy. If you all think we risk losing the support of Dagan if Bayard beats us there, then that's the call."

Cassia and Nien nodded along. Even though Cassia had suggested the idea, it had to be difficult for them to volunteer their own Society for siege by the Spear.

The decision was gut-wrenching, but once it was made, everyone moved fast. One good thing about choosing Dagan first was that the likely location of the crystals wasn't all that far from our Doorway, according to Veronica.

"The Deep is a huge chasm beneath the water. It's blacker than the blackest night you've ever seen, and we know there are deep-sea creatures down there that sometimes come to the edge of the chasm."

"Are they a danger to us?"

Veronica gave a fluid shrug.

"I hardly know. They're only ever seen at the edge of the Deep, and we don't spend a lot of time there. There's no need. We're not like the Crew. We live around the sea creatures, and we hunt when necessary, but we don't run into dangerous areas just for the fun of it."

"Until now," I muttered as I holstered daggers and my ax.

CHAPTER 8

Dagan's Doorway tunnel involved multiple chambers. We stood in one filled with air. Veronica and Thea passed out reeds to everyone. They were the only way for other Societals to breathe on Dagan. I wasn't a fan; it never felt that they gave you quite enough air to be comfortable, but it was a far better alternative to drowning. Another problem presented by the cramped chamber was having everyone pile in from the Doorway. We'd kept the group fairly lean compared to the Rift, but we'd still have to bring multiple rounds of Societals through all the chambers.

Our group moved from the first to the second. The door sealed shut behind us, and I clamped my reed between my teeth, trying to keep calm as water flooded the compartment.

I hadn't been looking forward to Dagan. The underwater planet had been off-putting to me from the get-go. Even growing up in Verkent, I'd been fascinated but terrified by the stories of Societals surviving so deep beneath the waves. Just the thought of it made me want to clutch at my throat and gasp for air. The water sloshed against my knees as it rose.

"Didn't miss this experience, huh?" Hale turned his head and smirked at me, holding his reed up between two fingers before popping it back in his mouth. I took my own out briefly to respond.

"I already hate this. Just don't tell Veronica."

The Dagan in question walked around the group, ensuring everyone had reeds and giving instructions.

"The pressure on this planet is nothing like what Earth or other Societies would experience so far down. That being said, it does get uncomfortable in the Deep. Not insurmountable, or deadly, but unpleasant. If you have to ascend, do so slowly. Only those of us with gills will be able to speak to one another once we're under, so it's important you stick close to us." Her bright blue eyes flashed as she made her way through the crowd.

The not-speaking part had me even more concerned. Yes, it was true I had been able to achieve projection without speaking before, but it was harder. Who knew how many crystals were in the deep, and how much energy they would take to fuse? How were the others supposed to do it? I wasn't having much luck untangling what percentage of our efforts could be attributed to their projection and how much was funneling straight through me. If they were responsible for much of our success, would the lack of speaking prevent them from helping?

I envisioned a massive wall of crystals deep under the waves, and having to tackle it alone.

Then there was the fact that we were only here first so they wouldn't be easily won over by Bayard. It was another fringe Society that was admittedly under-appreciated by many of the 'prettier' groups. Not everyone wanted oily sludge coating their skin, spiny teeth protruding from their mouths, or clouded eyes. If the Coalition had been truly balanced, and didn't just appear that way, this whole thing could have been avoided.

The door to the chamber opened, releasing us into the sea.

"We're well away from the largest domes, but we will pass a few smaller ones to get from here to the Deep," Veronica warned as she started swimming, her webbed hands and feet propelling her.

Most Dagan lived under massive domes. They didn't need them to contain air; they needed them to keep some of the more dangerous creatures in the water out. Thea swam along next to Sarah. The two had experienced a falling-out when Thea chose Dagan, but they'd patched things up. I listened in on their one-sided conversation.

"When I first came, I worried I'd made a huge mistake. You were so mad at me, and I had a hard time Assimilating. For weeks I swam around with a reed in my mouth. It was awful, feeling like I couldn't breathe and not being able to talk to anyone."

I could only imagine. Thea had to be tougher than she looked, to have made it through.

"But now I'm shocked I ever lived anywhere else. This is so much more freeing than Earth, or the Hub. And so much more comfortable than Tundra." Thea shivered, sending bubbles off her oily skin in waves. Marx grinned around his reed next to her, and she rolled her eyes. He made his emerald marks flash in response.

She giggled.

I looked over at Fell, and I understood the others' flirtation. My love for him was one of the few things keeping me afloat.

After a while we approached the first dome.

Veronica waved, and we followed her past it. I treaded water for a few moments, making sure we had everyone accounted for. Some took to the water like, well, fish. Others, not so much. Hok flailed around with his large limbs, struggling to make any forward progress. Sarah kicked up behind him, legs fluttering back and forth in symmetrical movements. She'd been loath to leave Charles back on Tundra, but she was doing just fine with the swimming portion of things. Digit had stayed behind as well, with Nix volunteering to hang out there and assist the techie with some plans.

"Crew belong on the water, not under it," Nix had reasoned.

Something hit me in the arm, and I nearly spat out my reed. I turned, readying myself for an attack, but it was just Hale. He pointed with fervor to the dome behind us. Several of the others had stopped and were treading water alongside us as they looked as well.

Rows of Dagan were behind the dome, glowing as they stared back at us.

Veronica swam forward, putting her hand on the dome. She stayed there for several seconds before turning around.

"I don't think they'll try to stop us. But I don't think they'll come help us, either. A lot of the Clan joined Bayard because they were bitter about their lot in the Coalition, but Dagan are mostly fine to be overlooked. Societals thought of Rift as the most mysterious planet, but I think Dagan might be the most isolated."

She cast another glance at the dome as we swam on and left it behind us.

Soon the water went from dark to pitch black. My body tensed.

"We're here. The edge of the Deep."

Veronica's voice shook just a bit as she swam out over the edge. I could barely see it under her glowing shape, but when I followed her, I felt it.

The water was frigid over the chasm.

Fear threatened to swallow me. My instinct for self-preservation urged me to turn around instead of swimming down into the Deep.

The darkness receded just a trace amount. Through the water, Fell reached out, clasping one of my hands in his own and squeezing. I turned toward him, nodding as my hair floated around my face. We could do this.

I kicked furiously, following Veronica and the other Dagan, who lit the way. Between them and those of us from the Rift, we were able to see.

After a while, Veronica stopped on a sandy outcropping. The Dagan in the group were able to stand, planting their oily feet.

The rest of us could merely float. This threw into sharp relief the benefit of Society-specific Assimilations—how those valued by the group as a whole or the Hub weren't necessarily the ones needed if you actually lived on the planets.

Veronica waved, and I looked over the edge to see faint lights farther below us. It had to be outcroppings of crystals.

Fell squeezed my forearm; his lips were curved upward around his reed, no doubt his attempt at a reassuring smile. He tugged, and we swam downward to the lights. I longed to take a deep breath, to steady myself, but such things weren't possible with the reed.

The other Riftians followed us. Vanya frowned around the edges of her reed, leafy green marks flickering and shaking. I doubted she wanted to stay in the dark, watery chasm any longer than necessary. Hok's silvery marks remained steady, but his jaw was tense. Silas's expression was blank. He held Vanya's hand as they swam out to join our line. Crimson lights wove into the water around him as we prepared to work on the crystals.

To my surprise, when I pressed the crystals on this planet, they were more malleable. They softened and smoothed into the walls of the Deep.

As we'd done before, we moved carefully, section by section. Veronica and the others stood watch over us, but Bayard and the Spear hadn't given any indication they were here.

We were getting closer. I'd have guessed we'd made it through eighty percent of the work when several small, glowing orbs rose in the water from under us. They reminded me of a fortune teller's ball, floating in the water in front of our faces. I was transfixed, overcome by a strong urge to reach out and touch them. Movement in the water caught my attention, and I flicked my eyes over to see Veronica throwing an arm out, eyes wide as she shouted.

"Get out! That's a —"

I glanced back in front of me as a row of lights behind the orbs illuminated, revealing a creature of the deep: a massive fish, with spiny teeth the size of my leg protruding from its bottom jaw. Its eyes were cloudy and greyed over. I froze, and Fell tugged me up as I began to sink.

I kicked my legs as the creature started to shake, vibrating and sending a powerful current to push against us. The line of Riftians broke as we were hit, and the creature let out a hideous sound. Ear-splitting, grating, and high-pitched. Fell pulled me out the way as its spiny teeth closed over empty water. He wrapped his arms around me, blue-purple marks brightening as he hauled us out of the creature's path.

I wanted to do nothing so much as scream, but I clamped my teeth instead, terrified of what would happen if I let the reed out of my mouth. Near us I sensed a thrashing movement, and I saw Silas tugging on Vanya, whose eyes were rolling back. She'd done what I'd avoided, and her mouth was open. Her reed floated near her, just out of her reach. I pulled on Fell, pointing toward the floating Riftian. He kicked with me, and we dodged as the massive fish snapped toward us again.

It turned away from us for a moment, and I saw that behind us the Dagan were creating a distraction. They were flickering, their neon patterns popping off and on like a light, rhythmically. The fish turned and swam at them. They'd given us time. Silas was breathing against Vanya's mouth, pushing air into her lungs. I snatched the reed and shoved it against her mouth when he put his own back in to take a breath. Vanya shuddered, sucking air in through the small breathing instrument. Her eyes went wide, head rolling as she looked around us. Silas pulled her into a hug. Fell pointed to where the Dagan were swimming around the large, glowing fish, pelting it with puffer darts that seemed to be having little, if any, impact.

The four of us had turned to swim toward them when I heard a yelp. Vanya clutched her hands against her face, pushing her reed back into her mouth before it was lost again. I looked down to see the tip of a tentacle tugging on her ankle, pulling her into the dark beneath us.

"There's something else down there! Out of the chasm!" Thea yelled above us, orange marks glowing and drawing attention to one of the creatures as another tentacle shot in her direction. She squealed as she swam around it. The tentacle slammed onto the wall of the chasm, sliding and leaving a slimy coating over the newly formed rivulets of glowing crystal veins.

Silas shot past me on one side, Fell on the other, as they swam after Vanya. I could see her green markings glowing below us, growing more distant by the second. I kicked after them as Hale swam past me. Crew residents were the next-best swimmers to Dagan, and he showed it.

Above us, I heard Veronica shouting.

"Whatever you do, don't stab it! A lot of the things with tentacles down here have poisonous ink!"

She was swimming for us, and as she passed me she grabbed my arm without a word, helping to haul me along. Beside us, Thea kicked past, hauling Marx as he swam.

When we reached the creature, it had Vanya wrapped in one tentacle and was slapping at the assorted Societals with others.

"Don't do that!" Veronica warned. Silas had his sword held high and was hacking away at the tentacle holding Vanya. Her eyes were wide and panicked, and she coughed around her reed, trying to shove it back into her mouth. Marx joined them, wrapping his hands around the creature's tentacle and prying it loose while Silas hacked away. Another tentacle slapped at his face, leaving a large red welt. With a last blow, Silas sliced the edge of the tentacle off, and Marx yanked Vanya free.

Her head lolled. She was unconscious.

"We've got to get her out of here!" Thea insisted.

Below us, the creature began to rumble.

CHAPTER 9

With a loud spurt the tentacled creature did just what Veronica had predicted. Ink spilled into the water around us. As Silas and Marx pulled Vanya up, I saw vibrant emerald light flare. New markings, small and intricate, wove their way under Marx's left eye and across his cheekbone.

I'd have gone in for a closer look if not for the spreading ink.

"Don't panic! Everyone hold your breath and kick up as fast as you can. It's only harmful if you ingest it!" Veronica called.

I looked between the spreading ink and the remaining crystals. The other Riftians were either fleeing or helping others to do so.

I wished I could take a steadying breath, but the reed wouldn't allow it. I threw my arms out, using projection to transform the crystals into glowing veins on the walls of the chasm. Knowing we had no time, I forced as much energy as I could into the effort. It felt like something forceful slammed into me, and cold beyond the chill of the Deep waters wove through my own veins.

The remaining crystals flared with light, fusing into the wall.

My arms dropped, limp and sore. Fell grabbed hold of my body-suit, tugging me up.

Veronica and Thea practically pushed Silas and Marx out of the way as they went over and grabbed Vanya by the arms. The men released her, and the two glowing Dagan hauled her upward through the water.

The rest of us kicked furiously for the surface.

When we reached the edge of the Deep we didn't stop. The whole group struggled to follow Veronica as Thea and the other Dagan with us shouted encouragement.

"Get to the surface! We'll go to one of the isles!" one of them shouted.

As we passed the edge of the Deep, tentacles slammed onto the seafloor as one of the creatures pulled itself from the frigid waters into the warmer seas. I turned my focus up, aiming for an orange and purple sky I could see faintly through the water above me.

Whether the creature had stopped pursuing us of its own accord or we had managed to outpace it, I wasn't sure. When I reached the surface, I pulled the reed from my mouth, clenching it in one fist to avoid losing it as I sucked in lungfuls of air.

Just as during my first visit to Dagan, the sky overhead was turbulent and stormy. Black clouds rolled and thunder echoed overhead. The one good thing was that I saw none of the large, pterodactyl-like predators in the skies this day. Vanya floated in Veronica's arms.

"This way!" Thea yelled, pointing to the nearest tiny island. We swam, she and Veronica each hauling one of Vanya's arms.

"Brace yourselves!" one of the Dagan called out just before a wave slammed into me. I shoved the reed back in my mouth, tumbling under the waters. When I broke the surface again I looked frantically for Fell. He surfaced not far from me and was staring up and over my shoulder. I spun and located the source of the wave. One of the huge whale-like creatures the Dagan called an omnidon had slammed its tail on the surface.

Kicking for all I was worth, I managed to make it to the island, even with my tired arms. Fell helped pull me onto the sands. I was gasping and sputtering. Fell's breath was even beside me, so quiet I had to strain to hear it above my own. Further down the shoreline, Veronica supported Vanya, who sat up and coughed water onto the sands. Vanya threw herself into Silas's arms, openly weeping. Her leg had circular welts on it from where the creature had grabbed hold.

"She's alive," I reassured myself.

Thea and the other Dagan waited at the edge of the sands, still submerged in the water at the beach's edge.

"Think you got enough of the crystals?" Hale leaned over me, offering his hand. I took it, and he yanked me upright.

"I think I got them all," I muttered, but he was already walking over to Fell.

"Forest walker?" Hale approached Fell and gave him his arm. I knew my Connected had no need of the help, but he took it all the same.

"Still like to swim, then?" Hale asked me, grinning. His smile faltered at whatever expression I gave him in response.

I shook wet blond strands, sending water flying onto us both.

"I don't think I'm voluntarily going back into that water ever again," I joked.

In front of me, Fell and Hale were wide-eyed.

"What?"

Hale reached out, tugging a strand of my hair forward.

It was white.

"But that's not—"

"It's what happened to Ama. Just before she created the Doorway. Her markings and hair turned white, then translucent, and then she faded away." Fell's voice was hollow, his hands clenched into fists at his side.

Faded. I'd tried to picture her ascending to the skies of the planet where she'd grown up. Not that the wording changed her fate.

"I had to. If I hadn't, there would have been too many loose crystals for Bayard to harvest or destroy. It was necessary." I scrambled for an excuse that made sense.

It had been the right thing to do, but I understood Fell's response.

I hadn't even realized that I'd been pushing myself too far. If I wasn't careful, I could fade away like the Reader. We still had five Societies left. Not to mention Tundra, and I hadn't even managed to salvage any crystals from the Deep for them.

"All right," Veronica shouted from the water where she'd joined the other Dagan. "We'll circle below and monitor the omnidon pod. Once they're gone, we can all head back to the Doorway."

I groaned, throwing myself back on the sand as the Dagan disappeared beneath the waves.

"Can I speak with you?" A shadow fell over me, and I looked up to see Nien staring down at me over his warthog-like tusks. His plated face made it harder to read his expressions than some Societals.

I rolled to my side and pushed myself up. My marks flickered a few times before settling; the only sign, I hoped, that I was annoyed. Fell reached for my hand.

"Do you want me to go with you?"

I glanced at Nien, who was frowning in my Connected's direction. In a move more Sarah, or Hale, than myself, I gave in to a desire to annoy him. It might have been petty, and I'd forgiven him, but I couldn't pretend that what he had done to me didn't still bother me.

"Yes. Come with us, please." I tightened my grip in Fell's hand.

We strode across the small island until we were reasonably secluded. The others were still in sight. This island didn't allow us much more space than that, but I doubted we'd be overheard above all the other conversations on the other side of the beach.

"You know what my mark says." Nien didn't waste any time dancing around the reason for his conversation.

"Yes. *Necessary sacrifice.* You want me to interpret it for you?"

He held his arm in front of him, staring at the glowing canary yellow marking in question.

"Is it any different than what I'm thinking? Does it mean I'm going to die? In the Twilight Grove, I second-guessed myself because I wasn't sure if I was supposed to be throwing myself in front of someone. Just now in the Deep, I considered swimming directly into the creature's jaws so the others could get away."

"Why didn't you?" Fell asked.

If the question had been presented by Hale, I would have assumed the intent was snarky. From the forest walker? He had to be genuinely curious.

Nien looked at me when he answered.

"If my purpose is to die for this cause, I want to do it at the right time."

The answer hit me like a falling Riftian tree. His voice didn't shake. He was more than willing to face death; he just wanted to make sure he didn't mess it up.

"It's possible that it means you're supposed to die. Ama had much more experience than me. Lifetimes of being able to guess at the meanings of the markings and then to see how they bore themselves out in reality. I don't have that advantage. The marking might even refer to something you've already done. Going undercover with the Spear; even what you did to me. Those could count as a sacrifice, depending on how you look at them."

"But it's not likely."

"If I had to guess, I would say you are right. This fight will still take something from you, and it might be your life. I wouldn't go around looking for moments to throw yourself into danger. I think you'll wait until the opportunity is in front of you, and then it will come down to you making a *choice.*"

I wasn't able to keep the lingering bitterness out of my voice, but I tried. Not well enough though. Nien flinched, just a bit.

"I know you want an apology; I still can't give it. At least not the one you'd like."

"Don't betray us. That will be enough of an apology."

I wasn't certain why I said it. Maybe I was paranoid after Bayard, and Juliard, and the news of my father. In spite of his faults, I trusted Nien. Then again, my judgment wasn't foolproof.

Nien pulled his arm back as Marx wandered over.

"Looks like you're discussing markings." He pointed at Nien's arms and then at his own face.

"Any chance you could help me decipher this one, Reader?"

The word hit me like a physical force. With Nien, it was different. I'd seen the marking on his back when Ama had been around, on the Hub. This was the first time a Riftian was bringing me a new marking to interpret, because I was *the* Reader.

"Of course," I sputtered as Nien retreated back to the group.

I leaned in, grabbing Marx by the chin and tilting his face back and forth to make sure I didn't miss any of the small, intricate swirls and swoops that made up the markings on his cheekbone.

"Well?" he asked, dancing on his feet when I let go of his face. I'd been on the other side of this experience; waiting for the results of your markings was nerve-wracking. Probably even worse now that we were revealing them to all the other Societals. Good for Marx. Otherwise he'd have needed a mask each time he'd visited the others.

"It says: 'Two destinies. Two worlds.'"

He frowned, one eyebrow drawing downward.

"What's that mean?"

When Ama pronounced her verdict on something, it sounded sage and wise. When I did it, I realized how vague the statements could be. I didn't have her lifetimes of experience to draw on. I just had the memory of her books, and my own instinct.

I looked behind him. Thea was across the island, watching us intently.

"Well, I'd say one of the worlds is the Rift, and the destiny would be your work as a maker. The other destiny will be another calling you feel drawn to."

He looked over his shoulder at Thea, flashing a smile in her direction.

"And the world? Does it mean Dagan?" He grimaced. He might like Thea, but this Society took some getting used to.

"Maybe. It could mean many things. Why not wait until we've gone through all the Societies to make that determination?" I responded as I fought for a delay. Maybe it would become clearer with time.

I blew out a breath as he smiled, accepting the non-answer.

"Wonderful. I haven't had a new marking in years. This is fantastic. Just, really amazing. Thank you, Reader." He ran back to the rest of the group.

"You did well," Fell complimented me.

"I didn't know what to say. I just made some of it up as I went. I mean, not made it up out of nowhere. I just used the markings and my common sense and the best guess I had."

"Do you want to know a secret?" Fell leaned closer to me, eyes gleaming as he whispered.

I nodded.

"I'm pretty sure Ama did the same thing."

CHAPTER 10

t took hours for the omnidon pod to swim to a safe distance, allowing us back in the water.

By the time we exited the Doorway onto Tundra, people were grumbling. Coming home to a snowy and icy planet while still sopping wet did nothing to improve anyone's mood. Those of us who had gone to Dagan crowded around a fire in one of the tents, smoke venting out a hole in the top. Fell wrapped a blanket over me, covering my hair and handing me a cup of something hot and sweet.

"Hot chocolate?" I questioned him.

"Something from Rover. You'd have to ask them," he responded.

I took another sip and was able to taste the slight difference. It had a more bitter taste than what I was used to back on Earth. The drink was a welcome escape from the cold, nonetheless.

"Where to next?" he asked me after I'd taken my first few sips.

It would come down to a vote, but we both knew that since I was the one interpreting the journals and overseeing the crystals, I'd get more of a say. Back on the Hub, it had been nearly impossible to get the Societals to agree. Now, in spite of the bickering that still broke out, we worked together. As nice as it was, the added pressure on me to make the right decision was something I could have done without.

I sighed, sidestepping.

"We didn't see any Spear members on Dagan. That means we've lost the Canopy."

"Maybe, maybe not. We won't know that until we go there. Are you rethinking saving that Society for last?"

"No. If Bayard did go there, then there's no sense in our running into a trap. That doesn't make me feel any better about it. While it's not because of any particular strategy, I'll admit that I also don't want to go to Crew next. I need a break from water for a bit."

I'd have to ask Digit where the next closest Societies were for Bayard. If he'd beat us to Canopy, and then moved on to Dagan, would that buy us more time? Just the idea of going back beneath the water was overwhelming, but I wasn't going to risk my best friend's home over my fears.

"I want to go to Kite next. Does that make me selfish?"

Fell knew of my affinity for the Society. If it hadn't been for Nien's meddling, I'd have been wearing a pair of wings instead of opal markings.

"Not at all. Any particular reason?"

"This just feels right. And, while I don't want to, I need to speak with Sybil."

He put an arm around me as I scooted closer.

His silence felt like an invitation.

"She and Pim were both in Verkent together their whole lives." The conspiracy—or not-so conspiracy, since the Societies were real—group I'd grown up in had also had many Societal descendants in its midst. Not that we knew at the time that we came from the Societies.

Pim and Sybil had both been married before. Each of their spouses had passed away. They'd been dating for years before they would admit it to anyone in Verkent. I thought they brought out the best in each other. Pim kept Sybil active and engaged with others, with his endless tech tinkering and desire to converse on anything and everything. Sybil kept Pim grounded and single-handedly grandmothered most of Verkent. With her interest in gardening, she'd always brought fresh food to the meetings. During the years after Juliard and I had our falling out, I'd missed her snacks and warm smiles.

Now I'd probably be the one erasing that smile for good.

The thought made me want to insist on saving Kite for last, but that also made me all the more certain it should go next.

She deserved to know.

I brought the idea to the others later that evening, once everyone was dry and in a slightly better mood.

"With the Doorways, we don't really have to consider distance," Digit informed us as she typed away at her tablet, "but if we did, it wouldn't matter much. From the system where Lone, Rift, Dagan, and Canopy are, those containing the remaining Societies are roughly equidistant, in different directions."

"The Spear will probably waste time going to Dagan anyway. I only wish we could be there to see their faces when they realize you beat them to it." Sarah grinned. The Serpentina held out her arm, and Charles slid back up her shoulder and into the relative warmth of her hair.

This time we didn't even take a whole night of rest.

Vanya declared that, other than being shaken up, she was more than well enough to travel.

The Kite contingent's best guess for the location of their crystals was their extensions. The bits of rock floating over their small planet were abundant, and they used them as secondary living spaces and for all sorts of other purposes.

"We've got hundreds. But there are some that form a ring around the planet pretty far up in the atmosphere," Ryshal informed everyone. "I'd bet they'll be there. They're incredibly hard to reach, even for us. The air is thin, and it's cold enough to form frost on your wings."

"More cold," Sarah groused, Charles hissing his displeasure at her side.

"Can we fly up there ourselves?" Silas asked. When visiting Kite, anyone without wings got weights to make up for the lack of gravity, paired with fake wings that resembled a two-sided hang-glider to allow them flight.

Acaius shook his head, opening and closing his black dragon wings.

"That material wouldn't hold up at those altitudes. We'll have to carry you."

All that remained was to determine pairs and logistics. Each Riftian would go with a Kite escort, and anyone not from those two Societies who went along would watch out for us from below.

"I'll take care of leading a group to the Kites' largest city and letting Nimue know that the Spear may be on our tail," Dex volunteered. Nix and Hale readily agreed to go with him to warn Kite's queen that she might have to prepare to defend her Society after we'd left.

It was decided that most of the Kites could simply hold their Riftian counterpart. I was paired with Ryshal, and our situation was a bit trickier. With his bat wings running the span of his arms I'd have to be strapped in, since he couldn't hold me and fly at the same time.

"I always liked my wings, but I hate that they're hindering us now," Ryshal grouched as Marx and a couple of Crew created a harness for me to take along.

"We'll be below, hoping for the opportunity to face off against some Spear," Everleigh promised.

She hadn't had much to say since Karo's death. At least this was giving her something to focus on.

"Tell Nimue she might need to have people evacuate from

the main planet up to the extensions," Shawd warned everyone. He and Cassius had befriended one another without the twin realizing Shawd was already a member of the resistance.

"Nimue may already have a plan in place when it comes to the Spear, but someone should give her the ideas all the same," Silas agreed.

Before the sun was even up we'd formed a line in front of Kite's Doorway, readying ourselves for another crystal attempt.

"Two down. Five to go," I tried to encourage myself. The number still felt insurmountable, but with each Society it would get better and better.

"Two Societies saved. The Spear can fight them, but they can't destroy or control their Assimilations. That victory is immeasurable," Fell reminded me.

"You always know just what to say."

Before stepping through the Doorway, I leaned on my toes and kissed the forest walker.

When we emerged on the other side, I let out a sigh at the relative warmth on Kite.

"It's good to be home." Cassius puffed out his chest and took a deep breath through his nose as we exited Kite's Doorway tunnel.

Shawd walked by, fluffing out his tan and blue wings. Ryshal and Acaius were doing something similar, stretching and flapping.

Iduna, a former Hub instructor of ours, walked by them and sniffed derisively as she gave her grey feathers only the smallest of shakes.

"Unnecessary blustering," she declared. I still didn't care much for her, but I caught the smallest bit of a smile on the edge of her lips. Maybe we were winning her over.

The rest of the Societals wandered the perimeter of the extension we'd landed on. The Kites' actual planet was by far the smallest of all Societies, but the floating chunks of rock and land tethered by vines or with waterfalls created more space.

Marx leaned over the edge. You could just see the cloud cover over the planet below.

"Going all the way down there, are you?" Marx asked. Thea strode over to the edge next to him, and when she hesitated to look over he offered her a hand.

"I won't let you fall," he promised.

The Kites carried all the Societals except the Riftians down to the planet's surface.

"Once you're done warning Nimue, have some of the residents down there give you a ride back up," Acaius instructed, "and if any of them would like to join us, let them know we could use the help."

When he was done, he walked over to Fell and me.

"We might be going to the wrong place." I chewed my bottom lip.

Acaius shook his head.

"I doubt it. With Kite being so small, I feel we would have noticed if they were somewhere on the planet itself. And you said they'd all been placed in portions of the Societies that were treacherous and difficult to reach. Our destination checks those boxes."

He gazed up at the sky above us. It was likely that in all the remaining Societies it would be just as tricky, if not trickier, to reach our destinations.

"When you put it that way, I'd say we're headed to the right place," I acknowledged.

Once Hale, Nix, and the others had been dropped off below, all the Kites returned for the Riftians.

"Ready!" Ryshal announced as he made his way over to me.

"Why *do* you all stretch your wings so thoroughly? Iduna said it was just showing off, but does it serve a purpose?" I asked him.

"Comfort," he explained as the others helped strap me in so

my back was against his chest. "The other planets have more gravity than ours. It makes us feel heavy."

I hadn't even considered this.

Fell walked over, standing in front of me and buckling a portion of the harness that held me to Ryshal. I stared past him to the edge of the extension.

"It's bothering you, being here," the forest walker observed, "but I have confidence. I think you'll be just as successful here as in the Rift."

I sighed.

"This is where Pim was," I reminded Fell.

"He meant a lot to you. And you haven't had the opportunity to truly grieve."

"It's not just that. I still don't know what to say to Sybil."

She had the most beautiful set of blue monarch wings, and an easy smile. Just imagining what this news would do to her shattered me. Fell was right; I hadn't had my own chance to grieve Pim. I didn't know how I would put someone else in a similar position. Pim's death was what had set off my first real attempt at conscious projection. In a way, we owed this entire plan to him.

"You will say something from the heart. You always do. I don't know what happens after all this. I only want you to know that if we survive, it will be because you saved us. We never could have gotten this far without you."

Acaius joined us and grabbed Fell under his shoulders. The two Kites and my Connected ran through a final review of the plan.

While they were talking, I gazed at the Society that had meant so much to Pim.

"I'm sorry I couldn't save you," I whispered.

When the Kites took off, the initial ascent wasn't bad. I gave Fell a nervous smile.

Cassius flew holding Silas, and his friend Shawd was carrying Marx. We had enough Kites for each Riftian. Even small, fairy-winged Tibby was carrying Vanya, although she looked a bit absurd since the Riftian was twice her height. Her green wings flapped furiously.

I had to bite back a smirk when I saw massive, muscled Hok being held by Iduna. She was stern, and frankly rude much of the time. She had no fondness for Earthers, so it was just as well that she wasn't carrying one of us. She might have been tempted to drop us from the sky. Then again, she'd acknowledged us as real Societals because we'd Assimilated, so perhaps not.

The farther up we got, the chillier it became. I conversed with Ryshal about the view, the colors of the flowers on extensions we passed, anything to distract myself. I made it a point to not look down, even someone without a natural fear of heights would have been nervous at that height.

After a while the extensions became sparser, and those present had different plant matter entirely. Gone were the vibrant wildflowers with birds and butterflies flitting through the petals. In their place were long grasses that leaned and swayed over the edges of the extensions. Several of the extensions still had waterfalls, the liquid a fine mist as we flew under it.

Once we'd passed even those and my teeth were chattering, we reached smaller extensions that were more akin to how I pictured an asteroid. I clutched at the harness that held me to Ryshal and gasped when my fingers wiped frost off the material.

"H-h-how much, f-further?" I managed. Ryshal hadn't complained, but I could feel him shivering against my back. He wasn't any more comfortable than I was, though I imagined he might be warmer with his constantly moving wings.

"There!" He pointed ahead of us, and we swooped sideways to land on one of the extensions.

"Sorry, the cold and altitude are making me a bit light-headed," he explained when we slammed into the extension and made a hard landing.

"That's fine," I squeaked as I unbuckled myself.

I counted every winged Societal and their charges. They'd all made it, even Tibby, with her frail-looking translucent green wings. Vanya stepped away from the girl, shaking bits of ice out of her hair.

"I'd just as soon never do that again," Vanya admitted, walking to the edge of the extension and peering down.

I stared at the ground beneath our feet.

"Acaius, I don't see anything."

Without a word, he pointed up, staring above our current extension. There were more overhead, small and circling us.

"The outer ring."

The underside of the extensions above us glittered and gleamed with crystals. They were a sparkling array of colors, but several bore patterns within them reminiscent of some Kite wings.

My breath caught when I spotted a crystal above us whose base was deep gray, then faded to near-white at the edge, like smoke rising. Pim.

"I will make this right," I promised, looking up at the colors that reminded me of my friend.

I watched the rotation of the small extensions above our heads.

"I think we'll need to link arms and work on each extension as it passes by," I told the group.

"How long will that take?" one of the newer Riftian resistance members asked, and I turned to see his arms wrapped around himself.

"The extensions are moving fast, and the planet's not large. That will help. We could work in shifts?"

Acaius shot me an apologetic glance, not mentioning the detail I knew. The others could rest. I would need to keep going.

I looked at the gathered Riftians.

"Everyone, link arms."

CHAPTER 11

n the end, I was wrong. I did have to rest. The whole group had huddled together at one point, trying to catch some miserable bits of sleep in the cold. Several of the Kites had stood around the group of us, their wings held open to block us from the chill as we snatched a bit of sleep.

We'd been up again for a few hours. After a while, the extensions that rolled by had crystals that had already been fused into them; small, glowing veins running through the rock.

"Could we have missed any?" I questioned as I stared up at the fifth extension in a row that we'd already worked on.

"No. I've been keeping track," Acaius said. He and a few of the others had also flown up and extracted some whole crystals for me to take back to Tundra.

"If it helps, I will stay here to monitor the entirety of the rotation while you all go back to Kite and get some real rest."

I jumped at the sound of a voice as cold as our surroundings. Iduna, once again showing her softer side.

"Thank you," I offered the stern woman. She just gave a terse nod and pursed her lips.

"Guess that means I'm staying as well," Hok grumbled, his silver markings flickering as he shivered.

"Oh no, you don't have to, I could—"

He held out a hand to cut me off.

"I don't mind, Kena. We all know you need the rest." Hok cast a pointed glance at the white strand of hair that framed my face. Word had gotten out, then. I wasn't surprised. It wasn't like I could hide it. At least I hadn't had to push myself to that extent on Kite.

"We'll warm up and wait for you down on Kite," Ryshal promised them as I got strapped in. "Once you've confirmed there are no more crystals to fuse, we'll all head back to Tundra."

Every incremental bit of warmth on the way down was a welcome reprieve from the icier air. My breaths came easier, and I realized just how little oxygen there had been on the extensions. It was enough to make me lightheaded, and I sagged against Ryshal, glad that we weren't dependent on me to stay aloft.

The lightheadedness and the fatigue combined with the rhythmic beating of Ryshal's wings had almost lulled me into sleep when my ears caught raised voices from below.

"Something's wrong!" I yelled to Ryshal. "Dive faster!"

"The air is thin up here. If we go down that fast you could pass out," he argued back. I set my lips in a thin line, trying to sound like the authoritative Queen of the Alliance they'd all deemed me to be.

"Those are our allies down there. We go!"

He huffed, but we began to plummet. His bat-like wings were tucked in as we flew. He wasn't wrong; my vision went dark at the edges, and a wave of nausea swept in. I just barely managed to swallow it down. Ryshal landed at a run, and when we hit the ground I was already unbuckling myself. As soon as I was free, I took a few steps out of Ryshal's grasp, dizzy and weaving.

Something swung past my face and I ducked on instinct, my eyes scanning as an ax similar to my own swept so close that I felt a whoosh of air on my cheek.

"What?" I shook my head, and as my vision cleared I saw Fell barrel into the ax-wielder, fury in his eyes. When the forest walker stepped away from my assailant, I saw the white spear.

"That doesn't make sense," I reasoned aloud as Fell ran back over toward me, steps silent. "How did they catch up?"

We were the only ones with access to Tundra's Doorways, and they couldn't have found Ama's. Not unless Juliard had betrayed us after all. My stomach lurched again.

Fell grabbed me and gave me a light shake.

"Are you all right?" His hands ran over my arms, my torso, clutched at my face. "Did he hurt you?" His marks flared.

"No. No, I'm all right," I reassured him, and his marks dimmed again.

I felt for my ax, pulling it from its holster at my side and getting a grip on the handle with one arm, readying the other to throw out and project.

"Clear a path!" I screamed as Fell and I moved through a crowd of Spear members toward what appeared to be the center of the melee.

Several of them stopped and stepped back, giving the resistance members precious seconds to gain an advantage. I stumbled again, and Fell's arms were under mine, steadying me.

"Use the ax, unless absolutely necessary." He didn't often tell me what to do. Not since our forest walking lessons. I could hear the concern laced through his words as he brushed the strand of white hair back from my face.

Bitterness had me gripping the handle of my ax tighter. I'd finally embraced what I could do, and yet I wasn't able to use it to help us on a consistent basis. As powerful as my projection was, it had limits. I could either help save the Societies as a whole, or use it to save those who fought alongside me. I wasn't always going to have the energy to do both.

This realization was punctuated by the scream of a Clan resistance fighter going down. I spotted Dex stepping in front of the Societal, doing what he could to block any further damage.

At his side, Digit, looking more petite than ever next to the towering man, swung a cutlass at the advancing group of Spear.

"That's right! You want them, you go through me!"

She let out a scream, bellowing at her attackers. Even considering how small she was, a couple of them shied away for a moment, giving Dex a chance to launch himself at them.

For a moment, rage that seared like a burn consumed me. I wished we were on an extension so that I could instruct all the Spear to walk off the edge. The idea of them falling was satisfying.

I gasped, shaking the hateful thought loose. Ama had warned me, and I had to focus. My motivation was to save the Societals, not to destroy the Spear. That would be a byproduct, but I was choosing to let loyalty and compassion rule my actions, not hate.

Slowly but surely, we gained an advantage. There weren't that many Spear on Kite. One by one, they broke off and ran for a ship in the distance.

So they hadn't used Doorways. I saw only one ship, and no Bayard.

"Could they have split up?" I didn't say it loud enough for most to hear, but Fell was close, and with Riftian ears he caught the message.

"Possible. We'll have to ask Digit once we're back."

I noticed that as we fought, the Spear had been retreating closer and closer to the ship. When they weren't that far from its bay door, the remaining Spear members broke and ran.

"Wait!" Silas yelled at the group, giving voice to my own thoughts. "It's a trap; stay where you are!"

"The only people down here fighting have been Societals. There should also be Earthers on that ship, and the Earthers had guns," I called to the others.

A few paused, but many didn't heed either of us.

"Stop!" I yelled, running after the resistance members. "Stop! They—"

The last few Spear members made it to the hull of the ship. It lit up, and cracks echoed louder than any of the screams as gunfire peppered the ground.

Resistance members turned, fleeing. A few made it out of range, but at least a dozen had been hit.

A voice boomed from the ship, so loud that our enemy had to be using speakers somewhere.

"Give up the Puppet Master, or we level the city," it threatened. It didn't sound like Bayard, or my uncle. It might have been Kaiser. That's how he'd referred to me back in Twilight Grove. If it was, I knew he wasn't presenting an empty threat. He would do it.

I took a couple of steps forward. Fell grabbed my hand.

"You can't seriously be considering going in there."

I gave my head the slightest shake.

"No. The Spear lie and manipulate. I don't trust them to stick to their word, no matter what we do. If we want to beat them, we need to play their game."

I looked up at the ship, and shouted at the top of my voice.

"First give us a chance to retrieve our wounded. When they're off the field of battle, then I will surrender myself."

After a minute or two of silence, we got a response.

"You have until the sun dips below the horizon."

I looked up at the sky, noting the round, pale orb was nearly there already.

"We'd better get moving. I don't think they'll stick to this, any more than their original offer to spare the city. We need to help the wounded and evacuate at the same time."

"I'll see to it that all the wounded are taken care of," Fell volunteered.

"I'll go with several of the others to make sure Nimue evacuates the city," Silas added.

Once we'd moved the wounded out of range of the ship, we had another decision to make. Did we take them to the extensions, or back to Tundra?

"We should get them tended to here," Hok insisted, silver marks keeping a steady hum. "Tundra's too cold, and it's got limited supplies. The Kites have volunteered to help, and we should accept the assistance."

"Then, once they're recovered, having resistance members here who know how to get back to the Doorway will help, if for any reason the Kites do need to leave the Society entirely," Cassius added.

If it came to that, we'd have even bigger problems. Any Society we fused crystals on held no further usefulness to Bayard. He couldn't control the resource at that point, only the people.

"We go to the extensions," I decided.

The city was probably lost either way.

We were out of range when the edge of the sun dipped below the horizon, and the gunfire started again. It didn't take long to catch up to the resistance members and Kites who had evacuated the city while we'd been working to get the wounded.

There was a cluster of extensions all floating relatively close to one another.

We gathered with many of the others on the largest.

"This waterfall"—Cassius pointed to where water cascaded onto the edge of the extension from above—"is where Kites have to pass through in order to Assimilate their wings. That's the tradition, anyway."

Acaius tilted his head up.

"In theory, that water could come all the way from the outer extensions somehow. It might originate near the crystals, for all we know."

"And we don't think Bayard will think to look here?" Dex asked, trading looks with Silas.

Shawd frowned.

"Regardless of whose side they're on, I couldn't picture the Kites who have joined the Spear suggesting this location. It's a superstition. Bayard may be focusing on the crystals now, along with us, but the other Kites won't be. If the falls go, so do our wings. At least that's the legend. I don't think they'd risk it."

That would have to do. I certainly didn't have a better alternative for those who weren't willing to abandon their Society and go to Tundra.

"Fell!" Someone called out.

A Kite with soft canary-yellow wings and coarse red hair ran through the crowd toward us. Fell's mouth dropped open, and I glanced between the two of them.

"Alsey," he breathed out, running toward her and enveloping the woman in a hug.

I gasped. He'd told me of his sister who had died, and how her partner had been so devastated she'd abandoned Canopy shortly after.

As I looked closer, I saw the orange tiger-striped fur on the woman's cheeks and arms. When she smiled, her canines had a sharp edge.

Fell spoke to her, and after she nodded assent he reached out and held the edges of one wing. Fell gestured toward me, and Alsey broke out in another smile as she came over and wrapped her arms around me.

"So you're the Alliance Queen," she teased, smirking as she pulled away. I was certain I blushed.

"I'm not that important. I'm just another resistance member."

She shook her head.

"No. You're more than that. Fell is still my family, and that means you are a sister to me."

I was taken aback by the declaration, but I returned her hug.

"She has no idea the trouble she's just signed on for," Hale joked as he joined us.

He stared at Alsey.

"Two Assimilations?" he asked.

Before she could answer, a sob rent the air, and I looked over Alsey's shoulder and saw Sybil. The woman's knees gave out, and she collapsed against Silas. He patted her on the back, whispering something.

"Sybil!" Alsey and I yelled at the same time.

"You know her?" I asked my newfound family member.

"Yes. She's got a keen eye for plants. A love for growing things. She's like a Canopy resident in that way." Alsey smiled as she spoke of the older woman. "We bonded when she arrived here. She also keeps herself to herself, except for that man with the grey wings. Pim. But I don't engage much. I wasn't sure what people would think when they realized I had wings. Sybil stumbled upon me one day, gardening one of the extensions. She didn't give one jot whether I had fur and wings or not, as she put it. She only cared that I wasn't there disturbing the plants. When she realized I was the one who'd grown them, the friendship sort of happened on its own."

I threw my arms around Alsey, hugging her again. When I stepped back, I swiped a single tear off my cheek. Alsey looked between me and Sybil.

"The man. The one with the grey wings. Something happened, didn't it?"

"Yes."

Her face fell as I responded, and for a moment her lower lip wobbled and I thought she might cry. Then, she set her jaw, brows drawing down in a look of determination.

"I know what that's like. No one should face that alone. And she won't be. I promise you."

We made our way over to Sybil.

"I told her what happened, Kena. With Digit and Pim getting taken, you trying to get them out, what you did after, all of it," Silas confessed.

Sybil was still sobbing, but she threw her arms around me. I'd dreaded this moment. I'd been terrified Sybil would rage at me, blaming me for the loss of the man she loved. Instead, she was embracing me.

"Thank you," she said, sobbing against my chest. She

collapsed into me, which forced me to sit down with her still in my arms or risk falling over.

"Thank you," she kept repeating.

"But why? I didn't save him. I didn't do anything!" I protested, then slapped a hand over my mouth, mentally chastising myself for arguing with the grieving woman.

"You were with him. Someone who loved him was there with him at the end. That *is* important. He deserved that."

I broke down, crying against Sybil. I could hear the others in the background. I felt it when two hands were laid on my shoulder.

"It's not fair. And it's not okay, but *you* will be okay. You will not be alone," Alsey whispered to Sybil once the tears had subsided a bit and she was sniffling instead of wailing.

Alsey and Fell helped the older woman up, and I got to my feet to find Silas on one side of me and Hale on the other.

The reminder that I had so many people who cared might have sent me into another emotional spiral, but instead it bolstered me. There was that anger again, weaving in and around the sadness. Propping me up.

Alsey had promised to help. To stay and tend to the gardener, like Sybil did her own plants. I felt differently.

I was going to hunt Bayard down. I was going to make the Spear pay.

CHAPTER 12

Once we'd ensured Sybil was being looked after by Alsey and the wounded were settled in under the care of Nimue's menders, we'd made our way back through the Doorway to Tundra.

"There was only one ship," Silas said before the last of us had even made it from the Doorway onto the snow.

Fell nodded.

"He's right. They could have sent all their remaining ones to Kite, but they didn't. No Bayard, and no Juliard. That means—"

"They split up!" Hale finished, throwing a hand in the air.

Silas dipped his chin in Hale's direction.

"Precisely. Bayard made his priorities clear. He went to the Rift personally, but he chose to hedge his bets. We can't be certain how many working ships they have. It's possible they were able to fix the damage we did on Lone, but they might be down to just the few ships we didn't tamper with."

Digit beamed from her spot in the group, giving a thumbs-up around the circle. We all knew the truth. The others had helped her get into the ships unseen and find the tech rooms, but she'd done the work. She was the one who had shut down a number of the ships on Lone, making it possible for us to attempt a stand against them and diminish their might enough that we were able to get away safely.

Fell chuckled, and I turned wide eyes in his direction, as did the others. Typically, if he laughed, it was only in front of me.

He waved us off.

"I'm just thinking of what Bayard's reaction will be when he realizes we beat him again. To Rift and to Kite."

"I hope he chokes on the news." Vanya's voice dripped venom, and she spun one of her daggers in her hand, glaring at one as though Bayard's face was painted into the hilt.

I looked at the techie.

"Digit. Some of the others helped with different aspects of the ships' design, but you were in their systems; you know them better than anyone. Based on how far Kite is from Lone, is it even possible for them to have made the trip in this amount of time? Or do they have another means of travel?"

The others stopped chatting and making joking threats against Bayard as I asked the question. If he did have his own Doorways, I had to know.

Digit pulled out her pad, now kept in an ocala case strapped around her back. Marx winked at me when he caught me staring at it.

"Had to do something with my skills, since we aren't exactly working on any Twilight Grove ceremonies at the moment. I took some ocala when we left, and protecting the tech felt like the best use of the material."

He cast a glance around at the other Riftians.

"Maybe I should have asked before giving it to someone outside the Rift, but I'm also not apologizing."

"No. I think it's the perfect use of the materials. There's no point in all of us gatekeeping what we can contribute. Not anymore. We're all equal members of this team." Hok glanced over at Sarah, a bit of red creeping into his cheeks as his silver marks lit up. When they did, the marks began to spread.

A new marking, swirling and delicate, made its way up the

side of his neck. He put a hand over it. Even without being able to see it, I knew he had to feel it. New markings were warm and electrifying.

"Wow." Sarah leaned over, reaching out and pausing just before touching it. He gave a nod, and she ran her fingers over the swirls of the mark.

He looked over at me.

"Do you know what it says?"

"Yes." I looked around the circle; there were a lot of people present. Interpreting Riftian markings was traditionally a private thing, between the bearer and the Reader. Then again, the markings themselves had been hidden everywhere but the Rift before this. "Do you want me to interpret it for you?"

He tilted his head, maybe judging his options.

"Go ahead."

I moved over to him, and he craned his neck so I could see. They were more complicated, less straightforward than what Marx had. I was able to figure them out, but explaining what they meant was trickier. I didn't have Ama's knack for that yet.

"They talk about you as a steady presence. A grounding figure for others. It's sort of like leadership, like what Silas has, but a different kind. It's like, you influence by being a help, and a rock for others. And your voice is respected because of it."

I was afraid I'd fumbled it, but Hok was smiling.

Sarah flashed him a grin, scooting over to take a closer look.

"Got it!" Digit announced, waving her tablet in the air.

I jumped back, refocusing.

Digit held out the tablet, and I caught the scrawl of numbers, letters, and squiggles that I was sure fit into the equation somehow. They were all far over my head.

"That Spear ship *could* have made it to Kite straight from Lone. That is, if it left almost immediately after we did. Of course, I haven't tracked our travels down to the nearest minute, which made it more difficult. But I don't think I've lost track of the days. By my estimation, if they departed Lone the afternoon after we left, they'd have been able to make it if they pushed the ship to its limits. Honestly, the speed they would need to maintain would be potentially hazardous, so the move would be reckless, but it's possible. Without any secret Doorways."

I breathed out a sigh of relief. No new Doorways.

But that left another question.

"Why? Why risk it? The Rift made sense. Of course he'd go there first. But Canopy and Dagan are the other planets closest to where they were. Shouldn't he have sent all the ships there and tried to secure them before moving on?"

Fell frowned.

"Bayard knows you, Kena. He knows you wanted wings. Maybe *he* went to the Rift first because of its significance to him, but he also knew how much you loved the Kites. He sent people there to get ahead of you; to hurt you."

"And he knew about Pim," Silas reminded me, "what he meant to you as well. Bayard was with us after that. He knows how you are with people you love. Taking Pim's Society away from you would have been a devastating blow. He'll have been betting on that."

I saw flashes of light out of the corner or my eye as my opal marks flickered. Struggling to maintain control, I took a few deep breaths. It wasn't that the breathing itself helped so much as it slowed me down and gave me time to think.

Whatever Bayard had intended, he had failed. I'd beat him to Kite, just like I'd beat him to the Rift. He was already losing; he just hadn't admitted it yet.

"Do you think we should change our minds? Go to Canopy next? I know what we thought about him going to the closest places first, but if there's a chance we were wrong—"

"No," Nien spoke, pushing gently past a few of the others until he stood in the center of the group. "He may have sent some to Kite, but he personally stayed nearby on Rift. I'm willing to bet he *did* go to Dagan or Canopy next. If he chose Dagan, by now he's realized you were already there and he'll be scrambling. If he chose Canopy, he'll be headed to the other soon, to look for you. You all forget, but those of us who worked at the Hub or worked as delegates knew Bayard. He thought things through. He may have spared a ship or two to strike an emotional and petty blow at Kena, but he won't risk his victory over it."

Cassia walked up next to him.

"Nien is right. Not about Bayard; I don't know the Riftian well enough to say. But I stand by our earlier plan. Canopy will fight. Our residents can disappear into the surroundings, and there are plenty of plants and animals alike there that could kill the Spear for us. I put my faith in my community. We chose our path, if you'll all excuse the expression. We stand by it. So, where next?"

My initial thought was to go to Clan. More Spear members came from there than anywhere else, but Everleigh raised her hand and pushed her way to the group's center.

"I vote us. You've all heard what happened on Crew when the Spear overthrew the Coalition meeting. Ships containing Spear sympathizers attacked the rest of us who had welcomed the Earthers into our midst. Crew residents are brawlers. I'm certain there's been nothing but fighting since we left. I hate to admit this, but if we don't intervene sooner rather than later, the victor there will be decided before we ever arrive. It's possible the matter is already settled."

"Hale, Nix, what do you think?" I asked the pair.

Nix petted Kaos on the head absentmindedly, the black serpent cuddling into her.

"She's right. I could list several Crew who were against the Earthers, my ex included. We're a determined bunch. The environment will be our barrier to the crystals there, but it's the infighting amongst the citizens that we'll ultimately need to contend with."

"And the crystals? Where would they be?"

"Only one answer for that. Gotta be the Edge." Hale flashed me a smile.

"The way you're grinning is scaring me," I admitted as he rubbed his hands together. He looked positively gleeful.

"Do I even want to know?" I asked.

Hale just laughed.

"Probably not, but if we're all going there, I suppose you'd better."

The Edge sounded just as treacherous as the Deep when it came to the possibility of sea monsters, and much more terrifying once the Crew explained the terrain. At least Everleigh had begun to engage again, growing more spirited as she described our destination to us. Even though it sounded terrifying, I didn't take much convincing. If Bayard had sent people to Kite just to hurt me, it made sense he'd have someone waiting for us on Crew as well. He knew my best friend had Assimilated there.

"We're in for a fight. Once we come out of the Doorway, we'll need to keep our eyes open," Everleigh warned us.

"Bayard could be there waiting for us," Silas agreed.

Everleigh shook her head.

"I'm not talking about that, although it's a fair point. I'm talking about the anti-Earther ships. While it still makes less sense to me than a sea serpent as captain of a ship, the Societals with the heaviest prejudice against Earthers Assimilating were the ones most likely to join up with the Spear. They were fighting the resistance pretty hard just after Bayard and his lot disrupted the Coalition meeting. I doubt the time and tension have done anything to cool their tempers."

Sarah raised a scaly hand in the air, speaking before anyone acknowledged her.

"Yeah, quick question. Has anyone bothered to point out to these individuals that our side is the one using Assimilated Societals, and that it's their precious Spear who's aligned themselves with actual, aren't-Societals-and-never-will-be Earthers? Does that seem ridiculous to anyone else?" She threw her hands in the air as she finished the statement, huffing. Charles gave a small snort at her side. I hadn't even realized snakes could make such a noise.

Everleigh kneaded her temples while Nien stepped in.

"The Spear values strategy and the end game. They're a 'results justify the means' type of organization. They may not like Earthers, but in this case the Earthers aren't trying to join them, not really. They're using each other to achieve their aims. Once this war is done, if the Spear wins, presumably the Earthers will leave. They'll take our tech and whatever planet is offered by Bayard and that will be that. For the record, I don't think that's what *would* happen in the event we are defeated, but that's what they believe. They think they're keeping all the aspects of their old lives that they liked, and getting rid of the parts like Coalition control that they didn't."

Nien paced while he lectured, hands gesticulating as he spoke around his tusks.

Hale huffed at my side.

"Still a filthy bunch of hypocrites, if you ask me."

Nien shot him a glare. The instructor had to have enhanced hearing, because he always appeared to know when someone was gossiping around him. Whether he chose to acknowledge it was another matter.

In this case he did.

"They *are* hypocrites, but they don't care. If you feel it would help our cause, you're welcome to point that out to them."

Hale sat back, slouching and crossing his arms as he grumbled.

"Point made."

I didn't doubt Hale might mention to their faces what hypocrites the Spear were, but that was likely to be after he'd driven a dagger through a few of them, so I doubted it would help.

"To the Edge," Everleigh growled, giving Nien a small shove. "Once we've made it past potential anti-Earther or Spear ships and actually reached our destination, that's where the real work will begin. Crew's planet has a massive canyon running around about half its circumference that makes the whole thing less of a sphere and more of a unique—" she moved her hands around, trying to indicate some shape other than a circle. There were a few giggles, but I did my best to pay attention. She cleared her throat when she realized the visual wasn't helping.

"Well, regardless, the canyon means there's a massive set of falls dropping down. That's the Edge. There are some pretty large and vicious creatures roaming the waters just before the drop, picking off smaller sea creatures that get caught in the current. The crystals could be at the top, although quite frankly I don't know how anyone would've survived the many sets of teeth there. I think it's more likely the crystals are at the bottom of the falls, or behind the waterfall itself."

"Does this mean more swimming?" Vanya asked, voice high and tense.

She still had a few fading, circular welts from her incident on Dagan.

"I'm thinking it will mean more flying for most of you."

Everleigh laid out the rest of her ideas, and I prepared myself to risk our lives again.

CHAPTER 13

The Dagan were in the most danger with our plan. They'd readily agreed to Everleigh's suggestions, but that didn't ease all of the burden of responsibility I felt toward their safety.

"My ship, and a couple others, were docked by the Doorway to Tundra when we first made our way back to the Hub. Some of our crews should still be there. That will add to our numbers," Everleigh clarified as we lined up for the Doorway.

"Those of us on the ships can distract the sea creatures long enough for the Dagan to scan the waters at the top of the Edge, and then follow the falls to the seafloor at the bottom," Hale added as he relayed the idea to the rest of the group.

Meanwhile the Kites would fly Riftians down to the base of the falls. We'd be doing our best to find crystals at the shores, or look for a trail that could bring us up the side of the falls, and behind them if there really were any rocky caves there.

"Hidden treasure on the high seas. You really did become a pirate," I teased Hale.

He gave me a salute before walking through the Doorway.

"Three down," he reminded me before he stepped through as well.

Four to go.

We emerged onto one of the Crew's golden-sand islands. This one was large enough that getting to the docks required a small trek—an additional measure to give the Doorway some security.

"We should be fine getting to the ship. Karo and I each left ours docked at a small inlet that should provide some cover from passing ships. If the Spear had figured out where those were hiding, they'd have invaded Tundra by now," Captain Everleigh assured everyone.

Her words didn't bring me as much comfort as they appeared to give some of the others.

Nix and Hale walked beside me, hand in hand.

"She says that, but once we're in the open waters it's a whole different story. There'll be no hiding then," Nix warned.

I relayed the information to Hok, Vanya, Silas, Fell, Sarah, and Digit as they joined our growing group.

Silas put a hand to his chin, head tilting as he thought about it.

"I'd say we work with the strengths we have, and handle the rest when we get out to sea. If Bayard knew where the Doorway was and wanted to force your agreement, he could have gone to Tundra, taken the children and wounded captives, and destroyed most of the remaining Doorways. The fact that he didn't is at least something."

Fell and Vanya nodded as he said this.

Nix snorted into her hand.

"What? What's funny about that?" I demanded.

She held her hands up in mock surrender.

"Hey! I'm on your side. I agree. I just don't think that's why we won't get attacked. You all forget, we are not Riftians. If Crew members have a problem with each other, we handle it right then and there. Trust me, if those ships and Doorways had been found, the Spear-sympathizing Crew ships would have engaged them immediately. They wouldn't be waiting around."

Digit nodded in agreement.

"She's right. Crew are nothing if not direct."

Also bullheaded, rash, and dramatic, but I didn't add those last characteristics. The truth was, we needed people with all sorts of talents, which came with all sorts of drawbacks. No one was perfect.

"In that case, our focus should be on the destination of the crystals. Tell us what we're in for," Vanya instructed, green eyes flashing.

Digit pulled out her battered but functional tech pad.

"Right. Well, the Crew mainly keep detailed maps of the actual planet *on* their ships. You Riftians should appreciate a good secret," she said, winking at me. My opal marks flickered, thinking of how Riftians had kept the forested nature of our planet from the other Societals for generations. "But we Crew don't mind a bit of deception as well. Lucky for us, I remember all the needed information for my ship. I created myself a file I could access from the Hub's database and was able to access it from here."

"Do we even want to know how you managed that?" Hale rolled his eyes, but I could tell he was impressed.

Digit smirked at him.

"Probably not. The explanation would bore anyone except Pim to tears." Her voice faltered a bit as she mentioned him, and I felt myself get choked up as well, but Digit barreled on.

"Although, I have been teaching Nix some things. Crew ships sail all the way around the Edge rather than cross this thing. The mists created by the falls there, the sheer change in altitude, and many other factors would have made it hard for even a ship that could fly to navigate the area from top to bottom."

"Great. We're all going to die," Hale moaned. Nix elbowed him in the ribs, but she was smiling.

As we trudged toward the docks, I thought about Silas's words regarding the hidden Doorways. The same thought kept coming back to me, and I couldn't shake it. Juliard had left me, but he knew about the Doorway Ama had created. If he wanted

Bayard to win, if he wanted his *son* to win, he should have showed him. But if he'd wanted to help us, why was Bayard still alive?

Juliard hadn't always made sense to me at the best of times, and the situation had grown too complicated for me to guess at his motives, but I couldn't help trying. The best-case scenario I could picture was that Juliard thought Bayard was redeemable, and he was going to try to stop him peacefully, as his letter suggested. It wouldn't work. My father had been the one with the golden tongue, not Juliard. And Bayard was carrying around too much resentment for the father that had left him alone in the Rift. If anything, I thought it more likely Bayard would corrupt my uncle, no matter how pure his aims.

When we reached the docks, we found three ships there, anchored and undisturbed, under the two orange suns of the Crew skyline.

"What did I tell you? Safe and sound!" Everleigh observed. Crew members came out on the decks as we approached.

"How did they survive this whole time we've been gone?" Dex demanded as he watched the tattooed Societals gathering in front of the ships.

Everleigh just shrugged.

"Crew are hardy people. They could have survived much longer than this off the fish and the island. Our only problem will be that they're probably all itching to get back on the seas, and for a good fight. Which, now that I think of it, may come in handy."

I didn't care what fighting they did if it meant we had enough people to manage the ships. We divided ourselves among the three vessels. Two would be manned primarily by actual Crew residents. The rest of us made our way to the third, wooden-hulled ship—a familiar sight.

"The *Nimitz*," I sighed. It was the first Crew ship I'd ever been on. The delegate, Track, who had toured us around it had died at the hands of the Spear.

"You weren't tempted to Choose here? Even with your best friend?" Fell questioned as the others got us ready for the waves.

"The ship was too crowded and loud for me. A moot point when you think about it; here and on Tundra we're constantly surrounded by crowds and noise."

"That's not forever," he reminded me. His black hair was swept back by the wind as we began to move over the water.

"Even so, I think I found exactly where I needed to be."

We stood together, staring out across the waves. They reflected the soft light from the orange suns, and small, furred creatures that reminded me of an otter-dolphin cross leapt along with the ship. Part of me longed to stay there, leaning against Fell, but I had other things to do before we got to the Edge.

Once we were underway, I sought out Everleigh on the deck.

Nix and Hale followed me. Everleigh turned to me, head tilting as she took me in. I wasn't sure what the captain thought of me personally. Crew members supported a good fighter, and strong leaders, so at least she didn't think me weak. That didn't mean she agreed with all my calls.

"If we see approaching ships, how do we know if they're friend or foe?" I asked the captain.

Unlike the pirates I'd heard about growing up, these ships didn't fly flags. The only distinctions I could spot between Crew ships were in the materials. Some were metal and others wooden. I was certain, though, that those used to seeing them on a regular basis would be able to more easily identify the difference in vessels.

"Different shape and color sails on the wooden ships. Different tint to the metal on the others. Different shapes to the hull. Some ships have a figurehead on the front. All sorts of details like that. I assure you, we'll know who's who. And I have enough familiarity with all the other captains to guess at which would be sympathetic to our cause."

"I can think of one we ought to avoid," Nix grumbled beside the captain. "One of the metal ships, the *Wavecutter*, attacked us when we were fleeing toward Tundra. If we see that ship, we know to steer clear. Although that's me giving the answer the Queen of the Alliance might want. If it was just me making the call, I'd vote we fight them."

I was sure that would be her vote, and I avoided thanking her for putting the needs of the group first. She'd likely see it as sentimental drivel. But I did smile at her. She grinned back.

"Actually, I thought about using Nix's method, but I'm worried I might be going too far. I wanted to ask Everleigh for her opinion."

Everleigh blinked at me, and her form flickered as she shadowed under the sun. Her arms were covered in tattoos of sea serpents, knives, and even a map, but nothing to do with other ships.

"All right, Queen. You've got my attention."

"If these other ships, the anti-Earther and anti-resistance ones, find us, will they try to kill us?"

She laughed, snorting into her hand.

"*That's* what you felt you needed to ask me? Of course they will. Crew have always been fighters, and they'd be the first Society to raise the stakes in a situation like this. Yes, I can confirm on my word as a captain that if they come at us, it will be with deadly intent."

I sighed, hating what I was about to say next. My fists clenched at my sides; I opened them and flexed my fingers.

"Then what would you think about responding in kind?"

"How?" She leaned in. At her side, Nix had a smile plastered on her face, and Hale's eyebrows scrunched down as he frowned.

"Do captains have full control over their ship? Even if the others wanted to go against them and there was a mutiny, are there any safeguards?"

Everleigh shrugged.

"The sailors might overpower a captain eventually. In that scenario, were it me, I would go to the captain's quarters. Some of these ships may look old, but they all have Societal tech. Locked in the captain's quarters, I can control the whole ship if need be. It's for emergency situations specifically. It would let me get a distress call out to another vessel, or steer the ship to an inhabited port for help."

"Would it have to be a port, or could you steer it anywhere you wanted?"

"What are you—" Her eyes went wide. "Oh."

I nodded.

"Yes. I'm wondering if a captain could force their ship over the Edge. If they come after us, and someone gets me close to the captain, I think I could make them do that."

"Excellent idea!" Nix yelled, pumping a fist in the air.

"Kena." Hale's voice was nearly drowned out by his girl-friend's. I wasn't sure if he was surprised, or judging me. It was impossible to tell what was my own insecurity and what was the truth.

I just knew that, while the idea of risking that many lives turned my stomach, I would rather lose that many Spear than my friends.

"We'll see what we're up against. If it comes to that, I'll send for you," Everleigh responded. On a Crew ship, a captain's word was law.

To reach the Edge we sailed through the rest of the day, past the time when the green and blue lights waved above the ship at night, and into the next morning.

"How are you feeling?" Fell asked as I rolled to my side in our crowded bunk below deck and met his gaze.

"Refreshed," I responded, stretching.

We were halfway through a breakfast of fish jerky and toast when the yelling above deck started.

Fell and I emerged to see Crew running every which way, and the other Societals standing wide-eyed in the center of the activity, trying to stay out of the way as the tattooed Crew residents rushed past them.

"That'll be my ex." Nix pointed to a metal ship splitting the waters and headed straight for us.

"Still, it's three to one. They must be out of their minds," Digit observed as the ship crept closer.

Everleigh caught my eye. She shook her head.

"We're nearing the Edge. The other two ships can hold them off." Everleigh was glaring at the *Wavecutter* as she yelled more orders to her crew.

We were leaving the others to fend for themselves. It had to be a hard call for her to make, but if the *Wavecutter* followed us to the Edge, they might figure out what we were up to. For all her bluster, it looked like she didn't want to force my hand unless absolutely necessary.

The Kites moved around the deck, stretching out their wings and getting ready alongside the Riftians.

Nix rushed up to us.

"Wait! Before you go, fly me onto the deck of one of the other ships!" Nix instructed Cassius, the closest Kite in reach. Cassius looked over at me.

"What for?"

"Revenge." Nix rubbed her hands together, a violent smile on her face.

I was torn. She and Hale were the only Crew who were supposed to go with us, and we might need their knowledge when it came to the terrain.

Hale threw an arm around Nix's shoulders, leaning to whisper in her ear. I was close enough to catch it.

"You know how attractive I find your penchant for violence, but in this case, maybe we could table it for later? After we help out the Cloaks?" He used the nickname the other Societals had given Riftians. Her scowl morphed into a smile as she looked back up at him, catching him by surprise with a kiss before turning to the rest of us.

"If this doesn't prove my loyalty to the resistance, nothing will," she stated as she joined those of us gathering together on the deck.

The other two ships pulled and anchored facing one another, blocking the *Wavecutter* from pursuing us.

For a moment it looked like the metal ship might try to run the barricade, but as they got close, water shot into the skies.

A sea serpent larger even than the omnidons or tentacled creatures of the Deep raised its head from the water.

I stared, wide-eyed and stunned. As I glanced around the deck, the others wore similar expressions. All except the Crew.

Hale just shook his head, smiling as though he saw this sight every day.

"Never thought I'd be rooting for the sea serpent." Hale whistled as the creature slammed its tail into the metal ship.

We were out of sight before I could see who won.

CHAPTER 14

It was clear when we got close to the Edge. The thundering crash and roll of water going over the lip reached my ears even before I saw the top of the falls through the mist.

The sound became thunderous, loud enough that I saw Fell's mouth moving as he shouted at me, but I couldn't hear a thing. Near the bow of the ship, Everleigh stood, hands flashing as she signed to the Crew members around her. They sprinted to and fro across the deck.

"It's. Too. Loud. To. Use. Voices. Here." Hale leaned in close, cupping his hand over my ear as he shouted into it. "So. We. Use. Signs." Each word was punctuated by a deep breath. It was impressive, the ingenuity that the Crew displayed.

The Kites stood by their Riftian counterparts, and the few non-Riftians accompanying us, to act as our defenses. Fell strapped me in against Ryshal before going to Acaius.

My heart thundered along with the falls as we edged closer, but just when I thought we'd go crashing over the side, the ship stopped. We bobbed in the harsh current, stationary, as the mists coming off the falling water soaked us all.

At the helm, Everleigh waved her arms. Hale strode over, a

winged Kite behind him as he leaned over and yelled into my ear again.

"She says now!"

I tapped Ryshal's arm, and we shot into the air. The other Kites followed suit with their own charges. The Dagan dove off the edge of the ship. Veronica didn't even hesitate as she launched herself over the side and plummeted towards the raging waters. They might be used to the ominous deep seas of their own planet, but these falls had to be different.

Air rushed against my face, mist pelting me as Ryshal flew us over the top of the falls. We rose higher and higher, until the spray from the churning water was far below us. The sound echoed underneath Ryshal's wings, but I could hear him when he yelled in my ear.

"We're going to dive!" he warned me. He arced. I held back a scream as we were turned upside-down and I stared at clouds of spray below. For all we knew the falls were bottomless, and we really were going off the edge of the world.

Ryshal plummeted, speed increasing the closer we got to the edge of the falls. At one point he started to shake, his control wavering as the force behind the falls buffeted us. One of his wings jerked backward, and he grimaced. We started to spin.

I screamed. With a snap, Ryshal managed to get both wings back under control, and halfway down the falls he spread his wings and we started to glide. The noise was ear-splitting.

"Can you see anything?" he yelled, his dark hair plastered down and dripping from the spray.

"Just the others," I responded, relieved to see draconic wings in the distance. Fell was all right.

Though the falls had seemed to go on forever, Ryshal did get us to the bottom. We saw a sandy shoreline, but Ryshal flew us over the water, far enough from the falls that it leveled out. The water below us was as smooth as glass, but I didn't notice any glowing or glimmering.

"I can't see anything," I told him, relieved I no longer had to shout. Several other Kites came alongside us.

"Nothing. You?" Fell called.

I shook my head.

"Us either!" Nix shouted. Tibby held her.

We turned back toward the falls. As we got closer, the water below us bobbed and waved, dark rolls hiding who knew what sort of creatures. But no glowing. We slowed down as several oil-coated faces popped up above the water. Ryshal swooped down until his feet skirted the waves.

"We haven't seen anything down here! Sorry, Kena!" Veronica called.

"Are you all okay?" I called back. She shook her head, face drawing down in a frown.

"We're alive. But a couple of us hit the rocks; we have someone with a broken leg and a broken arm. They'll have to be transported back to the ship. The Edge is just as treacherous as the Crew indicated," she admitted.

Broken bones were bad, but a low cost considering what we'd risked. Several of the Kites landed, setting the Riftians down on the shore.

Something splashed, and I saw Thea pop up from the water.

"I saw a glowing thing! When I went over the falls!" she yelled. It was always hard to tell against their oily-coated skin, but it looked like something was wrong.

"Thea, are you bleeding?" I asked, and Ryshal obligingly flew us closer. Thea put her palm to her head, and it came away sticky.

"Just a small cut. I got lucky, really; I just missed an outcropping of jagged rocks. But I think that could help us. There's something behind those falls. A landing. Maybe another cave? You all need to check it out."

After how treacherous it had been just to get to the bottom of the falls, going through them was far down my list of desired activities, but it was the whole reason we'd come to Crew.

"Those from Dagan who need assistance, wait by the shore. Shawd and Cassius, can you take turns flying the injured back up? Steer clear of the falls," Fell instructed as the two Kites nodded and each grabbed onto an injured Dagan before shooting back into the sky.

"The rest of us should spread out and see if there's a path up the side of the falls. Maybe a walkway we can hike up from here," Silas told those gathered on the shore as Ryshal set us down and helped me unbuckle my harness, "Dagan, go back underwater, just in case the entrance is at the bottom of the falls. Don't risk it if the currents are too strong. Kites, fly near the base and see if you can spot any gaps on the edge of the falls where we could sneak through. The rest of us will walk around the shoreline at the edge and see if we can find a way in."

Fell came over to me, taking my hand in his as we started walking toward the falls.

During my months in the Rift, Fell had trained me on forest walking. He could scale any surface, moving silently and with apparent ease through any terrain. I didn't have a knack for it, and while I'd improved beyond many other Societals compared to him, I was still loud and clumsy. Which explained why he wasn't even breaking a sweat when, what felt like hours later, I was aching and soggy.

It was a relief when I heard a yell near us.

"Hey! Riftians! Crew!"

Cassius and Ryshal swooped down to us, the black bat wings and golden-flecked angel wings cutting a sharp contrast.

Cassius hovered in front of us while Ryshal flitted side to side.

"Find anything?" Cassius asked us. His wings were coated with droplets of water.

We all shook our heads.

"Hope you didn't spend your day on the same useless

endeavor we did. All we've got to show for our efforts is hunger," Nix complained to the flying Societals.

"And the joy of exercise," Hale added, rolling his eyes.

"We did find something," Ryshal volunteered. "About halfway down the falls there's that outcropping of rock that Thea mentioned. It splits the water, just for a second or so, then it comes back together again underneath. The current isn't even, so the gap doesn't always stay open for the same size or width of time."

"But," Cassius added, "we think we saw a cave behind the gap. There's definitely something there."

I groaned at Cassius's description.

Even if we had found a trail that led up and behind the falls, I couldn't imagine scaling halfway up and climbing back down again.

"What would you like us to do? Should we keep looking, or do we go through the falls?" Vanya questioned at my side. Her skin was coated in the same combination of sweat and misty saltwater as the rest of us.

I sighed, glancing back at the Kites.

"That's up to you. This occasional gap, was it big enough to fly us through? How long does it last?"

Ryshal shook his head.

"It's water. Water is unpredictable. There's short bursts when the current isn't as strong at that one spot where the rock splits the water. We'd need to go one at a time, flap in front waiting for the gap, and then fly through as fast as possible. I won't lie, it would be incredibly difficult."

Silas took a step forward, his crimson gaze locked on Cassius.

"With how strong the falls are, what do you think would happen if one of us got hit with them full force while we were going through?"

Cassius grimaced, running a hand down the feathers of one of his wings.

"We'd likely be forced down to the bottom of the falls. Either we'd get smashed on the rocks beneath or possibly drowned at the base, worst-case scenario."

Silas's lips were in a thin line, face tense as he nodded.

"And best case?"

"We have enough momentum to push through the waters and land behind them in the cave. Likely injured, and with no way to fly ourselves out."

More of the Kites joined us, flapping and glancing at one another.

"Who's the quickest, and who has the most durable wings?" Fell questioned, casting a twilight glance around the circle of Kites. The mist was coating his pale skin.

"Mine are the strongest," Acaius responded from behind Fell. "The leathery quality of the wings may fare better against the water as well."

"Great, who else?" Silas asked.

"Mine, actually," Cassius volunteered, the gold flecks on his wings glinting in the sun. "The feathers on mine are thicker and more durable than most."

"He's right," Shawd added, fluffing out his own tan-and-blue wings. "I'm afraid I won't be much help there. Mine are feeling waterlogged already. I'm not a great first choice."

Iduna pursed her lips, presenting the same sour-faced expression I'd seen on her when we'd first met.

"My wings are good for fighting, with their sharp edges, but the base of them isn't as durable. I'll go first if needed, but I doubt I'd be our strongest option."

"I'm the quickest," a small voice piped up, and I looked over to see Tibby. She was just as petite as Nix. "I can make it through, so I could go first." Her translucent green wings looked paper-thin, and it gave me the urge to order her to stay behind.

Then again, what would that accomplish? The Spear was full of bullies. Big and muscled Societals who looked tough but weren't skilled. And then there were people like Sarah with her serpent, Ariadna with her polar beast, even myself. We had all been underestimated. Who was I to deny Tibby?

"Anyone have any objections to Tibby starting us off?" Silas asked.

The Kites around the circle shook their heads.

"Maybe her unlucky passenger," Nix muttered.

"You can stay here. I could try going through by myself first, then come back for you," Tibby offered.

"And force you to make another trip? Absolutely not. Crew do not shy away from things like this. Although if I live through this, *someone*"—she looked at Hale—"had better recommend me for a mark."

In the Rift, glowing markings appeared on their own. On Crew, the black and white tattoos were earned.

"Deal," Hale promised.

The Kites grabbed their charges and flew us halfway up, in front of the falls. I held my breath when Tibby zoomed forward, Nix in her arms. They shot through the tiny gap created by the rocky outcropping, and into whatever was beyond.

"Did they make it?" I yelled.

Ryshal flew as close as we could get without being buffeted by the falls. Through the small gaps I saw Nix yelling something and waving her arms. At least she was moving.

Several of the others went through, including Acaius and Fell.

"Looks like it's our turn," Ryshal shouted in my ear when only a few Kites were left.

I slammed my eyes shut as he flew us toward the falls. Mist coated me as we sailed through the gap in the water. Ryshal folded his wings, tuck-and-rolling us on the ground instead of stopping us on our feet.

"Sorry! I wasn't sure how much space we'd have behind the water before we hit a wall," he explained as he righted us and helped me out of the harness.

"It's okay, I'm just glad we made i—"

"Wow." Hale's voice echoed as he spun a slow circle.

All around us on the walls were crystals growing like moss, or patches of grass at points along the cave floor.

CHAPTER 15

"**D**ang it!" There was a clatter as one of Dex's hooves rammed a piece of crystal, and a small bit went flying across the floor of the cave. The light inside dimmed and died within seconds. We'd brought the Clan resident along in case we needed to scale any rock walls, but his large, furry legs would be a hindrance with such tight maneuvering.

It just underscored why we had to project the crystals into the cave's surface, and what we risked if we failed.

"They're our colors." Nix's voice was hushed as she looked at the crystals. She was right. The crystals in the cave were the same blues and greens of the lights that filled Crew's sky at sunset. Soft orange, just like their two suns. Even stark white and black light that mimicked the tattoos the Crew covered themselves with.

"All right. Riftians, spread into a line. We'll go forward together. Careful with your steps, now!" Silas instructed. The Riftians moved into a line as the other Societals stepped back and out of the way.

"We'll watch the falls," Nix volunteered as she made her way over to the entrance, along with the Kites and non-Riftians.

My hands shook as I grabbed Fell on one side and Vanya on the other. We'd had a problem on every Society thus far. It made it hard to trust that this time would be any different.

"Kena." Hale squeezed my arm before joining the others. "Please. Be careful with my home."

"I will," I promised.

That was one thing I was growing more and more confident I could deliver on. Using projection on the crystals was draining, far more so than controlling people. Even so, I didn't have to feel conflicted about it, which made it far preferable.

"Ready!" I yelled, and Riftians nodded down the line. Vanya, Hok, Silas, Fell, Marx, and others I still didn't know well. All supporting me.

I threw my arm out at the first clump of crystals. Fell grabbed onto that arm, keeping the connection. It wasn't as if projection was a visible skill, but I felt it when it slammed into the crystal.

The blues, greens, and oranges shone bright. Then they began to fuse. We were careful with our steps, the line twisting and spinning but never breaking. After the first round, Silas gasped and stepped out of the line.

I rushed over to check, and his arm had new crimson markings crossing his right forearm. He waved me off.

"Later. We finish this first," he insisted.

We moved throughout the cave until every bit of crystal shone underneath a smooth surface like glass, as much a part of the planet as the cave itself.

"Done," I pronounced, letting out a huff. Fell eased me down to the newly smoothed floor of the cave. I had no idea how he was still standing.

"Kena," he said, voice catching. I turned to see something shimmering in his eyes. When I reached towards him I caught a tear.

"Wha—" I stared at my hands, where the tear clung to my

finger. My marks were flickering and shaking. Dim and pale in places.

I set my jaw, pursing my lips.

"It's all right. It costs what it costs," I told Fell, though I didn't feel as certain as I sounded. What if I gave too much too fast, and like Ama, I disappeared? *Ascended*. But there was nothing for it. We had no other way.

As I watched the tear fall, warmth began to spread through my limbs. My opal marks grew brighter again, and I smiled as I looked over at Fell, thinking of our matching 'soul' marking. The thing that signified us as Connected.

I leaned forward, grabbing onto his ocala tunic and pulling him toward me. Our mouths crashed together, and he reached one arm around my waist, hauling me against him. When he pulled away, I reached up to run a hand through his silky black hair, and he jumped back.

"Your hand!" Fell gasped.

New markings ran onto the back of my hands and to my fingertips, where they had previously ended at my wrists. Glowing opal brilliance. Different on each side. I was getting better at reading, and I caught snippets of what was on them without even trying.

Fell must have caught my look. He grabbed my hands, turning them in his own as he looked at the new markings.

"What do they mean?" he asked, voice firm.

"It doesn't seem fair, when I haven't even read Silas yet."

"Kena?"

I bit my lip. He wouldn't like it, but we'd promised to be open with each other. I couldn't lie.

"On the left," I started, "it speaks of selfless giving, for the greater good. Which makes sense, since that's what we're trying to do with the crystals."

The interpretation was too similar to my father's ring. It sat in one of my bodysuit pockets, the moon quartz I'd been gifted on Clan sat in another. Both reminders of original owners who had died. I glared down at my left hand.

"And on the right?" Fell demanded, his hold on my hands gentle even as he pressed the issue.

"It, um." I gulped. "It's about risk. Deadly risk."

"I won't let that happen," he promised, closing his hands over mine. "You just rest. We should be safe behind the falls for now."

The Kites and others monitored the falls while the Riftians slept between the crystals.

"I don't think it makes us quite as tired as you, but I'm thankful for a nap all the same," Silas admitted, sitting down next to me once we were readying to leave.

"Do you want me to read your new marks?" I asked.

He held out his arm.

I laughed when I got a good look at them.

"What? What's funny?"

I shook my head, blond and white hair falling in my face before I brushed it away.

"Your marks are very insistent. They're as mission-oriented as you are. You've already got multiple that indicate things to do with leading or leadership in some way, and this is more of the same. More of a similar nature, at least."

"Oh?"

"They tell about making decisions based on the good of those you feel responsible for."

"That is something I always strive to do." He looked down at the marks, and I saw his original grey eyes through the crimson glow.

"Silas? What was your gift from Ama?" I'd been wanting to ask, and I wasn't sure when I'd get another opportunity.

He smiled.

"She left me a book."

I frowned at him.

"Your gift was waiting in the training arena. I'd assumed another sword, a mace, or something like that."

He nodded along.

"So did I."

"Then why leave it in the arena? Is it a book on fighting? War strategies?" I guessed.

"No. It's a book titled *Hobbies of Riftians*, and it includes chapters on things like gardening, birding, and woodworking."

My mouth fell open.

He gave a deep laugh.

"I know. I was surprised, too, but I think the Reader was just as smart as she gave herself credit for. Ama knew that just because I was good at fighting, it didn't mean I wanted to spend my whole life doing it. It reminded me of the idea that all the fighting leads somewhere, like a peaceful time where I *could* pursue a hobby. Where people could be safe, and happy. That's what makes it worth it. I think she was trying to make sure I didn't forget that."

My marks glowed with the happy thought.

"Who knows. Maybe I'll even take up woodworking," he said as he pushed himself to his feet.

"All right everyone, follow my lead." Tibby did a bit of jogging in place, her wings fluttering rapidly behind her. It looked like the Kite version of psyching oneself up. Nix waited in front of her, flipping a dagger back and forth in her hands. When Tibby nodded, Nix walked over and let the smaller girl grab hold of her. We all stood in a line behind Tibby, and when she saw a break in the falls she scrambled, running forward and flicking her wings out before sailing through.

I waited as Acaius and Ryshal embraced before approaching them so I could get strapped in. Fell tightened the straps that held me to Ryshal, buckling them in place.

"That's four down," he reminded me. I sighed, giving a weak nod. The others were tired, but I ended each of these sessions ready to collapse. There was no doubt in my mind by this point that even if they helped, most of the ability was coming directly from me. I was draining myself first. I held my hand up to him, and he laced his fingers through mine, kissing the new marks on my fingers.

"Ready?" Acaius asked, approaching my Connected.

"Ready," Fell confirmed, letting the dragon-winged man scoop him under the arms. Unlike the other pairs, Fell was able to run with Acaius as they moved toward the falls and give them more momentum. One of the benefits, I supposed, of being a sure-footed forest walker.

Ryshal let out a sigh as the two sailed cleanly through an opening in the current.

"They made it." I didn't have to ask whether he was relieved. I was as well.

"Us up next?" I questioned instead. Ryshal clapped his hands together in front of our faces, his wings temporarily blocking my view.

"Yep, just have to wait for the opening."

It was harder to see from this side of the falls, but everyone had been okay so far.

Looking behind us, I saw the dwindling group waiting. Part of me wanted to suggest that we go last and ensure everyone made it through, but a larger part of me just wanted to get back to the ship. The short rest we'd taken hadn't been enough after fusing all the crystals. I found myself longing for my cramped quarters on the ship.

"Now!" Ryshal yelled. I snapped my head up to see a break in the falls as the water came down. Ryshal took off sprinting for the water and I did my best to keep up, my feet dragging. I was going too slow.

Behind us, Shawd started shouting, but the sound was muffled by the falls.

"Rysh—falls not—enough!"

Ryshal's wings snapped open. Another second and we'd be through.

Something slammed into Ryshal and we were sent tumbling. Logically, I knew there was no way to hear anything over the thundering falls, but I felt like I heard Fell screaming my name. One of Ryshal's wings hit me in the face as he flapped wildly and we continued to plummet. He tucked one arm in tight by his side, but the other fumbled in front of us.

I realized what he was doing as the buckle around my waist snapped open.

CHAPTER 16

fell, screaming the whole way down and sucking water into my lungs.

Any air left was knocked out of me as I hit something. The impact was strong enough that I couldn't tell whether I'd landed on the water or the rocks. I was still conscious, but in enough pain that I wished I wasn't.

Given what we were trying to accomplish, my thoughts should have been selfless. It wasn't even that I was afraid of death; I simply couldn't afford to die. Not with all the work we still had left to do. Instead, though, I found myself thinking of when I'd first been in the Rift. I'd fallen over the edge of a log saving Ariadna, and Fell had thrown himself off after me, keeping me safe. He'd told me about his sister who had died at the site of a waterfall on Canopy. All I could think was that I couldn't put him through a loss like that twice.

I spun under the water, kicking frantically and ignoring the pain as best I could. I couldn't tell if I was making any progress at all. The water churned, and it was impossible to even determine which way was up.

As I began to lose consciousness, there was a tug on my arm. Two hands grabbed and pulled, and someone else wrapped their arms around my center. I was propelled through the water. When we broke the surface, I tried to breathe but found myself hacking and heaving water out. My throat burned.

"It's all right. We've got you." Veronica's vibrant blue eyes were staring at me from where she pulled, and I looked back to see Thea, with her orange marks, kicking and pushing from where she held my torso. Wincing from the pain of moving my neck, I let the two women haul me to shore.

They laid me on the beach, and my voice rasped.

"Ryshal?"

The shore was a scene of chaos. I heard yelling. Farther down the beach, Hok was carrying someone from the water in his arms. Acaius was wailing as they set Ryshal on the beach. The bat-winged Kite wasn't moving.

"Kena!" Fell dropped to his knees at my side, hands fluttering over me like he was afraid he'd injure me if he made contact. Did I look that bad? He might not be wrong; I hurt almost everywhere.

"Ryshal," I managed again, lifting one arm. It moved, so at least it wasn't broken. I tried the other one, reaching across my chest to point down the beach. "Ryshal."

"I'll go see. Try not to move," Fell urged before sprinting down the beach. Sand sprayed from under his feet with the first few steps, revealing his emotions. His marks were shining like the lights that danced in the Crew skies at night.

I rolled my head back to where I could face the sky. That position hurt the least.

"Hey, kid."

I blinked my eyes open to find Silas kneeling over me. I did my best to give him a wry smile.

"You haven't called me a *kid* in years. How bad is it? Everyone's telling me to just stay still."

"Not to be the voice of dissent, but I think we should start moving you. Not all at once; don't sit up! But slowly. Try flexing your feet, roll your ankle."

The voices from Ryshal's direction grew louder, but I let myself focus on Silas and his instructions. One muscle, one movement at a time. It helped. I didn't even realize how close I'd been to panic until the emotion began to dissipate. We made it up to my torso, and Silas asked for my permission before pressing on my ribs to see if anything was damaged.

"You knew I was about to hyperventilate, didn't you?" My question came out hoarse.

"Hmm." The sound was noncommittal, but I took it as a yes. "I recognize the reaction when I see it."

He'd been similar after his first markings; on the verge of panic when crimson symbols the color of blood had covered his arm.

After he'd lost his leg, he'd been despondent, and numb.

"I think you've broken a rib or two. Also, not that I've ever thought of you as vain, but I'm going to warn you now before you see a mirror—you're bruised all to hell," he cautioned me.

I appreciated the blunt information, even more so when Hale and Nix ran over, skidding to a stop beside us.

"Your face! You look like someone's painted you purple and red!" Nix blurted.

Hale put a hand on her shoulder, grimacing at me before he managed to fix his face into a more neutral expression.

"A bit of blood, a bit of bruising. You'll wash off your face and I'm sure it'll look much better than it does now. Not that it looks bad. It looks—okay, well, it *does* look bad, but not as bad as you're thinking it looks. If you're thinking you look like your face got smashed all to bits, well, I mean it's not that—"

Sarah threw a hand in front of him as she joined us and took over.

"You look like you've been kicked in the face by a Clan resident's hooves. Several times. There. Now she's got the idea."

My head was pounding, and the panic over Ryshal was creeping back in when the others parted. Fell walked between them, back to his silent steps.

"Ryshal?"

His lips were pressed in a thin line, brows drawn.

"He'll live. Shawd threw himself into the water when he saw what happened and managed to haul Ryshal away from the rocks until the Dagan could get to them both. Shawd's ripped out several feathers, and he's pretty bruised but otherwise fine. We think Ryshal broke his clavicle, and one of his arms. The wing on that side is badly torn. I'm not sure it's going to be mendable." He finished the last sentence in a rush, each word clipped and tense, as though he hated relaying the information.

"When we were falling, he kept one arm out so he could unbuckle me."

"He said he didn't want to risk you drowning, stuck attached to him when you hit the water," Fell confirmed.

I went to shake my head, then realized how bad it would hurt and thought better of it.

"The falls shredded his wing because he saved me. That's what happened, isn't it?"

He didn't answer me directly.

"You have nothing to feel guilty about. He doesn't regret his actions. Kena, this isn't your fault."

I turned away from him, looking at Silas. I didn't say anything. I didn't need to. He could relate to what Ryshal would be going through better than any of us. Losing a wing, for a Kite, was as close to losing a limb as anyone here had experienced.

"I'll talk to him. Be there for him, if he wants me to," Silas confirmed. "Although you're the one with more luck cheering people up."

I wasn't so sure about that anymore. My role had certainly shifted since we'd left Earth.

"I can try, but I might leave the bad jokes to Hale," I managed, earning a grin from my best friend.

"Are you okay if we pick you up? Someone will need to carry you back to the ship."

It wouldn't be Ryshal. I doubted it would be Shawd either,

from what they'd said about his wings. Two Kites out of commission. I cared more about them because they were friends, but it was impossible to deny that it hurt our efforts as well. I didn't regret for a moment that I was Riftian, but the benefits of flying in and out of tight spots was undeniable.

The others left and came back with Cassius. He flexed his arms, and gave me a tight smile that was a bit too large on his face. I guessed they'd told him to try to keep a positive attitude, but I caught him glancing over his shoulder to where the others had situated Ryshal in a net of some sort, held between two of his fellow Kites as they lifted him into the air.

"Ready to help me time how fast an ascent I can manage?" Cassius asked me. Fell leveled a glare at him, but I recognized that he was probably trying to lighten the mood.

"If you don't make it to the top of the falls in under a minute flat, I'll be thoroughly disappointed," I warned him. His smile relaxed, becoming more natural as he kneeled down and scooped me up. Instead of having me stand against him, he held under my knees with one arm, and supported my shoulders with the other. It seemed no one trusted me on my feet just yet.

In spite of his words, Cassius was careful and steady as we flew up and over the falls.

Once we landed on the deck of the *Nimitz*, Cassius kept me in his arms, tucking his wings and walking us down the stairs below deck.

Everleigh caught up with us below. She sucked in a breath at the sight of me, and I knew, if a Crew member was put off by my appearance, then I had to be a sight.

"You're lucky we thought to bring a mender along," Everleigh declared, as though it had been her personal idea. The mender in question made her way over to us. She looked vaguely familiar: a Dagan woman who had treated some of the wounded back on the Hub.

Fell came in, along with Hale and Nix, while the mender bandaged me up.

"She needs rest," the Dagan mender told the others tersely, flashing her spiny teeth at them.

Hale held up his hands.

"No arguments from me."

"What happened with the *Wavecutter*, any word?" I asked Everleigh, wincing as the mender dabbed some sort of cream on a very sore cheek.

"You'll be happy to know that our other two ships, and a stray bit of luck with the sea serpent, sent them running." She grinned for a moment, then her face fell into a frown.

"What? I thought you said we won?"

She gave half a nod.

"We did. It's just that, Crew don't tend to run away. I'm happy about it; I'm just surprised."

"Maybe there was something wrong with their ship? They needed to get out of range from us to go repair it," Hale suggested.

Nix stuck one hand under her chin as Kaos slid up her arm.

"Yeah, maybe."

None of them looked convinced.

After another stern warning from the mender, everyone but Fell cleared out. He took a bunk across from me.

"I don't want to jostle you," he explained.

"I look that bad, huh?"

"You look injured, not *bad*. I would be attracted to you no matter what, but I have no desire to hurt you."

I couldn't argue with his logic. Even lying in the bunk hurt. When I tried to adjust the way I was positioned, I let out a hiss against the pain in my ribs. My left leg had also started to cramp horribly, and I could feel that it was swollen around my knee. I was shocked the ocala bodysuit had made it through unscathed —a testament to the durability of the material. I felt for the moon quartz I'd been given on Clan, relieved to feel it still nestled in the pocket over my chest. Using it, or even knowing how to use it, was still something I had to figure out, but I'd been given the indication it was important. The ring was still in a pocket as well, and part of me wished it had fallen into the sea.

Between the injuries and my exhaustion from using projection on Crew's crystals, I wasn't much use to anyone.

"Hey," I whispered to Fell, noticing he was frowning at me, "four down. Only three to go."

"Five, if you count Tundra," he pointed out.

I started to nod, then thought better of it.

"I'll take whatever wins I can get."

"You should try and sleep until we reach the Doorway," Fell suggested.

I was tired enough to try, but being sore almost everywhere made it more difficult. In spite of my pain, I'd almost managed to drift off to sleep when the door to our bunk area slammed open. I jolted up in bed, then grabbed my side with a groan.

"We have company." It was Nix, and behind her I spotted Dex, Hok, and Silas in the hall.

"The *Wavecutter* came back," Dex informed us.

"And there's another ship with it. They've sent over a message. Bayard is on board," Silas added.

My cousin had terrible timing.

"Has he attacked us?" Fell asked the group.

"No, but he's said that he will. He's demanded we give him what he wants, *immediately,* or face the consequences."

"What does he want?" I asked, already worried I knew the answer.

Silas scowled.

"You."

CHAPTER 17

We didn't meet Bayard's delusional timeline.

The wooden hull of the *Nimitz* shook as whatever Bayard's ship was using battered the sides of our vessel.

I limped up the stairs toward the deck, leaning heavily on the rail for balance. As I reached my arm out to grab the rail, I noticed the purple, blue, and red bruises that served as the current backdrop to my opal markings.

A figure darkened the door to the deck above. Hale.

"He's demanding to speak with you, or he'll continue battering us," my best friend informed me.

"So I've heard," I grunted as he offered me a hand.

My grip tightened as anger at the injustice of the entire affair pulsed through me. Bayard had seemed so steady, so intelligent and fair-minded. He'd fooled me as much as my father had. Each time I was reminded of their actions, I had to shove down the small part of me that understood. Understood the way the Coalition had limited choices even with their Choosing, understood the imbalance within a seemingly balanced system. I had to ignore the fact that my biggest complaint was their method of

violence and murder, as I used it to fight back against them—
dragging myself down to their level.

"You're not going to do it, right?" The ship swayed, but it
wasn't pitching back and forth with the same violence as
moments before.

"Go over to his ship, or try to send it over the Edge like I
promised Everleigh?"

"Either. It would be foolish to try the first, and you're not in
any shape to attempt the second."

He wasn't wrong about that part. If we'd landed on Rover or
Clan within seconds, I doubted I could do much to affect the
crystals, let alone a living being.

I looked around at everyone running over the deck. Captain
Everleigh made her way over to us, face stern.

"Another message demanding you go over to him. More
ships who will support us are on the way, but the one Bayard
has is one of the Crew's fastest. We might be able to make it
around him and *Wavecutter*, but he'd be on our tail and likely
follow us to the Doorway."

Silas scowled.

"That does limit our options."

"We could sail somewhere random until we lose him, try to
sink both his vessels, or let him destroy us." Everleigh rattled off
the choices. "Or Kena can send them over the Edge, but I warn
you, we've sailed away from it now."

"It would have been tough for me before. I don't think I
could do it right now. Not at a distance, not injured, and not to
Bayard." I glared down at the deck while admitting all the ways
I was limited.

"You can't be thinking of going over there." Hale reached
toward me, grabbing my hand where the new markings glowed.

"If you don't, he said he'll come over and take you," Everleigh admitted.

"Well, we're obviously not handing her over." Hok crossed

his arms over his chest, scowling down at Everleigh. The Crew captain scoffed.

"I may be the best captain the Crew has ever seen, but I can't make this ship move any faster than its limits."

"I'll go over to them. At the very least, it could buy you all some time to come up with a better plan."

"Kena, you can't." Fell crossed over to me, standing at my back with his hands hovering without holding me, as if he were aware the action would disturb every new bruise. I leaned back against him.

"If you go over to that ship, they'll never let you go," Silas concurred. Hok and Vanya nodded.

"We can't trust Bayard," Vanya agreed.

"And if you aren't forgetting all the many stunts we've pulled, along with the people we've killed, the rest of the Spear would probably love to get their hands on you as well, *Puppet Master*," Sarah reminded me, using the nickname some of the Spear had adopted.

"We can't trust Bayard. But we might be able to trust Juliard, and we can definitely trust in Bayard's greed." I looked around at the group, willing my marks not to flicker with my hesitance at what I was about to propose. "I'm going to go over there; one leader to another. We'll tell him the Queen of the Alliance is willing to meet with him. We'll offer a temporary truce. They have ceasefires in wars all the time, right?"

I cast a glance over at Silas.

"They have them on Earth, but that doesn't mean people honor them," he grumbled. "It's a risk, no matter what we do. We pulled this stunt on Kite already. Both sides reneged on their end of the bargain."

"Yes, but he wasn't *on* Kite. Maybe he doesn't know about that," I argued.

"A ceasefire only happens when both sides agree to the benefit. What's everyone getting out of this? If we're going to entertain this idea, we need solid terms to present to him before you go over there."

I thought it through for a few moments before giving a careful response.

"We'd both benefit from the time. We need it to tend to our wounded and regroup. He might also have questions about where we've been and where we're going. We aren't sure what he knows. We could give up one or two locations."

I didn't like making any concessions at all. It already felt like we were moving at a breakneck pace to outsmart and outmaneuver my cousin, but if he stopped us here or followed us to Tundra, the entire thing would be pointless.

"It won't be enough for him. Someone like Bayard is only satisfied with a complete victory." Dex was probably right. He was mostly comfortable to roll with whatever plan the others had come up with, but I'd learned that when he did contribute his own thoughts, it meant he'd considered them carefully.

"He is intelligent, though. He only offered this because he's not sure he can win without you. Otherwise, he'd just try to annihilate us here and now, but he knows better. He knows we have a chance of slipping away here. He's got to be getting scared, no matter how overconfident he was initially. He knows Kena and the rest of us could beat him. We just need something else to sweeten the deal here. We can't give him your knowledge about the crystals, but maybe something else." Vanya had her daggers out and was spinning them in her hands as she spoke.

"It could actually be good if we could probe a bit on that. Figure out just what he does and doesn't know about the crystals," Silas added.

As they spoke, the answer came to my mind, but I didn't like it. Not in the slightest. Still, if it gave us the bargaining power to get away, I knew it's what she would have wanted us to do. Survive.

"I can think of something. Ama's journal."

Fell moved around to where he faced me, kneeling in front of me and taking my hands in his.

"If he reads that, he'll get the information about the crystals anyway. Exactly what we're attempting to avoid."

I shook my head.

"Not if we're very careful. When Ama was working with the journals she was still experimenting and pushing her abilities. What if I could, with the other Riftians' help, obscure key pieces of information? We leave the bits about the original planets having difficulty Assimilating in. We leave in the parts about leaving Lone, Ama's regrets, all of it. We just take out what she did to save Assimilation on the planets. We leave that a mystery."

"You're suggesting we send you over there even more drained than you already are." He frowned.

"At least that way we aren't giving him the answer outright."

No one liked the idea, including me, but no one could think of anything better. Our ships were low on supplies after being docked at the Doorway's island for so long. We had multiple injured Dagan and Kites. The Riftians were tired. A chance to get away and regroup was the best we could hope for.

The intricate work on Ama's journals was tricky but effective. I slumped against Fell as I finished obscuring the last bit with direct reference to how the crystals functioned.

"I know it's there, but when I try to read, I just skip over those bits," he confirmed as his eyes scanned the page. He took the heavy book from me, flipping it shut.

"Then we're ready," Silas pronounced.

"One more thing. Could someone hand me my pack?" Hale reached over, passing the bag I'd kept Ama's journal in. I rummaged through it, pulling out the ocala and Lone-metal circlet crown my uncle had left me just before he'd abandoned us on Lone.

Maybe its presence would unnerve him, or play on whatever guilt and affection he had left regarding the niece he'd left behind. Maybe it would remind him that he'd already left me once, and he owed me.

At the very least, it was something to distract from the bruises that covered the rest of me. The crown and my blessedly intact ocala bodysuit looked like something the Queen of the Alliance might wear. My battered appearance, not so much.

"Let's get going, everyone!" Hale yelled at the resistance members.

I reached out and put a hand on his arm.

"No, Hale. I think, just the Riftians should go."

It was a hunch, playing into Bayard's prejudices. He *used* other Societals, but he thought he was better than all of them. It might help us if he thought we did, too.

"Then, do I count?" Nien strode over to us.

"No." He opened his mouth to protest my response, but I plowed on. "Not because of any feud between you and I. I'm not sure he even knows yet that your kind of second Assimilation is possible. We're already giving up the journal. I don't want to be the one to tell him."

"But my marking. What if it means you're going to need help?" he insisted, as he followed my limping gait across the deck.

"We have no idea what it means," I countered.

"But it could—"

"Why are you being so quick to throw your life away? If you cared so little for it, maybe we should have gone through Pim's cell in the prison and left you for last!"

Nien froze. I regretted the words the moment they were out of my mouth. The cell we'd come out in was random. There was no way to know it was Nien's.

"I am sorry about your friend," Nien offered, "but that means I should go."

"No. Only Riftians. And not because that's how I feel. Because that's how it will look to Bayard," I clarified.

My cousin had made this personal, and I had every intention of showing him which Riftian would come out on top.

CHAPTER 18

We didn't lower planks between the vessels. I wanted it to be as easy as possible for Everleigh to separate and flee if necessary, not that running was in her nature.

Acaius was gentle as he lifted me in his arms to take me to Bayard's ship. Our remaining uninjured Kites carried the rest of our party, leaving us on the deck of Bayard's ship and then flying to hover off the sides in case we needed a quick exit.

Before coming to the Societies, I'd had a few hobbies on Earth, but theater had never been one. While I appreciated the skill, I knew I wasn't much of an actress. Still, I did my best to stand tall and appear as unbothered as I could in my current state. Bayard would surely sniff out any weakness and exploit it. One thing I did have going for me was the support of those surrounding me. I didn't have to fake the genuine care we felt for each other. Bayard's alliances were based on fear and bribes. Ours were based on compassion and a desire to protect who and what we loved.

Bayard wasn't waiting on the deck when we landed. We were surrounded by Spear members standing evenly spaced around the deck. Most glared at us. In between their ranks I saw Earthers, several holding guns. I wished we could have destroyed those weapons, along with the operating capacity of all the ships on Lone, but we'd done what we could. Bayard came up the stairs and joined us on deck within minutes. He was flanked on one side by Kaiser, the leader of the Earth militants, while my uncle stood on the other, bronze marks glowing in a soft hum, with a golden scythe strapped to his back. I could see the grey sheen behind the bronze in his eyes as he sought me out, and I pointedly focused on Bayard instead.

"Cousin. I am delighted you agreed to this little meet. I wish you hadn't brought along an entourage, but given my superior forces I can see why you felt the need for added security."

Entourage was hardly an appropriate description for our group. I'd been right to think Bayard would home in on whom I had brought with me. Fell and Silas stood to my left. Vanya, Hok and Marx were at my right side.

Bayard ignored Fell and the weapons instructors entirely, but he did look over at Marx and address him.

"Maker. I do apologize for the destruction of your grove. When this is over, you would be spared if you'll agree to work with us to re-establish it. Ocala could have so many uses if it weren't being hoarded selfishly. One or two items per Riftian—what a dull system. Ocala should be distributed and used by those in power who need it and most deserve it."

Marx answered for himself.

"It's true the material does have many uses. Although I'll admit I'd never before seen it weaved with metal from Lone. Is it true the mines on Lone, and what was found there, had properties that rivaled the rarest of Clan gems? Who knows what the Queen of the Alliance can do with hers."

Marx tilted his head in my direction.

Bayard's marks flared to life, sapphire glow that had no right looking as beautiful as it did washing across the deck as he turned his scarred face and glared back in my direction. Behind him, Juliard's markings wavered for a moment.

"From Lone, you say? My, my, the Reader was full of surprises. And here I thought the mines were emptied out."

Bayard didn't so much as glance at my uncle, which told me he hadn't bothered to mention what he'd left for me. Bayard assumed it was from the Reader.

Juliard was staring hard at me, but his focus wasn't on the crown, or my bruises, it was on my hands.

Only the Reader could interpret the intricate meanings behind Riftian markings, but some Riftians were able to garner the basics behind symbols that appeared frequently enough on people's skin. I wasn't sure how common all my markings were, but the way Juliard scowled at my hands had me wondering if he had gleaned their meaning well enough.

If I didn't know better, I might have guessed he was concerned for me.

"Ready to share some of your good fortune, Kena? Show me just how it is that you've managed to exert such influence over my army and your enemies? Provide us the details on just how the planets maintain Assimilation, and how I can control the source?"

I clenched my fists at my sides, determined not to let him see me shake.

"You know I can't do that. I'm still not ready to hand over these worlds to you. In fact, I'd say we've been one step ahead of you since you left Lone, but this might give you a chance to catch up." I was trying to balance taunting him enough to bait his interest, without insulting him so much he'd refuse. The line was thin. Bayard was hard to fool, but he had to be growing more and more desperate if he was spending his time chasing us around the worlds instead of using his forces on a single Societal overtaking, as he'd planned to do. He wanted to take care of us first. He'd given away that much with his actions.

"Just what would put us on an even field, then, in your mind? I've been playing this game a lot longer than you, and I think you'll find I've learned more about the Societies in my life-time than you will probably ever know."

"You're right," I acknowledged, "but there was someone who knew more than either of us. I've got Ama's journal. It includes her memories of Lone, the formation of the Societies, the founding of the Coalition, the beginning of Assimilation, all of it."

His fingers twitched, marks shining just an iota brighter as he heard the news. He was interested, all right, but he had himself back under control. When he spoke, his tone was noncommittal. He didn't even look at me; he stared at the blue and green lights overhead, as if he didn't care one way or the other about what I had to offer.

"What are your terms?"

"You let us go, right now. We sail away. We take a week for a truce. No killing. Either side. In exchange, we give you the journal and leave here with no further losses, on your side or ours. And, I don't force your crew to throw themselves over the side of this ship."

I didn't have the strength to back up my words, but I put as much force behind them as I could muster, and I saw several of the Spear surrounding him shrink back.

"You're not going to give in to the Puppet Master! Let's kill them now and move on. If you'd listened to me and started raining heavy artillery down on the other planets, we could have claimed victory and been headed back to Earth by now."

Kaiser stomped up to where Bayard and Juliard were stand-ing. He was an all too familiar and unwelcome presence. His hair was in the same buzzcut as always. He'd originally purported to hate the Societals, and I still fully believed he did. But what he didn't hate were violence and money. Many of the Earther task force members had been tricked by the Spear or bribed by promised technology and new worlds. They wanted results, instantaneous results, which was a stereotype of Earthers as much as glowing eyes were a feature of Riftians.

"And if we headed back to Earth,"—I turned my attention to Kaiser, as much to annoy Bayard as anything else—"what would we find?"

Bayard opened his mouth, but Kaiser stepped in front of him, speaking before he could.

"You'd find what you deserve. A planet full of people who fear and loathe you. The task force has been hard at work on that. Everyone down there thinks you're all backstabbers and betrayers. We levied all sorts of taxes and fees from around the globe to afford this specially trained force and firepower. It will all pay off, of course, not that those people will see the benefits. Many pay the price, and few reap the rewards."

I couldn't tell if he was baiting me or was just that wretched.

"And to ensure you were never found out, you saw to it that the Earthers who came up here had no home if they returned."

He put a finger on his nose, then pointed it at me.

"Bingo. But who would have you now? The way you look? At least we've still got those normal boys able to go home. As soon as we can pick up the task force and them on Lone, we'll—"

"Enough." Bayard raised his voice.

And it was enough. So, Derek and Mancio, two Earther teens who had betrayed us, were still alive and well. And on Lone. Along with the task force. That meant Bayard had left at least a few ships there, if he didn't have the space to transport everyone. Digit's meddling had worked after all.

Bayard directed his ire at the Earther militant.

"I will decide what terms we do or don't agree to. Your opinion is unnecessary. You're here for your show of force, not your brains," Bayard snapped at the man. Kaiser went a peculiar shade of red and raised a fist, as though he were coming at Bayard, but then dropped it and backed away. Juliard had pulled out his scythe, slamming the handle onto the deck.

Bayard gave a cold smile in Kaiser's direction, then turned his attention back to me.

"You will remain here until I have thoroughly reviewed the journal and can confirm it has the information I need," Bayard countered.

I had anticipated this, and I shook my head.

"No. I will stay long enough for you to read the first entry to ensure we've given you something authentic. The rest is up to you."

"Done." He extended a hand, offering to shake the Earther way.

I had to put effort into keeping my face neutral. I'd expected far more pushback, if we got any agreement at all. In spite of my insistence we try this, I was fully prepared to flee back to our ship and run.

After a moment's hesitation, I took his hand. His scarred eyes lingered on my new markings, but then he dropped them.

"We'll go to the captain's quarters. Juliard, myself, you, and one of the Riftians. Bring the forest walker if you like."

It was all I'd been able to manage so far to hold the book while keeping myself upright. The thought of even a walk to his quarters made me want to weep, but that would just be inviting an attack.

I glanced at the Riftians to each side of me, hoping before I spoke that Fell would understand my strategy.

"Silas. Would you come with me?"

Silas was a trained soldier, and he didn't give any outward sign that he'd expected any differently. He just looked in my direction, face flat and expressionless as he answered.

"Of course, Kena."

We followed my uncle, Kaiser, and Bayard to the door leading below deck.

"After all, we Earthers have to stick together, don't we?" Silas added, earning a few jeers from the surrounding Spear. I looked back and saw him smirk as we descended the stairs, while behind us Kaiser's Earthers and the Spear began arguing.

CHAPTER 19

When we hit the bottom of the stairs, I caught my cousin scowling back at me. This wasn't going as he'd anticipated. Good. It would be better for us if I could keep him on his toes. One blessing of being on an enemy's ship, or any of the Crew ships, really, was that they were more spacious on the inside than any large ship I'd heard of back on Earth. The corridors allowed Silas and me to walk side by side. His crimson markings kept an even glow in the hallway, the colors mixing on the wall with Bayard's sapphire blue.

It was only when Bayard showed us into his quarters that I broke my stoic exterior and gasped. The office wasn't like the haphazard lodgings that I'd seen on Hale's ship. It was a near-replica of the delegate offices from the Hub. He'd styled it similar to Warrick's, with a large desk in the center and shelving on the walls, lined with books and objects whose uses and sentimentality I could only guess at.

"How long have you had this ship?" I couldn't help asking.

His eyes were dulled and the skin around them scarred red from Dagan puffer poison, but they still flashed a short blue gleam as he responded.

"How long has the resistance been around? How long were

Societals denied the right to go back to Lone? Some span of years in between those two, I'd say."

The cold, calculated Societal in front of me made me wonder how I ever mistook Bayard for anything but a villain.

"I respected you. I looked up to you," I admitted. I looked at him, and then to Juliard.

It was nothing they didn't already know. If it weren't for Fell, and my friends, I'd have been convinced that I only gave my heart and my trust to all the wrong people.

Bayard just scoffed.

"Now then, the journal. Hand it over, unless you'd like to tell me what you're doing with the crystals, or show me how to use projection to control people. Your *choice*."

I pulled the book from my satchel and handed it over, trying to keep the pain of losing it off my face.

Bayard grabbed at it greedily, clutching the book as he made his way to his desk. He scanned the symbols on the front, Lone writing.

"Yes, yes, there's the map." He'd recognized the map of Lone embossed on the book immediately. "But what of the crystals?"

He flipped open the cover and began to read, his eyes scanning the page with speed and flipping to the next. It should have been enough to convince him the tome was readable.

He waved a hand at the door of his quarters without glancing up.

"Block the doors."

From the hall, two Spear, a Kite whose wings couldn't quite expand to their full shimmering width in the space, and a Dagan armed with puffer darts, stood in front of the door. They parted to let Kaiser enter the room. He stood with a gun slung in front of him.

Silas glared down at the weapon.

"You really need that to win your fights?" he demanded of the Earther.

Kaiser scoffed.

"I'd be a fool not to use everything at my disposal. The guns, the recruits from Earth, the technology and land, from our good friends the Spear."

I didn't think Kaiser noticed when Bayard frowned. Behind the desk, Juliard tensed. They might be allies, but they weren't friends. It had to eat at Bayard, being tied to someone like Kaiser. The Earther's fight-craving and impulsive attitude would have prompted me to say he'd fit in with the Crew, at least when I first arrived at the Hub. Now, I knew enough about each Society to realize they were much more than the first impressions they gave. Kaiser didn't understand loyalty; he didn't understand any of the good qualities that would have made him fit with any Society.

Bayard flipped another couple of pages, taking his time.

"You've seen more than enough to know it's legitimate. You're coming dangerously close to breaking our deal and this truce." Silas's voice came out low, almost a growl.

Bayard paused, raising one eyebrow as he matched Silas's stare.

One advantage of Silas? Bayard didn't know him nearly as well as the other Riftians. Vanya, Hok, and Fell had felt even more betrayed by Bayard than me. They'd grown up training under him. The Riftian had only known Silas for a matter of months, and while Bayard had witnessed his skill during weapons training, I had no doubt that Silas hadn't shown the Riftian everything he knew. Bayard glanced down pointedly at Silas's leg. Another advantage. Bayard looked down on weakness. When Silas first lost his leg it was traumatic, and there was no denying that, but he didn't see it as a weakness anymore. Ama had provided him a special ocala prosthetic, and he'd adapted all his moves and balance.

"They have a point. This army is fractured enough as it is; if we want to have anything to hold together after this fight is over, we've got to start leading with some honor and decency," Juliard insisted from his son's side.

Bayard cut a gaze at my uncle that would have terrified a weaker man.

Perhaps he forgot that Juliard had been around longer than he had, and had used projection skillfully to hide himself in plain sight all those years. I hadn't. Which was why I was surprised when Juliard looked down in the face of his son's anger.

"Ultimately, though, it's up to you. This is your fight."

That wasn't the Juliard I knew.

"You're right. It *is* my fight. You and Uncle Tiberius had your chances, and you failed."

I swallowed anger and bile. Bayard had no right to speak of the man he'd killed, one crime on top of so many others.

Bayard closed the book, leaving it on the desk as he stood and walked over to me. He placed a hand on my shoulder, and I pulled away.

"Now then, cousin, Juliard does have a point. You're doing something to those crystals, and if you won't show me, then I'll just have to dog your steps until we find out. I had my own plans with the Societies, but finding out yours is more important. I've waited lifetimes; I've learned patience."

"That's just fine with me. As long as you remain one step behind me, you'll never win," I couldn't help snarking. It wasn't like me to talk before thinking, but staring into the face of the man who'd killed my father and cost me my friends, I found myself unable to contain *all* of my bitterness.

Bayard raised a hand as if he were going to slap me, his face tense. I didn't even flinch when he brought the hand down.

"Don't!" Juliard yelled behind him. Bayard's hand paused just before it made contact with my already bruised cheek. "What purpose would that serve? We've got what we need. The book. You'd already learned the crystals existed, because I told you about Ama's plans to bring something to Earth to enable Assimilation."

"You told me *something* existed. We had to follow my cousin to the Twilight Grove to figure out what it was. And the only ones we have lose their light and die the minute they're moved!"

Bayard took a few deep breaths, then smoothed his tunic.

"Be that as it may, I am a reasonable Societal. We've got the journal, and in her current state I doubt my cousin could fight off a young Blank, let alone those of us in this room. Kena, you may leave. *You*, however,"—he pointed at Silas—"will be staying right here. I wanted the forest walker, but anyone my cousin cares about will do."

"That's not what we discussed!" I snapped at Bayard, moving myself between him and Silas.

"Come now, Kena, you didn't really think I'd leave without some leverage."

No doubt it looked ridiculous—a bruised, thin woman blocking a large, muscled man. I wasn't letting anyone else go without a fight.

"Kena." Silas's voice was soft behind me, and unless I imagined it, he was touched by the gesture.

"You're stalling me today, Kena, but know this. For every one of my Spear that you harm, for every time you thwart me in the future, he will suffer. If I have to, I'll follow you to every Society, taking your friends as I go, until this ridiculous mission ceases. Then, after these delay tactics, I'll go back through the planets until I've conquered every single Society. The end result will be the same, but the extra suffering will be on your hands. Is that really what you want?"

He would do it, and he could do it, but he wasn't getting Silas.

Kaiser stepped forward and Silas wrapped his arms around me in a hug.

He spoke over my head.

"It will be okay, Kena."

Then Silas leaned forward, his whisper so quiet that even with enhanced Riftian hearing Bayard wouldn't have heard it across the room.

"Duck."

I let my knees give out; it was the easiest move I'd made all day. The difficult part was going to be getting back up.

Kaiser started to lower his gun in Silas's direction, but the Riftian slammed into Kaiser's chest before he got the chance. The gun went off, and my ears were ringing. A hole had been blown through the door of Bayard's office, and the Dagan guard was rolling on the ground and holding an injured leg.

The other guard ran in, his wings folded to fit in the space as he lunged at me. The next part was the hardest. I forced myself up, grabbing the daggers from where they were sheathed on my legs. The ax would have been better, but in my injured state the lighter daggers were easier to wield. I didn't stand a chance of winning with strength alone, and I wasn't particularly quick. I had to let the Kite get in a few more blows to get myself in position to make a few well-placed jabs.

"Run!" Silas yelled, grabbing me around the middle and hauling me past the injured Kite into the hall.

Two more Spear members, one from Dagan and one from Clan, rounded the corner into the hall, no doubt drawn by the shouting and the gunshot.

The Dagan opened his mouth, ready to spit darts at us.

"No!" I yelled, throwing an arm out. He stopped, clutching at his mouth that was no longer cooperating.

I was ready to collapse, as the command had sapped most of my remaining strength. We had to get through them.

"Let us pass, or I will make you swallow them," I threatened. The Dagan's clouded eyes went wide, and he practically shoved the other Spear member out of the way to let us through.

"You're building quite a reputation," Silas said, laughing, as he hooked my arm over his shoulder and helped haul me to the top of the steps. He propped me up as we got close to the deck, and I knew if we wanted to leave I'd need to walk on my own. The Spear on deck couldn't think me weak.

"Cousin!" Bayard's yell echoed behind us. I turned and saw

him pulling out a weapon. He, like a few Riftians, was a dual master. Often, he had a collapsible scythe similar to what Juliard wielded. But he also used throwing knives with great precision.

He moved to throw one, but a golden weapon sliced in front of him, blocking his throw.

Juliard moved around his son, not harming him, but fighting him off as he tried to follow us. He managed to shove Bayard off, throwing him through one of the open doors in the hall and slamming it shut.

"Juliard!" I yelled at him. Bayard would no doubt break out of the door within seconds, and if a real fight broke out between the two of them, I wasn't sure who would win.

"Go. We must do what we must do, and it costs what it costs," he yelled.

"Wha—"

"Move!" Silas shoved me up the stairs, farther and farther away from my uncle. I stumbled up the last step and Silas righted me as we reached the deck.

Between the slosh of the waves and the general din of Spear members running to and fro to complete jobs on the deck, our scuffle downstairs appeared to have gone mercifully unnoticed. The rest of the Riftians waited for us, staring down the Spear that surrounded the edges of the deck. The only signs of tension were their flickering marks and the way Fell's jaw was clenched shut, one hand hovering over a dagger.

Knowing we had limited time, I did my best to move quickly across the deck. As soon as we got within Riftian hearing range, I called out to the others.

"Signal."

As one, our markings flared into vibrant light. In this situation, letting tense emotions loose wasn't hard to do. Leafy green, liquid silver, twilight blue, opal, crimson, and emerald shone over the deck and to the sky.

Within moments I heard the flapping of wings, and then thuds as the Kites landed on the deck.

"Kena first," Fell told Acaius, who had already scooped me into his arms. We shot off the deck as below us the others were collected. Cassius hauled Hok up, muscles tensed as he lifted the larger man. Tibby pulled Vanya off the deck. The whir of her green wings mixed with the leafy glow of Vanya's markings as they soared from the ship. Kites I wasn't familiar with took the others; I was just thankful several new faces had joined us from Nimue's domain. Purple wings with a sheen more like silk than feathers blocked Fell's face as they flapped.

"The ships are on the move already; we'll catch up to them," Acaius yelled in my ear.

Good, they'd stuck to the plan. We'd told the others that as soon as the Riftians reached Bayard's ship, they were to start sailing away.

The figures below us were growing more and more distant, but with Riftian sight I was able to see well enough when Bayard burst onto the deck, sapphire markings shining as he yelled at his Spear crew.

I let out a sigh of relief when bronze light followed shortly after. I didn't know what Juliard had said or done, but at least Bayard had left him free and breathing.

"Hold on!" Acaius warned me as we swooped; an arrow whooshed past. I saw a few of the Earthers on deck raise guns, but Bayard waved them down. He still wanted me alive. That gave us an advantage. A couple of the soldiers disobeyed, firing wild shots into the sky.

In quick succession they fell to the deck, with Vanya's arrows through them.

The events of our time on Crew caught up to me. Once we were out of range of Bayard's ships, their metal hulls a blur in the distance for even Riftian vision, I closed my eyes. I let myself fall asleep, napping in Acaius's arms until we reached the *Nimitz*, then sailed for the Doorway.

CHAPTER 20

We sat on the snowy ground of Tundra, and Dex sharpened a sword, his movements even and methodical.

"There's nothing for it. I can't think of a single spot the crystals might be. It's not as if there's a lot of us to ask," he muttered, eyes focused on his task. His skin glinted with dried sweat, even in this snowy area. He was one of the Societals who had trained during every spare moment we had on Tundra. We didn't trust Bayard to give us a whole week of peace, but according to Digit, it wouldn't matter much.

"We'd still be able to beat him to Clan or Rover. My only caveat is that he might have a welcome party waiting for us like he did on Kite, but I'd be surprised if we saw Bayard himself," she had informed us.

We'd decided to chance at least a few days of recuperation. My side still ached over my healing ribs, but the menders had worked wonders on the rest of me. My left leg only hurt after being on it for a while, and the bruises were fading.

We were huddled around a fire, and I basked in the warm glow while the others debated whether Rover or Clan should be next on our list. I sported nothing new but my bruises, although several of the resistance had fresh black and white tattoos. Everleigh had declared that, after the events at the Edge and our saving of the crystals, such marks had been earned.

I wasn't surprised when Digit, Nix, and Hale had clusters and outlines of crystals placed on their arms. What had taken me aback was the number of others who'd taken Everleigh up on her offer. Several of the Kites, including Cassius, Shawd, and Acaius, had tattoos as well. Ryshal was still recovering, but he'd allowed them to tattoo a huge set of falls going down his uninjured arm. Even Hok and Vanya had agreed to crystals. Hok's was larger, fitting between some markings on his shoulder, and Vanya's was at her wrist.

The new tattoos made the group look even more united as they discussed potential strategies.

"He's right. There's a few dozen Clan with us, but none who claim to have any knowledge of where they might be hiding a bunch of crystals," Silas added.

Fell shook his head.

"Bayard knows he has a hold on that Society. If I were him, that's an area I'd have secured early on."

Vanya nodded, the braids on one side hitting her shoulder. Her leafy green marks glinted.

"He's nothing if not intelligent. We've already wasted enough time. He won't. He'll be shoring up whatever holds he does have. And that definitely includes the Clan. He's got the numbers. He can just plant his Clan Spear members all over the mountains and mines and defeat us that way. Without a destination in mind, we'd be just as likely to stumble upon Spear sympathizers as we would the crystals."

"No one wants to say it, but could we just cut our losses with that planet?" Nix asked. She raised her palms as several of the others shouted her down. "All right, all right, okay! Just a suggestion." Kaos slithered onto her shoulder and hissed at the Societals who were shouting at her. The serpent had really taken to her since her uncle Warrick's death. She was the first non-

Rover to have a serpent. Nien with his mark, the Crew tattoos, Nix with her serpent, and Alsey with her wings: we were changing the landscape the Coalition had created.

Across from Nix, Hok held Sarah's hands. Her serpent, Charles, blended in with his night-black hair as the snake wove between the strands.

"Maybe we're thinking about this all wrong. The Clan residents aren't like the rest of us. We've been thinking the crystals might be somewhere in the snowy mountains because it's the roughest terrain, right?" Hok gave Charles a pat on the head as several of us in the group nodded or murmured an affirmative response.

"But the Clan residents don't care. Even in Crew, where they're fearless, it wasn't about the danger of the location. It was about how much planning and plotting went into getting there. Crew are brave, but straightforward. We need to think like the Clan. Based on their lifestyle and values, where would the crystals be least likely to have been discovered?"

Fell's eyes got a shade brighter as he squeezed my hand.

"They're industrious. They're hard-working. Overlooked and under-appreciated by many other delegates when it came to Hub leadership. There's never been a Clan Magistrate." He tallied the items on his fingers.

"They don't care about that stuff, though," Dex interjected. "We aren't like that. We're more rugged and lower maintenance than most Societals. We care about function. Being useful."

"The gems!" I all but shouted as Dex stopped to stare at me. I felt my cheeks heat. "Sorry. But I think I've got an idea. When I was first there, our tour guide told us about how they hauled off most of the gems they mined and tossed them. That they sold them to other Societals but didn't care about them unless they served a purpose."

That same delegate had died for our cause. I owed him a great debt. He'd also given me a gem that *was* useful. At least according to him. A rose gold moon quartz that sat in the chest pocket of my bodysuit. I gave it a pat, reassuring myself of its continued presence. The crystals were our first priority, but if I could, I wanted to find out what it was for while we were on the mining planet.

"She's right," Dex allowed, shaking out his horns. "We keep the gems for bartering and trade with other planets, but unless they're dumping more cartfuls, they're largely ignored by the Clan residents themselves."

"Where do you keep the gems?" Silas demanded, eyes gleaming. "I think we've got our plan."

The following morning, we scrambled one by one out of the Doorway on Clan.

"Wow." Hale's mouth dropped open as he craned his neck over the edge of a very steep drop.

"We're inside the *peak* of one of the mountains. Stay back from the ledge," Dex cautioned, throwing wide arms out to prevent anyone else getting too close. The Doorway was at the top of a narrow set of stone stairs that led down into the darkness. I noted there wasn't so much as a handrail or support. Fear twisted my gut. When I fought, there was always the chance of death, but to an extent I could rely on my skills and my friends. If I took a wrong step and went tumbling into the deep dark of the mines? I couldn't argue with gravity.

"You think you could fly down and save us faster than we could fall?" Cassia asked her brother, nudging him with her elbow as she echoed my concerns. He gave her a wry smile.

"Please. With these wings?" He extended each one, and they glinted in the dark. "Piece of cake." His voice wavered on the last words as he stared over the edge himself.

"Just, um, how far down are we going?"

"It's really not any warmer here, is it?" Sarah grumped, wrapping a furred coat tighter around herself and her serpent. Dex shook his head.

"Nope. We're near the top of one of the snowy peaks. This peak has been mined out. That's why the resistance chose it for the Doorway. There's nothing valuable here. No reason anyone would come looking."

"Well, I vote we take turns going down on Kite-air." Hale gave a pointed look at the winged members of the party.

"Sorry. Not an option. There are bits of hanging chain, rocky overhangs, and who knows what else scattered around here. I wouldn't recommend the Kites unless someone actually is plummeting to their doom." The group's chatter went silent at Dex's words.

There was only one option: a long and tedious walk down to the base of the mountain.

By the end of the first day of traversing the stairs—and we'd only decided it was the end because we were exhausted and had come to a narrow ledge where we could lean and rest—Dex predicted we were maybe two-thirds of the way down.

"Just great. If we fall tomorrow, perhaps we'd only break something instead of dying." Nix wasn't the only one in a foul mood. The day had been grating on everyone. Fell and Dex, along with the few Clan who had joined us, tackled the stairs better than anyone else. The rest of us were on edge from a series of near-slips, trips, and tumbles. Cassius and Shawd might have been in the worst mood of all. They'd had to keep their wings tucked in tight all day, and I had no doubt they cramped terribly. Shawd still had a patchy spot on one wing, but he was able to fly, albeit with decreased balance. Ryshal was still healing, and Marx had decided to stay behind as well, citing work on a new ocala wing for the Kite.

As we readied for another day of trekking down the Clan stairs, I tried to find a way to lighten the mood.

"I would have thought Crew members would be used to steep drops," I teased Nix. She stood with her back pressed up against the rock, as far from the edge as she could get. She sneered at me.

"We're fearless when the occasion calls for it; doesn't mean I throw myself off the side of the ship just for the thrill of it. Although ..."

She smirked as she put a finger to her chin, possibly considering the scenario.

"Who are you, and what have you done with my best friend? You're growing a sense of humor," Hale joked with me as he threw his small pack over his shoulder. I held nothing but my weapons. Fell shouldered a small pack for us both. I planned to bring back more crystals for Tundra if possible.

"Maybe I can Assimilate sarcastic wit the same way some do wings," I suggested to Hale.

"The closer we get to the bottom, the quieter we should be," Dex warned. "There's no telling who's milling about down there. We don't want to give ourselves away."

We continued down the stairs for what felt like hours, but it was impossible to tell. With no sky overhead, and no routine, there was no way of judging. It was a relief when Dex whisper-yelled from the front of the line. I'd been in almost a trance as I wove my way down the steps in front of Fell, and I jumped at the sound.

"We're at the bottom. Don't lose your balance on that last step," Dex urged.

One by one, we hit the flat ground. We didn't have the illuminated headlamps Clan members often gave their visitors for the dark environment. Dex and the others who lived on the planet could see just fine on their own. The rest of us had to rely on the light put out by the Riftians' markings.

Dex led us straight into one of several tunnel entrances near where the stairs ended. The one he chose grew more and more cramped as we walked on.

"How much further?" Cassius demanded, his shimmering wings tucked in as far as they would go. His bottom feathers trailed the ground, and the swell of his wings brushed the rock above us.

"Now, brother, don't tell me you're not enjoying the adventure." Cassia flashed her fangs at him in a grin.

"You wouldn't be either, if you had wings. That I can promise you," Cassius grouched. The other Kites with us murmured agreement.

"We're close," Dex assured them.

He was right. Compared to the climb down, it took almost no time at all to make our way through the tunnel and to another cavern. This one was massive, but it was stuffed with piles and piles of glimmering gems.

CHAPTER 21

T he sheer amount of glittering jewels was staggering.

"We found it," Hale exclaimed.

"Hard not to think what this would be worth to Earthers," Sarah whispered as she stared up at the innumerable stacks.

The piles weren't organized in any particular way that I could see. Larger ones leaned and toppled onto smaller ones. Some held a singular shade, like gold. Others held a mix of ruby, emerald, and pink stones. There were narrow walkways between some of the piles, but I didn't like how precariously everything appeared to be stacked. One accidental bump and thousands of solid gems would be tumbling down on us. We'd entered on the widest path, which appeared to divide the room in half, with smaller, cleared trails winding between the stacks on the sides.

"Everyone watch your step," Fell warned the others as he stepped over a fallen gem the size of his head.

"Maybe you'd better go in front, along with Dex and the other Clan residents. You can help us find the safest areas to put our feet," I suggested.

He nodded, moving to where Dex stood discussing our options with the other Clan residents present.

"We'll split into groups. That will make the search quicker and decrease our chances of bumping into one another *and* the gems. They may look pretty, but any one of these piles could bury you alive," Dex warned.

"The weight would crush you before anyone could dig you out," another Clan resident confirmed.

"Lovely." Cassia rolled her eyes. Vanya chortled at her side.

I joined Fell's group, and we made our way along a path that took us left.

"They couldn't put just one of these crystal things anywhere easy to reach," Digit grouched from beside me.

I cast a questioning glance at her.

"Sorry. I'm just sick of this whole thing, and the lack of sleep is getting to me. I don't really see the point of all these jewels. They'd be so valuable on Earth, and up here they're just piles of heavy trash that could crush us."

I moved to pat her shoulder, meaning to be comforting.

My hand stopped before it made contact.

"Wait. Digit, you're a genius!"

She scoffed, a smile playing at the edge of her lips. She reached up, her blue circuitry tattoos contrasting against her Crew ones as she smoothed her short hair down with one hand.

"Tell me something I don't know. But why this time, specifically?"

"The weight!" I realized how loud I was being and lowered my voice, trying again. "The weight. These piles of gems would have been heavy enough to crush and crack the crystals. The Clan might not care about things just because they're pretty, but they *do* care about function. They wouldn't risk losing the key to their Assimilation that way. Residents now have no clue, but the individuals who helped Ama place them would have been well aware of their value. I'll bet they started building the piles as a distraction. The gems might even be more than just a deterrent because Clan won't care about them. They're a defense. Who's going to go past this many piles? You'd take what you could and leave if you thought they were valuable, and ignore them entirely if you didn't."

"So the gems are—" Hale led me to the point. He and Nix made up the rest of our small group.

"On the edges of the room. The sides furthest from the entrance, I'd guess," I finished.

Fell led us along a few more winding paths before we managed to make it to the wall of the cave, where rock rose behind the piles, and sure enough, I saw dazzling light that looked almost like the gems, but that in fact came from crystals.

Hale and Nix broke off, going after the others and bringing them back to us.

"I've never seen anything like this," Dex breathed out as his group joined us.

The crystals on each planet had shone with colors like its inhabitants: stark black and white mixed with sky colors for Crew; the astounding array of colors for Riftian markings. The Kites' crystals had imitated the colors of their green vines and the multihued patterns of their wings.

"They don't look like all the gems. They look like us." One of the Clan members looked awed, eyes wide, as she approached the crystals with her arms outstretched.

The crystals were shining, beautiful, and filled with neutral colors: the greys and blacks of the rock within the mines, the browns and taupes of furred Clan legs, the colors of their horns and their hooves. A couple of the Clan who were with us had tears running down their faces.

"No one ever values us for what we are," Dex explained. After a few more moments of gazing at the crystals, Dex shuffled the Clan residents and non-Riftians away to give us room to work.

"We'll guard the paths leading here," he promised.

As before, the Riftians formed a line, careful not to bump the piles behind us as we began to work our way around the rim of the cavern wall.

I was huffing, my breath coming in short bursts, by the time we'd fused most of the crystals. I'd also tucked some away for Tundra. Fell had a sheen of sweat on his forehead. Hok looked woozy, wobbling a bit as Sarah ran to brace him under his arms. Under different circumstances it would have been comical to see the thin woman supporting such a massive, muscled frame. Silas and Vanya were leaning against one another for support as we continued.

"Just a few more attempts and we'll be done," I encouraged everyone. I felt wrung-out and trampled on, but it wouldn't help to let them know that.

"Kena," Fell whispered, pulling up a strand of my hair. I grabbed at the hunk he held in his hand, his fingers closing around a single piece. It had gone stark white, like the pieces before.

"Next is translucent," he reminded me.

What scared me more is that I hadn't even noticed it happening. I'd been too focused. I'd thought I had enough strength. My Crew injuries and confrontation with Bayard must have taken more out of me than I realized.

My fingers shook as I reached out and held the strand. I stared for a few moments, quiet, my lips pursed, before dropping the hair and running my hands through it to put it back in place.

"It doesn't matter. It's just hair. Ama ascended. She died. She gave everything for these people. If I go grey a bit early, where's the harm?"

He frowned at me but took my arm and turned back to the crystals. We both had to know what I wasn't saying. It wasn't just a hair. It was a price being paid, one small piece of me at a time. In truth, I had worried the cost would be much higher and that I wouldn't be able to finish what I needed to do. The white and translucent strand had shaken me, but if that was all it took to save Clan, how could I deny them?

"Kena, do you need to stop? We can try to find another way," Hok offered. Sarah nodded along beside him.

"Yeah, Queenie. You don't have to carry all of this."

It was a nice gesture, but it was false. We had no other plan.

At the rate it was going, no matter how tired it made me, I'd still be left with plenty of myself when we were done. I wasn't worried about losing myself *that* way; it was my emotions that had taken the biggest battering. I'd let every hair on my head go tundra-snow white before I endured another loss of friends or family.

We were on the next to last bit of crystal when Acaius rounded one of the piles, sprinting for all he was worth, his wings snapped tight against his back to avoid any accidents.

"We're not alone. They're here," he hissed as he slid up next to us.

"Kena, you'd better hurry, we—" Cassius came running from another direction, and as he did the edge of his longest feather tapped a hot pink gem. Just one. I held my breath as it slid from the pile. It clinked and echoed as it fell down the stack, landing with a hard thud on the ground.

I let out a breath when nothing worse happened.

"We've only got one or two sections left," I promised, throwing my arms out and going back to work.

I heard shouting in the direction from which the men had run in.

"They know we're here!" Acaius turned his back to us, snapping his wings open to block us from any oncoming Spear, but none came.

Instead, we heard pounding, and cracking.

Hale and Nix rounded a pile, sprinting to us with Digit behind them.

"They're hammering the walls! I think they're trying to cause the piles to give way!"

Hale had no sooner spoken than I heard the clinking and ringing of gems cascading down. The piles near us shook and trembled.

"Run!" Cassius shouted as the pile behind him began to tumble. Fell shoved me, forcing my body out of the way as the mountain of discarded wealth rained down. The gems from the first pile crashed into the surrounding ones as they went, creating a chain reaction. It was an avalanche of jewels, and we were no better off in here than if we'd been in a real avalanche out in the snowy mountain peaks of Clan.

"Fell, the bag!" Without breaking stride, he looped around and grabbed the pack he'd carried with us. Before starting our work fusing the crystals, we'd dug some out and put them in the pack to transport back to Tundra. He caught up to me and grabbed my hand as we kept running.

I turned to look behind me as we fled, a rainbow of potential death flowing after us like a river.

"Cassius!" Fell yelled, his voice rising to a volume he almost never used. "Take her!"

The Kites had given up staying on the ground, our cover already blown.

Overhead, Acaius was flapping hard to stay aloft as he held Digit under one arm and Nix under the other.

Cassius dove, scooping me around the middle.

"No, I—" My arm was wrenched from Fell's as Cassius pulled me away from my Connected. He swooped again, grabbing his sister with his other arm.

"Fell!" I screamed as a crush of gems tumbled toward him and he leapt up another pile, trying to get out of the way.

"It's no good—the way we came in is blocked!" Cassius yelled over the noise as he wheeled and turned toward the other entrance. The one the Spear must have used.

The only benefit to the avalanche was that, just as quickly as they ran in, our enemy turned to run out again. The Spear already in the room were caught as much as we were.

"What do you want me to do?" Cassius asked as we began to descend. He swooped to the side as several darts sailed in our direction. Most of the gathered Spear blocking our escape were Clan, but a few Dagan were scattered among them, poisoned darts at the ready. With the weight of two passengers, his movements were unsteady, and one dart just barely missed his wings.

Other Kites circled hesitantly near us.

"Drop me in the front," I instructed. "Don't land. Then turn around and go back for Fell."

"Are you sure?"

"Yes!" I urged.

"I'm sorry, Kena," he said, voice soft as we got close and he let me go. I couldn't help screeching as I plummeted, but managed, thanks to Fell's training, to tuck-and -roll as I landed. I was tired and bruised, my ribs screamed at me, but I came up running. I heard the thuds of several others landing behind me.

"Run!" I threw my arm out, projecting at the Spear with all the energy I had left. Two of the three dart-throwers turned and ran away, along with a few Clan.

"Drop them!" I yelled at the last Dagan. She tossed the poisoned darts aside.

The Clan members scrambled back and out of the tunnel as I surged forward, arms raised.

"It's the Puppet Master," one yelled.

"She burned Kidan alive!" another screamed back. I faltered, lowering my hand for a moment.

Murderer.

They hadn't said it, but I still thought it.

The Spear saw themselves as liberators, correcting a broken system. In their eyes, *I* was the villain.

Bayard and those closest to him were the ones manipulating everyone.

Still, they had been killing us indiscriminately.

Was there really a victory if we weren't willing to respond to violence with violence?

Maybe there was, but we didn't have time to find that way.

I squared my shoulders and marched forward again with one hand raised. I would send every one of them back into the avalanche of gems they'd created, if that's what it took.

CHAPTER 22

We fled into the tunnel behind the Spear. A few of the Clan in front of me lowered their horns and started to charge. I opened my mouth to send them running past us into the avalanche.

"Ahh!" A yell sounded overhead as Iduna swooped in, dropping Vanya just before barreling into and knocking over three Clan members. Vanya was right on her heels, daggers out and slashing at the rest of the line.

The remainder of our attackers scattered, fleeing away from us and down the tunnels. Whether they'd been with Bayard on Lone and he'd sent a ship, or they were Clan members who had remained here since before the Hub had been destroyed, it didn't matter. I wasn't interested in chasing them down. I just wanted everyone out safely so we could survive for the next Society.

Five down. Two to go, I reminded myself.

Hok walked up to me, Sarah at his side and still supporting him under one arm.

"We should stay in the tunnel. Wait out this avalanche, and when it's done we dig our way back out to the exit. It's either that or find another path to the Doorway." Hok's brows were drawn down into a scowl as he surveyed the still-tumbling gems in the cavern behind us.

Relief shot through me as Cassius swooped into the tunnel with Fell in his arms. My Connected sported several new bruises on his cheek and arms but looked otherwise unharmed. I threw my arms around him, then stepped back to address the others.

"Did anyone get left behind?"

Silas raised an arm, tallying everyone off as he conducted a headcount.

"All here," he confirmed.

Before we could discuss our options, several Spear members re-emerged into the tunnel. Silas's arm shot out, sword in hand, and sliced an incoming Spear across the stomach.

"Leave!" I screamed, throwing my arm out. My ears picked up the sound of running as I collapsed into Fell's arms.

The markings at the edges of my fingertips were white, the opal light flickering up to my knuckles.

"We need another way out." Fell held me firmly under my shoulders, avoiding my injured ribs.

"If we go back through the room with the crystals, we're liable to get buried," Dex agreed.

"Then we find a different way. The peak with the Doorway had multiple tunnels leading to it. We need to find another one," Vanya urged.

Dex nodded.

"Clan residents Assimilate a keen sense of direction. You have to, when you can't rely on the sky to guide you. I know what direction we need to go. That should be enough to help me navigate the other tunnels."

We followed Dex, managing to get through three turns to new tunnels without running into any Spear.

"It's no good—we won't fit," Cassius informed Dex partway through the fourth tunnel. It had become narrower and narrower, and the Kites' wings couldn't squeeze enough to fit.

We backtracked out, and Dex found an alternative. We were

in the middle of the new tunnel when we saw someone run past the exit we were headed toward.

"Spear!" Cassia growled over her fangs.

The Clan waiting for us at the end of the tunnel started yelling back. I heard the words *puppet master* thrown in. They didn't shoot darts or arrows. They didn't even throw spears. Instead, they used the same strategy they had in the cavern with the crystals. They began using their hooves to kick at the tunnel, and mallets to hammer at the walls.

The rock above us began to shake, pebbles under our feet trembling. A cracking noise sounded, and a long fissure worked its way down the side of the tunnel. They were trying to bury us alive.

"Everybody out!" Silas shouted, leading everyone back the way we'd come in.

"Move!" Hok echoed, scooping Tibby under one arm and hauling Sarah along with the other as he sprinted away from the rocks that had begun to crumble and fall.

Lungs burning, a cutting pain hitting my side with every breath, I ran. Fell tugged me along, and Vanya helped him. I'd never have made it on my own.

I heard a scream, and as I looked back I saw Digit trip over a rolling rock and go tumbling. Her pants were torn, her knees skinned. She'd landed on her hands, and I heard another cry of pain as the impact jolted through her damaged fingers on one hand.

Breaking free of Fell and Vanya, I sprinted back towards Digit, arms reaching out, longing to be able to move the boulders the way I controlled the other Societals. And I tried.

"Stop!" I screamed at the falling rocks, but they disobeyed, continuing on their path of construction with abandon.

The ground around us shuddered. A piece of rock fell from the ceiling and shattered where I'd been standing moments before.

"Digit!" I yelled as she pulled herself up and began moving toward us.

A crack echoed overhead, and she looked up. I did the same and saw an arc of rock break loose from the ceiling. Digit threw her arms over her head as a blur ran toward her. Dex, moving faster on his hooves than I'd ever seen him. He leapt off boulders, climbing them as they fell. He threw himself at her, wrapping his arms around her. They skidded across the ground, and he opened his arms and shoved her toward us as the ceiling gave way.

"No!" My screams were drowned out by the roar of crumbling rock cascading from the ceiling. When the sound had subsided to small clatters as pebbles rolled down the pile of downed rock and the dust cleared, the tunnel between us and the Spear was filled with rock from floor to ceiling.

Sticking out from the pile was a hand, and one twisted horn.

"No!" I cried, clenching my fists.

"What? What happened?" Digit sat, covered in dust, in a daze.

Silas ran past her, all but shoving her aside as he began heaving rocks off the pile.

"Dex! Hold on, buddy, I'll get you out!"

Hok joined him, tossing huge stones as if they weighed nothing. Others stepped up to help. Within minutes we had Dex out, but it was too late.

Silas and Hok pulled the lifeless body from the rubble.

"He shouldn't have done that." Digit's voice was monotone, hollow, as they set Dex against the rocks. Her eyes widened as she walked toward the battered body of her friend. "He shouldn't have. Why did he do that?"

Silas's face was crumpled, his eyes wet. Hok placed a hand on his shoulder, and the two of them stepped back as Digit approached. She reached her injured hand out, bent fingers stroking Dex's bloodied face.

"We can still help you navigate back to the Doorway," one of the other Clan residents with us piped up. I was ashamed to admit I didn't even know her name. She had light grey, furred legs. Her hooves clacked in the tunnel, and her ears were long and furred, like a goat's.

I looked back and forth between her and where some of the others knelt over Dex. Silas often helped in decisions like these, but he was staring at Dex. I made the decision.

"We don't leave without him. Hok, can you and Silas help carry him?"

"We can. It would be easier if we had something to drag." Hok looked around him.

"I bet we can help with that," Nix set her pack down and began ripping. I left her to it.

"Is there a way to get there without risking more situations like this in the tunnel? I'm sorry, I don't know your name." I turned my attention back to the Clan woman who had offered to help us.

"Begtas," she volunteered, "and yes. Sort of. We can move upward. We'd still be in the tunnels for a bit, but then we'd let out into the snow on the side of the mountain. Once there, we could make our way to the top and get to the Doorway from the outside."

No one made a quip or complaint about more cold weather when I relayed the decision to the group. My throat was tight, but I kept the tears locked away. This was no place to break down.

Between the others, they'd created a makeshift travois using the torn pack, Hok's fighting staff, and a spear one of the Clan on our side carried.

As we got started, following Begtas and the others, the group was somber and quiet.

"Very close now," Begtas informed us from the front of the group as we made our way up.

The air got colder and colder, and I started to hear the howling of wind. After a while, snow began blowing into the tunnel. I clasped my arms, shivering.

"One more turn should do it, I think!" Begtas encouraged us as we walked into the frigid air of the Clan's snowy peaks. When we came to the end of the tunnel, Begtas stepped onto a snowy ledge. It was hard to see anything else as my eyes adjusted to the brightness.

Our guide squealed, arms wheeling. Fell surged forward, grabbing her arm and hauling her back. Several Clan members blocked our exit, hopping down onto the ledge.

"We don't know how you've managed it, but Bayard sent specific instructions that you not leave this Society. All except the Puppet Master. We'll take her with us," the one in front stated. He had long, bovine ears. One was torn, like Cassia's. His horns were long and straight, coming out on the sides of his head. He shook them back and forth at us.

"And if you're thinking of running, there's more of us at the other end of the tunnel," one of the others by his side added. They all had white spears emblazoned somewhere on their clothes or weapons.

I was so tired of seeing that symbol, and so tired of fighting. They smirked at us, taunting us as we stood, trapped in the tunnel.

I counted six of them. We outnumbered them, but it didn't matter. They'd proven that already with Dex. They knew the mountain better than we did.

In spite of all that, I saw a solution.

It was a narrow ledge.

I sighed, feeling the anger flow through me, but it was chased by weariness. With Kidan, I'd let anger and desperation control my actions. With my offer to Everleigh, I'd made a calculated and strategic decision. In this scenario, I simply didn't have the energy or time to think of a better alternative.

I threw out my hand, aware of the chill this time that shot through my fingertips, and I pushed my projection to its limits.

"Jump."

I didn't want to look at their faces, but I watched them anyway. Saw their eyes go wide, their mouths open in surprise or to scream as, one by one, they turned and leapt off the ledge.

CHAPTER 23

held my hand out in front of me as I stepped out onto the snowy ledge. My arm shook, and my newest markings were white all the way to the base of my fingertips. No other Clan residents waited to jump us that I could see in the blowing snow. My ears didn't pick up anything. I lowered my arm to my side and moved up the path so the others could make their way to the ledge.

My hands were numb in the cold, and it matched the rest of me.

"Wow." Nix leaned over the edge but held onto Hale to keep herself steady.

"Good job, Queen!" Sarah thumped me on the shoulder as she strode by.

"Where now?" I asked, trying to keep myself focused on anything other than what I'd just done. Begtas was staring over the side of the ledge, but at my question she shook her head.

"Right. We continue up this way. I can lead." She climbed up the snows and worked her way around Sarah with ease. She began leading a line on the narrow path.

"We could have outfought them with our numbers," Hok

observed as he walked by. He hauled the travois, and Silas walked behind it.

"Without any of us getting killed? Are you sure?" I countered.

Hok opened his mouth, but Fell cut him off.

"Leave it."

Silas paused, then came to stand by me at the ledge. Fell had made his way to my side. I saw Silas give him a nod, and the forest walker swapped him places behind the travois and left the two of us on the ledge.

I waited for the others to make their way past us before I spoke.

"After the Hub was destroyed, when I sent Kidan into the fire, you told me a story."

"I did," Silas agreed.

I took a deep breath.

"You said that sometimes in battles like this, we kill for what *could* happen. We do it to prevent worse things after bad things have already happened. You also said that, in your situation, you'd done the right thing."

"Yes, I did. And I still feel that way."

I turned to him. I couldn't muster up the energy to feel regret, but I wasn't sure I liked the cold chill that took its place.

"Did I do the right thing?"

He sighed. His brown hair stirred in the snowy breeze. It had grown longer since everything had started.

"Sometimes—" he started, then let out another sigh. "Sometimes, there isn't a right answer, as much as people like to believe there always should be. Sometimes there is only death, and the question of who can avoid it, and who can't. Today, you helped us stay alive. I'd say that's what you should be thinking about, but I know it's not that simple."

I shook my head, stumbling forward a bit as the energy-drain of what I'd done and my healing injuries caught up with me.

Silas reached out, his hand gentle as he caught me and steadied me.

"Are you all right?"

I knew he meant more than just whether or not I could make it up the mountain.

I shook my head.

"No. I don't think I am."

"Come on. I'll help you up the path." I took the hand he offered me.

We were halfway to the group when I spoke again.

"Silas."

"Hmm?"

"They killed Dex."

"Yes, they did."

None of it made sense to me. Why the Spear was willing to murder over their complaints. I hadn't figured it out in all the time I'd known about them, and I wasn't any closer to doing so when we caught up to the others.

The rest of the walk over the mountainside was a quiet one, aside from chattering teeth and the odd screech or roar that Begtas told us belonged to local mountain creatures.

Fell made his way back down the line and walked with me. Silas moved back to the travois.

"I'm always here for you, Kena," he promised before walking ahead.

Fell pulled a Riftian cloak out of his pack and wrapped it around me.

Other than the cloak, the forest walker was strangely distant. Our group found the peak and a way in. We clambered through one last tunnel and made our way to the Doorway. I let the others go through first. Fell and were last, and the inside of the mountain felt empty and enormous around us.

"If you're mad about what I did—"

His marks brightened for a moment before dying back down to a soft hum.

"I'm not mad about the Spear."

"Then why—"

"What you did was foolish!"

After feeling numb the entire walk back, my emotions slammed into me. Grief fought with defensiveness. My eyes watered, and I crossed my arms over my chest, glaring at Fell as though they were his fault.

"So you *are* mad! You think I'm a killer. That I'm as bad as my father."

His eyes went wide and he stepped back as if I'd slapped him.

"Is that what you think? *That's* what you're worried about?"

He surged forward, taking my hands in his and holding my fingers out where I could see the white markings.

"I'm not worried about anyone but you. Look at what you're doing to yourself!"

"They had killed Dex! We've lost Pim; we've lost Warrick! They've hurt so many people. Cassia's ear, Ryshal's wings—"

"That was the falls."

"It's still their fault! We never would have had to go after the crystals if it weren't for the Spear. We wouldn't have been so rushed if Bayard wasn't on our tail this whole time. This whole, stupid system relied on the Choosing. I don't feel like I've had a choice. If I hadn't done what I did, more of us could have died. I'm done holding back!"

Fell was pacing, only a few steps each way on the narrow ledge. He looked more frustrated than I'd ever seen him, his marks flickering and flashing. He started to reach for me at one point, then snatched his hand back.

"You don't have the energy to use projection on the crystals *and* on the Spear. You want a choice. That's it. You can't have both."

I kept my arms crossed but stared down at my boots while I spoke, a bit ashamed of what I had to say.

"We talked about this. We talked about sacrificing everything to save the Societies. *That* is my choice. If I have to ascend into nothingness like Ama to have both, then that's what I'll do. I can't keep letting harm come to people I care about when I know I could help."

"I've changed my mind. That's one choice I can't make. I won't let you sacrifice yourself."

"It's not up to you!" I tried to take the bite out of my tone as I stepped closer, grabbing his hands again. "Fell, please. I love you. I *need* to know I have your support. I can't do this without it."

He gulped as he pulled his hands away.

"Not for this. If I have to pick, I'm going to protect you over everyone else."

I huffed.

"You've known some of these people your entire life. You've known me for months."

"I'm not Connected to any of them!"

We'd never fought in such a way, and it didn't seem like we were getting anywhere. I gave some ground.

"I will try, Fell. I will try to focus on the crystals. That's where I'll put the majority of my energy. And I will hope that's enough. But when Bayard comes for us, I'll do whatever it takes to keep the others safe."

He was still scowling, but he moved over to me and wrapped me in his arms. I sank into him, comforted by his warmth in spite of our argument.

"And I will do whatever it takes to keep *you* safe. No matter the cost," he promised.

When we made it through the Doorway back to Tundra, I just wanted to be alone, but I found Begtas waiting for me.

"Could we have a word?"

I nodded, following her past the tents and across the snowy fields. I stared longingly at a large tent where smoke billowed from the top and the smell of warm food wafted out.

"Dex was your friend," Begtas stated once we were away from the others.

"He was my friend," I acknowledged, unable to say more without becoming emotional. I pulled the moon quartz out of my pocket and rolled it in my palm.

"We respected him, at least those of us who opposed the Spear. I want to help."

She pointed at the gem in my hand.

"Do you know what it is?"

"I do," I allowed again, leaving my answers short. I didn't intend to be rude; I simply didn't have it in me to open up to anyone else. Not at that moment. When I got close to people, they were in danger. That's one thing I was learning.

"And do you know what it does?" she pressed.

I shook my head, hair that needed a wash swinging over my shoulder. I didn't bother sliding it back behind my ear as I typically would. It could stay. What was the point of it all, anyway? I stared down at the quartz, and Begtas grabbed it.

She held it up in front of me.

"Would you *like* to know what it does?"

I chewed my bottom lip but nodded.

"Moon quartz is rare. It's unique, and powerful. It amplifies and enhances Assimilations." She paused, glancing back toward me.

"It can be broken down and melded into something new. Used in the construction of weapons or armor. That's a popular choice, given you'd have permanent use of it that way, but there's another option."

She held the moon quartz back out to me, and I took it and slid it back down in my pocket.

"What's that?"

"The other manner of using moon quartz is far more

powerful but rarely done. It's a scarce resource, and you know how all Societies are about those. The Clan even more so. We'd generally say there's no reason to waste something so valuable on only a few uses, when you could have something that lasted a lifetime."

"I'm listening."

"It can be ingested. Ground into a powder and swallowed. Whatever Assimilated features you have will be tripled, ten-fold, a hundred-fold. Who knows for sure? It's dependent on the person and ability and has only been taken that way a handful of times, always with great effects. Someone once ingested it and used their strength to stop a whole mine from collapsing."

Then it could have saved Dex if I'd known better?

She must have caught my expression.

"It wouldn't have helped you. It's still in one piece. You need a Clan resident with the proper tools to grind it for you."

"And that would be you?"

"No, but a couple of the others brought tools that could do it. We would be happy to offer our services to the Queen of the Alliance. We'll melt it down and forge it into a weapon, or we'll make you the powder. It's up to you."

After everything I'd said to Fell about choices, a new one was being presented. I didn't have to think twice. I already had daggers, an ax, and projection. I didn't need more weapons to carry.

"The powder," I responded, handing the moon quartz back over to her.

Begtas took the gem with her to some of the other Clan members, and I made my way into the food tent.

The meal for the evening was a spiced meat of some kind with a plate of vegetables from the wildflower fields. I was just glad it was warm.

"What did Begtas want?" Hale asked as I sat down next to him.

"Just to talk about Dex." Lying to my best friend made me queasy, but I'd already argued with Fell.

Part of me wanted to tell them about the powder. Depending on how many uses it rendered, I could share it with my friends. It could help them. The other part of me wanted to take it all, go through a Doorway, and hunt down Bayard myself.

CHAPTER 24

After a night's rest, I was still feeling jumpy. I moved carefully out of Fell's arms and exited the tent. I'd promised him to look out for myself, but there was nothing he or anyone else could say that would change my mind. As we got closer and closer to finishing all of this, I got more and more anxious.

Five down. Five down. Five down, I reminded myself over and over, as I paced outside the tent. I wanted to track down Begtas and ask after the moon quartz powder, but most of the people on Tundra weren't yet awake. I spotted Ariadna wandering between the tents. The polar beast was chomping loudly on something nearby.

"Ariadna!" I waved a hand, running over to her.

Her purple eyes lit up.

"Oh, hey, Kena." She smiled at me. No *Queen of the Alliance*, no awkward tension. She still treated me as she had when we both went to the Rift. As a friend. Even after having to hide in the walls of the Hub, fight Spear members, and whatever attack had resulted in her facial scars, she was still all kindness and optimism.

"Ariadna, would you like to fight?"

Her purple markings flickered. Ama had been the one to read them, but they spoke of her gentle and caring nature. Animals and growing things. They fit her perfectly. Still, she wielded a flail and mace with precision when she needed to.

"I, I don't know. I guess I should keep up with it. Do you need me to go to Rover with you?"

She thought I was trying to pressure her into joining us. It was true that every Riftian helped, but the Tundra housed a good number of the children and wounded. Along with that, we picked up more and more Societals on each new visit for the crystals. The tent city was growing by the day.

"No," I assured her, "I understand you're needed here. A fierce Riftian and a polar beast? Who better to look after everyone?"

Her shoulders relaxed and she smiled.

"Oh, good. It's not that I wouldn't go. I would. I just, would rather help things grow than ..."

"Cause people to die?"

"Or have to see it. I worry about Vanya every time you all leave, but I also know she'll be more focused if she's not spending all her effort guarding me."

It was true. If Ariadna had come along, Vanya would have used her energy to guard her little sister.

"Then, if it's just for fun and exercise?"

"Oh, fighting, yes! Let me grab my mace."

When Ariadna returned, we walked to a group of snowy circles that had been set up for training. I wasn't surprised to find Hok and Sarah already there, along with Cassius and Cassia.

The Serpentina wore caps on her deadly nails as she lashed out at Cassius. He flicked and flexed his wings out of the way. He dropped to a knee, swinging one wing and knocking her feet out from under her. She landed with a huff but rolled before he could bring his fist down. She shot upward, and they stopped, both breathing heavily, with Sarah's capped fingernails at his throat.

He broke into a grin, offering her a handshake.

"Very good!"

"All right, step aside, amateurs. Our turn." Cassia strode into the circle along with Hok, who spun his fighting staff in his hands. Ariadna and I took the circle to their left.

"Ready?" I asked her. She gave a nervous nod, chewing her lip. I pulled out my ax, appreciating the familiar feel of it in my hand.

We faced each other for a few moments; then Sarah hooted from the side.

"Come on! No more dilly-dallying. Ready, set, go!" She waved her arms.

Ariadna stopped chewing her lip; the light from her marks grew steady and her hand tightened on her weapon. I fixed my grip on my own weapon and charged.

Later, I lounged on top of a cloak spread over a pile of snow. The weather was still frigid, but sweat plastered white hair to my forehead.

"That was fun!" Ariadna quipped next to me, smiling at the group that had grown since we'd started.

"Yeah, fun," Sarah muttered as she rubbed at a large bruise from where Ariadna's mace had whacked against her Riftian shield.

Ariadna's smile faltered.

"Sorry, I didn't mean—"

Sarah put up a hand.

"Think nothing of it. I respect the skill."

Ariadna's smile settled back into place.

Some of the others brought over breakfast. A delicious array of breads and fruits. As he sat down, Fell handed me a roll he explained came from a Crew recipe.

"About what I said on Clan," he started, "I can't think of anything worse than losing you to this. But I know I can't understand the position you've been put in. None of the rest of us have been able to do what you can. Not with others, and not with the crystals. Not without your help."

"I'm not trying to get myself hurt, and I'm not pushing for this because I want to. I'm pushing for this because I can't stand the thought of losing you, either. Every resistance member that goes down, every crystal we miss, feels like a weight in my chest."

He sighed.

"I could remind you that it's not your fault, but I hear what you're saying. All I can do is promise that I'll continue to support you."

I leaned against him, relaxing at the conciliatory words. It wasn't solved, but it wouldn't get solved until we'd won. At least things felt calm between us again.

Across the group, Sarah shoved a large piece of blue and white fruit into her mouth. When she was done she wiped her hands in the snow before standing up.

"Well, I guess Rover's up next."

"What about the Canopy?" Cassia questioned.

The Serpentina gave Cassia an up and down glance, Charles emerging from her hair and flicking his tongue.

"Fair enough. In the end, it doesn't make too much difference, I suppose."

I was a bit surprised she'd yielded.

Cassia crossed her arms, then laughed.

"I'm only giving you a rough time. As much as I want to go home, I agreed to the strategy of saving Canopy for last. Just don't get us killed by any giant snakes or bugs. I'm going to be very upset if I'm dead before I make it back to Canopy."

A few of the others chuckled, and a few grimaced. Sarah took the comment in stride.

"I'll do my best to keep Rover a snake-free zone for you." She rolled her eyes, but grinned. "I'd like to take Sorvay back, and I think it would help the people there to see a Serpentina. There hasn't been one in ages."

Behind Sarah, the RiC himself came forward. Sorvay was the Rover in Charge, although Sarah's Serpentina status seemed to place her above him. He'd been injured early on in our fight. He leaned against a wooden cane, and his snake Eldonio was wrapped around it.

"We're headed to the canyons," Sorvay stated. I frowned, wracking my brain. I knew they'd been mentioned in some of our pre-Choosing lectures, but there had been so many details about each Society that I struggled to place them.

Something hit me in the arm, and I looked over to see Hale nudging me with his elbow.

"Dinosaurs," he muttered out the side of his mouth.

My skin went clammy.

He was right. We'd been told by Nien that large, reptilian creatures similar to Earth dinosaurs still roamed the canyons of Rover, along with massive snakes. It was the last thing I wanted to see, after our encounter with the creatures on Dagan.

I looked across the circle until I spotted my previous Earther instructor. Nien was easy enough to find, with his protruding tusks and singular, glowing Riftian mark. He dipped his chin when he caught me looking.

"Rover it is, then. Everyone, grab your gear and meet over by their Doorway as soon as you're able," Silas instructed.

As the others broke apart to gather their things, I strode across the snow until I was planted chest to chest in front of the instructor.

"You taught us about the canyons a bit in your lessons, I believe?"

He gave a curt nod. I recalled the conversation. Nien, like

many on Canopy, had an affinity for animals. It had been a lecture where he'd appeared particularly interested and alive. Maybe that was my opening.

"I don't suppose you could give us any more information about what we may be up against?"

I paused, but he didn't respond right away.

"It would help the Riftians if we knew what to expect. And would help those guarding us even more, I'm sure."

It rankled that, while I worked on the crystals, the other Societals were responsible for looking after us. In part, because I hated needing help and knew many of the other Riftians felt the same. In part, because it put the others at risk, when we were the ones who would most likely remain safe. I hated that, even when saving the Societies, we were perpetuating a system that separated people based on Assimilation.

"Information could help," he allowed but said nothing further. I rubbed a hand against my forehead before running it through my hair.

"Nien. Please. I'm really trying here. Extending an olive branch. Taking it is the least you could do, all things considered."

He puffed up his chest, snorting over his tusks.

"The least I could do?" he sputtered. "I offered to give my life for this cause. Of all the—" He stopped and took a deep breath, then another, letting the air whoosh over his tusks in a slow exhale.

"You're right," he acknowledged. "Whether I meant to or not, I caused harm. To you. If supplying you with information on the creatures on Rover can help reverse the damage, I can do that."

It turned out that, once he got going on the topic, he became much more relaxed. He smiled as he waved his arms around, imitating the various beasts said to reside in the canyons.

"Some feathered, some leather-skinned. Huge teeth and claws. Some lumbering along the sands and some sliding through it like massive snakes. A true sight to behold!" he explained, arms pointing out as he pretended to weave like a serpent.

"And with our luck, are they all the Societal-eating kind?" Nix interjected, winking at me as Nien sputtered.

"She's right. The way things are going for us, one of these beasts is going to turn out to be some sort of crystal-guarding monstrosity," Hale added as he joined us. I noted several others had gathered around the instructor and myself.

"Just one?" I teased him.

Nien ran a hand through his coarse, wiry black hair.

"Well, there could be a few complications, it's true," he admitted. "At least they don't fly like the sky beasts on Dagan! But several of the species are quick, and just as many can crush you with no more effort than taking a step."

"How big are we talking?" Cassius questioned, flexing his gold-flecked wings. "Like, horse big? Elephant big? Bigger?"

Lucky for us, Nien had a fascination with Earth and had educated himself regarding our animal species.

"Some are elephant-sized," Nien responded.

"Well, that's something. At least, it's not all of them that are massive," Cassius stated.

"Though many are far larger," Nien finished with a mad grin. I could tell he enjoyed the animals, perhaps more than the rest of us.

"That's great. Just perfect." Cassius threw his arms up. "Sea serpents. Underwater beasts. Dinosaurs. Tell me, are there any planets here *not* trying to kill us all while we're trying to save them? You might all remember, Kite didn't present nearly this many issues."

He was right. Kite had butterflies and flitting birds. It had herbivorous creatures that resembled giraffes. All in all, a much tamer planet.

Cassia stepped forward and placed a placating hand on her brother's arm.

"The planets have no opinion one way or the other," she

reminded him. "They existed before the Societals' arrival, and as long as Bayard doesn't destroy them they'll likely remain long after the last Societal has died."

Her statement was equal parts comforting and anxiety-inducing.

CHAPTER 25

T he change from the frigid Tundra climate directly into the searing Rover suns was the harshest Doorway transition yet. The short tunnel that encased Rover's Doorway didn't do anything to protect us from the heat. It created an oven.

"Why would you make it metal?" Hale complained as he shoved his way out onto the open sands. They were even hotter.

"It's sweltering here!" Veronica lamented, her gelatinous coating starting to ooze into the sands and leaving a sticky, inky trail.

"It's uncomfortable," Cassius agreed, wincing and shaking his hand as some small bug stung him and flew off. He began fanning himself with his own feathers.

"Rovers are tough. You learn to tolerate the elements, even if you never learn to love them," Sorvay responded. The Rover leader still walked with a cane. Sarah had suggested to him that he stay in one of Rover's towns, but he had declined.

Sorvay pointed toward the flying bug with his cane, and when it landed at the edge his snake, Eldonio, snapped it up.

"A zapper. It'll sting and your finger might blister, but count yourself lucky. It's one of the least venomous things here."

"Wonderful," Hale grumbled, as if he'd personally been the one stung. "Deadly bugs."

I chose not to remind him that he lived on a planet full of equally terrifying sea monsters.

"Oh, look over here! Sand sweepers! How thrilling!" Nien leaned over what at first appeared to be a writhing pile of sand. Upon closer inspection it was clear it was a pile of interlocked snakes, only a shade or two off of the color of the shifting sands they inhabited.

"Those *are* dangerous. And we've got limited antivenom supplies. I'd recommend staying away," Sorvay cautioned, taking a wide path around the snakes. I followed suit. Nien gave a small frown and shrugged before joining the rest of us.

"Just be thankful we're not going to Temple Sands," Sarah's friend Saf grumbled, giving her feathered serpent a pat on the head.

"What's wrong with Temple Sands?" I almost didn't want to know, but all the Rovers around us tensed a bit; if it scared them, it scared me.

Sarah frowned.

"Part of the Assimilation process here. Now that we know about the crystals, I wonder if it's even a necessary one, or just something born out of tradition. The location is just east of the canyons, so the proximity would make sense."

"It's somewhere you go? A pilgrimage or something?" I guessed.

She shook her head.

"It's something you do. A serpent lives under the sands. Just as large as the sea monsters of Crew. You descend into the sands and it comes out, looping around you. It moves so fast it creates a tornado of sand, the red dirt tearing at your face and stinging your eyes. There's no way out. The serpent rises and rises until its head touches the sky."

"And then?" Nix leaned forward, eyes going wider and wider as the story continued.

Sarah sighed.

"Then the serpent drops the sand. It buries you alive. The theory is that a real Rover is able to dig themselves out, but not everyone makes it. Someone always dies."

Nix's expression drooped.

"Someone is *always* dying in the Societies." Digit had a tear trailing down her cheek that she didn't bother to wipe off, but she swiped at her nose and sniffled.

It did feel that way. When we'd first arrived at the Hub, we'd thought Assimilating and joining a Society was a given. It was only after they had us all up at the station that it was revealed that people who didn't manage to Assimilate were killed, and that there were people who didn't Assimilate every year. We'd since found out that was yet another trick of the Spear. A substance they'd slipped to people to somehow suppress the traits. A way to sow additional unrest against the Coalition, when friends and family were killed in the name of population control.

Ama's journals hadn't mentioned how the superstitions and rituals surrounding Assimilation on the Societies took place. It was very possible even she didn't know. In the Rift, Assimilations just showed up. In places like Crew, the tattoos were provided by Societals and earned, and Assimilations like shadowing in the sun and tolerance to the harsh salt water grew over time.

But in other Societies, like Kite and Rover, there were key events instigated by the Societals themselves.

"Shawd?" I turned to the Kite, healed enough now to join us. One wing was still missing feathers, but the menders had patched it enough that he could fly, although they had recommended he not hold any of us for a while.

"Yes, Queen?" He winked at me, lifting the mood just a bit.

"Acaius mentioned something about the waterfall you go under for Assimilation on Kite. Do you think it could be coming from the crystals?"

He put a hand to his chin, shaking out his wings behind him. "Very possible."

It was as if, unwittingly, some of the Societals had stumbled upon places close to the crystals and then built whole superstitions around them.

The heat beat down on us as we marched across the dunes.

"I take back what I said about Temple Sands," Sarah stated as we crested another dune.

"Because it wasn't so bad?" Hale questioned, voice raising hopefully.

"No. Because we're here."

Sorvay caught up, slamming his cane into the sand.

He started down the other side of the dune.

"We don't have to go *through* Temple Sands, do we?" Tibby asked, fluttering on green wings at the RiC's side. Several of the Kites had alternated between walking and flying.

The RiC shook his head.

"We'll go around."

I moved alongside Acaius, his leathery wings dragging in the sand.

"Which is worse?" I asked him.

"When I'm walking, I think walking. It's sweltering and the sand irritates my wings. But when I'm flying I think flying. The movement of my wings ought to create a breeze, but the air itself here is too hot. I'm just fanning myself with fire."

"How is Ryshal?" I glanced back to where he walked with Cassius and Shawd. He was laughing, but his eyes looked sad. I wasn't sure if I was imagining things.

I'd checked in on him on Tundra, but we hadn't had much to say to one another. I'd thanked him for saving my life, and he'd told me he'd do it again, but he'd stared at his ruined wing while saying it.

Acaius presented half a smile.

"Getting better. He's frustrated that he's still not quite well enough to try his new prosthetic. Marx recommended waiting until the wounds on his arms are less raw," he shared, shaking sand out of one wing.

"So the makers were able to fashion him a wing?"

Acaius nodded.

"Oh, yes. Marx did excellent work, with some of his friends. He and Thea were very kind to him. They'll be welcome in our home any time, as are you, by the way."

I thought it might be his way of letting me know he didn't blame me, even though Ryshal had shredded his wing making sure I was free of my harness.

"Acaius, if it had been up to me, in the falls—"

He put a hand in front of my mouth, then blushed.

"I'm sorry, that was rude. It's just, you don't owe me an explanation. I know if you'd had the choice you'd have told him to tuck both wings in. You easily could have drowned, and the hopes of the Societies would have died with you. He did what he believed in, and what he thought was best."

I looked behind us. Fell was walking and chatting with Hok, Vanya, and Silas. Even so, I'd seen him scanning our perimeter. I knew he was looking out for me.

"If *you* could have decided, if you had to pick between saving Ryshal and saving me ..." I realized what I was doing. "I'm sorry, Acaius. That wasn't fair to ask."

He glanced between me and Fell behind us.

"I think I see where you're going with this. The forest walker is normally at your side. You want to save the Societies, and he wants to save you. Do I have the gist of it?"

"You've nailed it," I admitted.

He blinked purple eyes back at me.

"I agree with you both."

"You can't do that!"

He laughed, throwing his head back.

"I can do what I like, and I agree with both of you. I feel the same about Ryshal. I care about him, first and foremost. *He* cares about the resistance, and you as its leader, and his friend. I respect his decision. He respects mine. He knows I'll do anything to support him, including letting him risk his own life, but that if it's within my power I'm going to save him."

"So if you had been able to intervene?"

He stopped walking, and I stopped beside him. He stared directly into my eyes.

"I'd have tried to fly you both out, but if it had been one or the other, I would have saved him."

The answer was a relief, somehow.

"Thank you."

He laughed.

"I wasn't sure whether you might hit me for such an admission. You do know I consider you a friend."

"Yes. But being Queen of the Alliance is enough pressure. Fell risking everyone for me is hard to swallow. I wouldn't want to think anyone else is willing to take the same risk. Somehow, it takes some of the pressure off."

"Glad I could help."

Fell joined me again after Acaius took back to the skies.

"Hold my hand?" I asked, looking up at him.

His marks glowed as he smiled.

"Of course."

"We should get there soon, everyone! We'll check the rim of the canyon now, then descend into it after nightfall if the crystals aren't up top."

"Climbing at night?" Nix questioned.

"It's just a smidge cooler that way," Sarah explained, "and I hate to tell you, but we have some nocturnal creepies and crawlies that come out in the sand at night. You won't be sad to get moving again."

When we reached them, the canyons took my breath away. I didn't even have the words to describe them. They were enormous, and ancient. Layers upon layers of slightly varied colors of red dirt climbing to the sky, and huge fissures carved between them.

"We're climbing all the way down that?" Hale craned his neck over the edge, taking in the vastness of the landmark.

Sorvay nodded.

"Yes, we are."

We didn't manage to find any crystals along the rim of the canyon, not that I had expected to. That would have been simple, and this had been anything but simple.

I found myself thinking that if Ama were with us, I'd have given her a hard time over how tricky the placement of all the crystals had been. The thought brought a smile to my face.

We treated the canyon like everything else; we took shifts.

Some walked the rim in case we'd missed crystals. Some stood watch, and others rested. It was only because I knew Sarah was watching over me, along with Charles, for snakes in the sands, that I was able to nap at all.

The sky overhead never grew dark. It just shifted from a light sky blue to a more vibrant and darker blue. I sat looking at it once I awoke.

"Yep. You get one color here. Blue, and then more blue. And don't even think of hoping for shade clouds," Sarah quipped when she saw me looking.

I rolled up the cloak that I'd had underneath me as we got ready to descend.

"Everyone, listen up!" Sorvay stood at the front of the crowd. His scaled green skin held scars, and his gold-rimmed eyes flashed. Sarah had said he was the youngest ruler of the Rovers ever, but I could see how he'd gotten the position. Though injured and frail, he still spoke with authority and assurance as he looked down at the canyon.

"I'm not going to lie. This is a treacherous climb down. Take your time. Rovers, Kites, and Clan residents, disperse yourself among the others to try and help them down. We'll be dealing not only with the terrain, and the heat once it's daytime again, but the beasts. There are still serpents and sand scorpions to contend with, but the creatures in the canyons are different. If we see any, try to stay out of sight. If they spot us, make for the edges of the canyon and do your best to find a path upward. Most of them don't climb well. If you stay on the floor of the canyon, you're likely to get crushed."

He turned and led us down.

"Someone needs to give him a lesson in motivational speaking," Hale whispered to me.

"He might be harsh, but he's not wrong," Nien said.

"The instructor's right," Sarah added, "Sorvay is a straight-shooter. If he's making it sound this intense, it's because it is. We'd all better be ready."

The others spread out, alternating between the Societals Sorvay had mentioned and those of us who didn't have Assimilations that would help our balance.

Fell walked in front of me and Acaius behind as we descended into the canyon.

CHAPTER 26

The sky was back to a pale blue, the heat at its peak by the time we reached the bottom of the canyons. The ground beneath us looked like dry, cracked clay. It had a similar reddish tint to the sands in the dunes, but it flaked away under our feet. Sand blew over the surface.

"Could there have been water down here at some point?" I asked as I picked up a crumbling bit of dirt.

"If there was, it's been lifetimes ago. Our only water now comes from the oases," Sorvay informed me.

"That, and canteens," Sarah added as she opened the one slung over her shoulder and took a long sip. It was tempting to grab it and pour the water over myself, but I resisted.

We followed Sorvay through the morning. After hours wandering the twists and turns of the canyon floors with no sign of crystals, I was ready to abandon the plan entirely and find one of the oases he'd mentioned.

He led us through a long stretch of wide canyon. The air was so hot it shimmered in front of us. Hale shadowed beside me.

"At least you won't get sunburned," I allowed, mightily jealous.

"I'd help you if I could. I know the heat's miserable."

The Dagan were dripping inky drops of sweat. Some of the Canopy and Clan with us had begged for a rest in the shadow that one of the rocky paths above us created. Those with fur were hotter than the rest of us.

"How can it be this hot down here? You'd think that, this far from the sun, it would be cooler!" Veronica complained as she slumped against a canyon wall. Begtas slammed her hoof into the rock just next to Veronica's head, and the former Earther jumped.

"Sorry—sun scorpion," Begtas explained as she pulled her hoof back to reveal the crushed and deadly bug.

I jumped up from where I'd been leaning against the wall, staring ahead of us at all the ground we had left to cover. Somewhere ahead there appeared to be large, shadowy things. Trees, maybe? Was it possible there was an oasis on the canyon floor after all?

I took a step or two closer, squinting against the light as I peered into the distance.

"At least sun scorpions and a few snakes are *all* we've run into. I'd take that over the dinosaurs any day, right, Kena?"

My mind struggled to put together what I was seeing in the distance. The blobs were getting closer. Was I so dehydrated that I was hallucinating? The trees looked like they were moving.

"Are those—?" Saf stood next to me, peering into the distance with eyes less blinded by the sun. She gulped.

"This is one of those 'it's right behind me' type moments, isn't it?" Hale guessed.

Sorvay and Sarah made their way over. Sarah cursed, and Sorvay started shuffling around, rousing everyone.

"If I'm not very much mistaken, that is a charging herd of mammoths," Nien shared as he looked past us all, grinning at the oncoming beasts that were most decidedly not trees.

They had a lumbering gait but moved quickly. The closer they got, the more detail I could see. They had tree-trunk-sized legs that were leathery, dried and wrinkled. One flicked a long tail behind it as it ran, and that, along with the spikes down its back, reminded me of a stegosaurus. The horn protruding from its head, though, was like that of a rhinoceros. The closer it got, the bigger it seemed to get. The beast had to be twice the height of an elephant, easily.

"That's not a mammoth!" I yelled as we sprinted.

"That's what we call it, but no matter what you want to name it, it could crush us all." Sorvay was prodding people with his cane to move faster.

"Stars help us." Vanya stared up at the massive beasts as she ran behind us, picking up speed with each step. "Why are they coming after us?"

She was sprinting alongside me now, readying her bow. For once, I doubted it would do any good at all.

"I'm going to guess,"—Nien huffed alongside her—"they're stampeding because of the clampers hunting them." The Societal instructor pointed at several blue shapes looping around the back end of the herd of stampeding mammoths.

The clampers were the most mammalian in shape of the animals I'd seen on Rover. Bodies much smaller than the mammoths, roughly the size of a horse. Four legs, with what looked like paws and talons at their ends. Their skin was leathery, like a Rover's, and the same shade of deep blue as their sky at night. The tails were whiplike, with a tuft of fur on the end. The clampers' snouts were like a canine's, long and thin, with sharpened teeth hanging over their bottom jaws. Their name, if I had to guess, must have referred to the two extra limbs hanging off their shoulders that ended in pincers like a scorpion's.

"For the record, I like those even less than the mammoths!" Vanya shouted as she picked up her pace. "And where is a path out of here?"

In the distance, I saw a narrow ledge we could use to climb out. Too far.

"Is anything on this ship-forsaken planet *not* predatory?" Hale griped as he kept pace with me.

"How do we bring them down?" Captain Everleigh shouted at the RiC, turning as if she planned to face the things.

"Rovers don't hunt them. Some creatures are higher on the food chain than us, and we leave them alone unless necessary," the RiC argued, tugging the captain along.

"I would say it's going to become necessary!" Silas shouted.

I didn't blame most of the Kites for taking to the air. There weren't enough of them to lift us all, anyway. Not before we got trampled.

"Acaius! Can you all fly ahead and scout for a way out?" I yelled to him. He was one of the few winged beings still on the ground, staying beside Ryshal.

"You'll watch him?" Acaius questioned.

"We leave no one behind," Fell assured him.

Acaius shot into the air, black wings snapping open as he flew overhead. I marveled at him. He'd already admitted to me that he valued Ryshal's life more than anyone's, and he trusted us to keep him safe. I wasn't going to let him down.

Without so much as a misstep, Fell weaved over to Ryshal and pulled the Kite's winged arm around himself, steadying them both as he continued to run. I fell for him even more in that moment. I'd been fortunate to have people that cared about me all my life. My family clearly had its complications, but I'd always had Hale. I'd had Pim. And while I wasn't ready to address the rest of my complicated feelings, my father had truly loved me in spite of other faults. So it was perhaps easy to take for granted the way Fell treated me.

But the way he treated others? The way he stepped in to help was one of the many things that had won me over. He didn't hesitate to assist, and he never demanded credit or expressed a desire to be in charge.

Some of the Kites had circled back to scoop up the slower members of our group.

"We're not all going to make it." Veronica was huffing by my side. The red dirt stuck to the oily substance she was covered in, coating her in a thin, powdery residue.

In front of us was a dead end. A massive canyon wall loomed over us.

The charging mammoths were gaining ground.

I dug my heels in, stopping and spinning. Fell stopped beside me.

"Get him out," Fell instructed as he handed Ryshal off to Hok. Hok gave a sharp nod, not slowing as he hauled the shorter man along with him.

Fell grabbed my hand, seeming to sense what I wanted to do without having to ask.

"Kena, what are you—" Hale's voice reached me as he broke off the question to yell. The thundering beasts were almost on us.

It wasn't even a plan, not really. It was a last hope. The clampers may have been the predators, but the mammoths far outnumbered them. Maybe we could use one problem to solve the other. I squeezed Fell's hand tight with my left, and threw my right out in front of me.

"Turn around!" I screamed with all the force I could muster.

For a moment I was convinced I'd made the wrong call. They were moving too fast, and they were too close. I could see the lines of dirt coating the first mammoth. A breeze hit my cheek as it turned its head sharply and cantered away from us.

Several more of the mammoths skidded and slid as they took sharp turns and moved back toward the clampers they'd been running from. I didn't have time to celebrate; the group was immense, and I had to repeat the instruction over and over again. Some of the other Riftians had caught on to what I was doing and linked arms to help. Silas wrapped his hand around the wrist I held aloft, and Vanya held his hand on the other side. Marx linked his arm with hers. I felt my strength increase when they held onto me.

The mammoths and clampers roared and squealed. The larger mammoths trampled over their would-be attackers, crushing several of the clampers into the dirt.

Even with everyone's help, I was growing weary when we got to the end of the mammoth herd.

"Turn ar—"

I'd been too slow, and as the last mammoth moved to turn, it collided with the line, sending me flying backward.

I landed with a thud on the ground, groaning as I rolled to my feet. I clutched at my side, worried I might have re-broken a rib. I heard yelling and the sound of metal on metal as weapons were unsheathed.

I struggled to my feet.

"Fell!" My voice was hoarse, but I pushed it to its limits despite the pain in my side.

"Kena," he responded from my side. His hand closed over mine, and as he pulled me toward him I yelped.

"Are you hurt?" Only then did tension creep into his voice.

"I don't think I can project anymore," I admitted. He reached out, pulling on another strand of my hair. A whole new chunk on the left side was stark white. The marks on my right wrist were the same. There wasn't time to worry about the implications.

Looking past him, I saw several clampers had made it past the rows of stampeding mammoths. They had climbed the sides of the canyon walls and were now surrounding us.

The clampers began hissing and clicking their pincers.

"I thought you said most of the creatures couldn't climb well," Vanya shouted to Sorvay, holding her daggers up.

"This would be one of the exceptions," he responded, "and you should know, the tuft on their tails isn't fur. It's a bundle of thin barbs. If one breaks the skin, it will release a toxin that temporarily paralyzes you."

"Oh, great. Because with the sharp teeth and scorpion pincers, I was thinking to myself, you know what they need?

More weapons as body parts!" Hale's voice rose with his rant. The hissing of the clampers got louder.

Charles, Sorvay's snake Eldonio, Kaos on Nix's shoulder, and Saf's serpents responded. The snakes slid down and coiled in the dirt defensively in front of their respective Rovers.

"That can't be good," Nix muttered as she glanced down at Kaos.

Overhead, I saw Kites coming back for us, and a shadow blocked out the light.

"Their wings aren't big enough to do that!" I put a hand over my brow and squinted upward.

"That's not the Kites," Sarah breathed.

"This canyon wall must butt up to Temple Sands," Sorvay added.

Some of the clampers on the canyon walls started to scurry away from us, running up and out of the canyon as a massive serpent's head emerged over the lip of the canyon. The rest circled back behind us, blocking any attempt by us to run from the serpent.

It slid down the wall, snapping up one of the clampers as it went. The scales of the serpent shifted in color as it moved, from gold to turquoise to the rusty shade of the sands.

"Kena, any chance of an assist here?" Hale's voice shook.

I tried. I threw out my hands, marks flickering before I'd even done anything.

"Stop!" My eyelids fluttered, and I swayed with the effort. The snake didn't even pause. Fell grabbed me under the shoulders to prevent me from falling over.

"We'll need to take it out ourselves," Fell instructed the others.

"Well,"—Vanya nocked one of her arrows—"looks like it's time to hunt."

"No! We do this the Rover way. Stay very still. Wait to see what it does," Sorvay insisted.

The serpent had hauled the entirety of its body down the canyon wall and started to circle around us.

CHAPTER 27

The serpent's body encircled our group, ensnaring a few of the clampers along with us. But it was the serpent the predators were focused on now, not us.

"It's going to try to bury us," Sarah observed, voice hushed.

The snake circled faster and faster. Though we weren't in the dunes, sand swirled around us, rising from the base of the canyon and off the walls. The serpent's head rose higher and higher, until it loomed over us, again blocking out the suns.

"Get ready!" Sorvay called.

The snake stopped moving, and as canyon grit rained down on us I spotted glimmering light through the scaly twists of its body. The whirlwind motion had pulled layers of surface soil off the canyon walls, exposing what lay beneath—crystals.

I tried to shout to the others, but the instant I opened my mouth it was filled with red sand. Hacking and coughing, I slammed my eyes shut and threw my arms over my head at the onslaught of debris.

The serpent didn't drop enough sand on us to bury us completely, but when I opened my eyes again the shower of grit had buried my feet and accumulated all the way up to my knees. The serpent wove around us, chasing down and consuming the remaining clampers. Wide-eyed, I watched it go, leaving us unharmed.

"And here I thought that serpent wasn't a fan of Rovers, given that it tries to bury us alive every year. I may have misjudged it," Sarah quipped as she and Charles dug themselves from a drift of red sand.

"The walls." Silas pointed, gesturing to the same thing I'd noticed earlier. Now that they were stripped of the loose layers of sand, the glowing crystals were well exposed.

Some were the red of the Rover sands and others the blues of its sky. A few were the pinks of their oases, according to Saf and Sarah.

"I don't think the serpent is coming back," Sorvay said as we watched the edge of its tail whip out of sight around a bend in the canyon.

"Not that I don't trust your judgment, but let's assume you're wrong and work fast," Hale urged.

First, we harvested some crystals to take back with us, and then we started on the walls.

"Only one more Society after this," Hale reminded me when I took a break to guzzle water from one of the canteens.

I frowned at a fused vein of crystal that glimmered with intermingled pink and blue. I expected Canopy to be the toughest. The longer we waited to go there, the more opportunity it gave the Spear to shore up defenses, or find the Doorways to Tundra, or raise more Earther reinforcements. There were too many possibilities, all of them bad.

I dusted my hands off and stood over the others as they rested in the sun, the non-Riftians spread out around us, keeping watch.

"Everyone ready to keep going?" I asked, impatient to be finished.

Vanya groaned, but she pushed herself up all the same. We made it through a few more clusters before Sorvay came running back as fast as his cane would allow.

"Wrap it up!" he yelled.

Behind him, in the distance, I saw the familiar blue outline of clampers.

"Guess they're still hungry, since you had their last dinner trample them," Sarah muttered.

I looked back and forth between the advancing clampers and the remaining crystals. Enough that it would take our group several more rounds working together to finish fusing them. The Temple Sands serpent was nowhere in sight, and I didn't see any mammoths either.

We heard the now familiar hissing and clacking pincers as the clampers drew closer.

"Grab onto me!" I shouted at the other Riftians. Fell scowled, looking like he might refuse what he suspected I was going to attempt. But he clamped a hand over my shoulder. Vanya and Silas lunged for me, slapping their hands over my arms. The Riftians crowded around me, and the others tightened a circle around us.

"Get ready to fly us out!" I called up to the circling Kites.

Then, I threw my arms out at the remaining crystals. For a moment, all the power coming from the other Riftians buoyed me, and then, just as quickly, it was gone.

I fell backward with a gasp as the crystals in front of me flattened and smoothed into a vein that traveled under the dusty surface to convey the transformation to all the nearby clusters.

I laughed, looking up at the sky as the Kites swooped down to carry us out and away from the clampers before they could reach us.

"We did it. We did it! Six down."

"Yes, six down. One to go. But not before you've had a chance to recuperate," Fell declared as he scooped me up under my shoulders and helped me into Acaius's arms.

The world spun a bit as I was lifted.

Fell hadn't said anything else, but I wondered why his voice had sounded so sad. I looked down and saw no new white markings.

I twisted my head to look at Fell as we hovered above him.

"What?"

"The ones on your back. They're white." He pointed where the markings ran between my shoulder blades and to a downward point, visible in the cut of my bodysuit.

"All of them?"

"Most of them," he responded grimly.

"It will be worth it. It *is* worth it," I insisted, as Cassius picked him up.

The Kites flew us to the rim of the canyon.

"We can stop at an oasis not far from here," Sorvay directed everyone once it appeared the clampers had finally given up the chase.

Sarah stomped over to me, holding out a hand. "Thanks, Queenie," she said, before pulling me into a hug. When she backed away, she kept a hand on me to steady me and sighed.

"No one else is going to say anything? Fine, I'll say it. We all see what Kena is doing to herself here, right? And no one is going to step in? No one?"

Several of the others looked at the ground.

"Sarah"—Hok reached for her—"don't."

"Just because we were asked not to? Like she thinks none of us have noticed anything? She's not dumb!"

Actually, I hadn't thought about how no one aside from my closest friends had anything to say regarding my markings or my hair. What was there to say? I had to do what I had to do.

"Who asked you not to say anything?" I looked around the group. My stomach dropped when I got to Fell, but he held his hands up.

"I may hate that you're doing this to yourself, but I will always be honest with you about it."

Hale blushed as he raised a hand. "It was me. I'm sorry,

Kena. I know you. I've known you your whole life. I knew the stress of this had to be killing you."

Nix elbowed him in the ribs, hard.

"Right. Sorry. Poor choice of words. I knew it bothered you. We all saw Ama. We knew what you were risking, but I also knew you were determined to do it. I didn't want anyone saying something stupid to you and making it worse." He shot Sarah a glare, but the Serpentina shot him one right back.

"Look. We appreciate it. We all do, but if it's going to hurt you, we'll just take Bayard on first and finish up when he's gone, right? Right?"

Cassia stepped forward, scratching at her ruined ear with a taloned hand.

"If you need a break, we understand. We'll find another way, or we'll wait. You don't have to go to Canopy."

The others began nodding.

"And that goes for facing down Bayard as well. We can handle that," Vanya assured me, patting one of her daggers where it was holstered at her side.

"We certainly can. He won't know what hit him." Sarah flashed her nails again, and this time they swirled with black venom.

They were all looking at me as though waiting for a response.

"Look. I appreciate what you're all doing, I really do. And Hale, thank you for trying to spare my feelings." He blushed and muttered something about "best friend."

"No more secrets, though. Not from me, either. Yes, saving the crystals and Assimilation is costing me. I'm worried about what will happen if I push myself too far, but I don't want to lose because I didn't push myself far enough. Once we're back to Tundra, I want to continue with what we've done this whole time. Tend to any wounds, rest up, and then head back out to Canopy as soon as we're able."

"You do realize Bayard has had plenty of time to shore up his defenses there," Silas reminded me. "We might be walking into a trap. This could be Lone all over again."

I dipped my chin in his direction.

"It could be, but it will also be the last place on our list. After we get to the crystals there, all that's left is Bayard himself." *And the rest of the Spear, and the Earthers, and what to do with Lone, and how to rebuild the Hub. And, and, and.* It was better not to think of it.

"We've been gaining people in every Society. We might outnumber the Spear by now. We can take Bayard." Nix pumped a fist in the air.

"That's what I like to hear!" Sarah clapped me on the back.

Digit whooped beside them, smiling for the first time since Dex's death.

"Six down." I just had to hold on for one more Society.

Acaius swooped over the water of the oasis, his wings coated and glinting with red dirt.

"Remind me again why the rest of you can't just grow your own wings?" Shawd asked after taking a large swallow from a canteen.

I was lying against the trunk of one of the trees, resting, while Silas kept an eye out for any threats. The shade was blissfully cool. Vanya was scanning our surroundings for any deadly serpents or bugs.

"We'll head out soon," Fell informed me. "Anything you need?"

"Do we have the crystals in your pack and Silas's?"

"We do," he confirmed.

I closed my eyes, halfway back to sleep.

"Then I'm good."

I didn't mention to him that during my earlier napping I'd had a horrible dream in which my marks went Tundra-snow white and disappeared, before I was dropped back on Earth with no way to reach the Societies again. That was one fear I wasn't worried would come true. Earth wouldn't have taken us back if we'd begged. Not after what Kaiser and the task force had been telling them. I was familiar enough with rumors to know we wouldn't be able to talk our way out of Earth's hatred without a whole lot of effort.

"Would you ever go? To Earth? To visit? If it were a possibility?" I strung the half-questions together until they formed a single point. I didn't open my eyes, and while I couldn't hear his steps, I felt the comfort of my Connected's presence as he crouched next to me and responded.

"I would, but I'd want to make sure no one was going to attack us first. Which, in the current circumstances, sounds like it might be impossible."

I cracked one eye open.

"One battle at a time. First the crystals, then the Spear, then we handle Earth."

In truth, I had no plans for them. As far as I was concerned, someone else could come up with that plan.

Sorvay and a few of the others had gone to the nearest Rover settlement to give the same warning we'd provided the Societals on the other planets, and to hopefully bring back more recruits for the resistance. We needed everyone we could get.

When they returned, several of the new Rovers went around patching up anyone who'd been hurt in our ordeal with the clampers and the Temple Sands serpent. Sorvay made his way over, gesturing to our most recent additions.

"I'm glad I convinced a couple of menders to come with me. They'll get everyone fixed up. We have fewer menders on Rover than any other Society, but they're the best."

"They'd have to be, if they're caring for people on a planet where everything is trying to kill you," Nix grumped, giving Kaos a pat.

Sorvay sighed.

"You're not wrong. Rovers value toughness and tenacity. It's hard to find individuals who Assimilate here and are willing to admit they *want* to be menders. I think we've only got any at all because they can pass it off as an interest in venoms, antivenoms, that sort of thing."

"Maybe we all have a few things that need to change," I suggested as I helped an injured Crew resident limp over to a tree to sit down.

When we got back to Tundra, I was shocked again at the stark difference in the Societies' temperatures. My teeth chattered so hard I could hear them knocking together. Ariadna and several of the others were on standby, passing out cloaks and blankets.

"Here you go." She handed me a fluffy cream blanket, and with a sigh I wrapped it around myself.

I lay on the floor of our tent with Fell later that day, curled up against him.

"Do you think we should be out training before the last Society?" I asked him.

"I'm not going to train, and you're not going to, either. We're supposed to rest. What would you like to do with the time?"

I leaned over him, kissing him, before bringing my head back down to his chest.

"I just want to be here. To be here together, and pretend that outside this tent it's a different world. No Spear, no death, and no decimated Hub. Just us, on the Rift, with no plans for the day except a nice walk through the woods."

I couldn't see his face from my position, but his markings warmed and glowed.

"I like the sound of that. When this is over, we'll do that. I promise."

I wanted to tell him not to make promises he wasn't sure he could keep, but that would have spoiled the moment.

Instead, I just let him hold me.

CHAPTER 28

There were no more debates or discussions to be had. There was only one Society left. The others were chatting about what to do once we finished the crystals there while we packed. I didn't join in. I'd already made up my mind. Crystals first, Bayard next. There was no other option. If my cousin didn't make an appearance on Canopy, I would track him down.

I was under no illusion that I'd go alone. My friends would come with me. The only real boundary I had was that I wasn't going to let them stop me. My hand closed over my ax, gripping it for reassurance as we waited in line, once again, for a Doorway.

"We've almost done it," Hale observed from his place in front of me.

"Almost," I agreed.

It didn't feel that way. My plans for after the crystals were overwhelming. I forced myself to go back to my mantra.

"Six down. One to go." Only by compartmentalizing the tasks could I face them.

I couldn't help thinking about Lone as we stepped through the Doorway and onto the surface of Canopy. Even with what was ahead of us, it was impossible not to be in awe of the lush landscape.

Vibrant, jewel tones of greens, oranges, blues, and yellows, of trees, vines, and flowers. Magentas and purples that were brighter than could be believed. Shades so saturated they didn't even exist on Earth.

I turned a slow circle, eyes up and arms spread with my palms lifted, as it started to rain. A soft mist at first, and within seconds a downpour. I opened my mouth, letting the drops slide down my throat, laughing.

"Kena?" Fell tapped me on the shoulder. "Are you all right?"

I swept an arm out across the landscape.

"Look at this. How did we ever confuse Lone for this place?" We'd known the moment we'd landed there that something was wrong. It had just been our own desperate hope that had us thinking for even a moment we'd been on Canopy. This planet couldn't be copied. Couldn't be imitated.

None of them could. All the Societies had their own problems, but they were also unspeakably beautiful; mesmerizing and wonderful in their own ways.

Cassia took a deep breath at our side, then let it out slowly, smiling over her fangs at the landscape.

"I missed this place."

Her brother clapped her on the shoulder.

"Just for you, I'm willing to give this planet my vote for second-best Society," he teased.

When I'd been debating just before the Choosing, Canopy had made it into my top three. I'd eliminated Dagan, Clan, and Rover without much difficulty. Crew I had never desired to be a part of, although I'd hated giving up my proximity to Hale. It had come down in the end to Canopy or Kite, and I'd favored wings. Not that my decision had mattered in the end.

I glanced over at Su Jin. The former Earther had mainly stayed on Tundra, helping the menders with the wounded. Even so, she hadn't been able to resist returning to her chosen Society.

She flickered as she attempted to camouflage. Her eyes were closed, her face raised to the sun as she smiled.

"It's like coming home."

"Where's the Spear?" Captain Everleigh demanded, a cutlass at the ready.

"Yeah. They have some payback coming." Digit scowled at the plants around us.

"It is disconcerting," I admitted to Cassia. "We thought Bayard would go here directly after the Rift. It was closer. Do we have any word from the residents here?"

Cassia shook her head.

"None. A few came through the Doorway to Tundra, but no one has reported seeing him. Some resistance members came here to warn them, but as far as I know, Bayard hasn't attacked."

That worried me more than if he had. We hadn't seen him since Crew. That couldn't be good. I went over and over Ama's journal in my mind. He might have managed to undo my hasty projection. But even then, what could he gain? He'd been behind us the entire time. He couldn't take any crystals for himself on the other Societies. That only left Canopy. Unless he *had* decided to throw that idea away entirely and go straight for the people. It was possible he'd moved in behind us and already started killing residents of the Societies we'd left behind.

"Surely not," I thought aloud. "If he'd gone after the others, we'd have heard something. Someone would have made it through the Doorway and warned us, right?"

"Most likely," Silas responded as he caught the direction of my thinking. "The best thing we can do is get through the crystals here quickly."

Near us, the Canopy residents were still happily chatting away about their Society.

"And this isn't even the best part. Just wait until we get to the Wilds! I've been wanting an excuse to go." Cassia practically glowed as she spoke of it.

"Wait. Pause on that. Hold up!" Hale waved his arms as he walked between the two ecstatic Canopy residents.

"What do you mean? Haven't you been there before? I thought we knew where it was," he questioned.

"One of you has been to this place, right?" Hok demanded. He held his fighting staff at his side.

"We've been to the edge of it. All Canopy residents know where it is, but that's only so we are aware of the boundary and can protect it. All Societies have methods for preservation and care of their planets. This is ours. The Wilds comprise a good third of the planet, and the area has been left completely untouched. No one is allowed beyond the borders except the creatures that live within its bounds," Cassia informed us.

"But, a few of us have been able to observe the edges for scientific purposes. Don't worry. I know exactly where we're headed." Nien made his way to the front of the group.

"Glad we have Nien for this," Hale grumbled.

So was I.

"Well," Silas sighed, "we've had a lot less to go on before. At least we know where it is. Lead the way."

"That's all you're going to say! A third of the planet," Hale moaned as we fell into step beside our Canopy guides.

"This will definitely make it difficult to find what you're looking for, Kena. That's a huge space to be looking through. All I have on the map is a broad swath of wilderness. We were depending on the Societals here to know more," Digit informed me.

Maybe we should have called for Alsey. Fell's sister-in-law had lived on Canopy for years. But I wouldn't have wanted her taken away from Sybil, either. We'd just have to figure it out.

We were so close. We would find it. We had to.

"Six down. One to go."

I repeated it again under my breath as we walked.

Then Bayard. Assimilation was seen by him as their most

valuable resource, and if he couldn't control it, he'd have to win by force alone. Kaiser's way.

The idea brought out a mix of satisfaction and fear in me. The more small victories we took, the closer we were driving him to the edge. I was growing more and more certain he would default to wiping everyone out.

The Canopy was yet another Society where the resistance's desire to keep the Doorways hidden aided us. It took only a couple of hours to reach the edges of the Wilds. In fairness, that was also probably because of its sheer size.

"We're at the far west end of the Wilds," Nien informed us. "I vote we make a sweep from west to east."

"Given the sheer size, we'll probably also need to work on a north to south grid as well," Silas added. "Unless, Kena, you'd like to go straight to the center? It's possible they would have put the crystals there, if they were truly trying to keep them as hidden as possible."

I gave it some thought before we entered the vast wilderness in front of us.

"Cassia, as far as you know, the Canopy residents respect the rule about not entering the Wilds?" I turned to her.

"Absolutely. Given what's happened, I can't speak for the Spear, but I can for us. From my first day here, it was drilled into us that Wilds acts as a sanctuary for the plants and animals that were here long before us."

That was good enough for me.

"Although." I turned to see Su Jin, her head tilted. She chewed at her bottom lip with a prolonged canine.

"Yes?" Silas pressed her.

"It is possible that if they were hiding from the Spear, some of the residents may have fled to the Wilds for refuge," she allowed.

Cassia glared at the plants in front of us.

"True. But even if they did, these would be residents sympathetic to us. And they would do nothing to damage the environment or the crystals. We consider it an honor to care for Canopy. *Real* Canopy residents wouldn't do anything to cause harm."

I could guess who she considered false residents of Canopy, and I'd bet all of them had white spears emblazoned on their attire.

"All right, then. We'll start here and work our way across. If the residents here consider the area a safe haven, there'd be no reason to put the crystals in the center. They would look at the entire area as having equal value."

Silas dipped his chin in acknowledgement.

Cassia, Su Jin, Nien, and the other resistance members from Canopy gathered groups of us together. They warned about careful steps and making an attempt to leave no trace, and then they led us into the lush trees.

The Wilds was an apt name for the area. Cassia had been right. It was almost a Society unto itself, untouched by outside influence. I marveled at a tree that had small orbs hanging off it in strands, each filled with glowing liquid. Some sort of willow.

"We have some like that in the areas of Canopy where people live," Cassia informed me. "The liquid is good for medicinal purposes. It expedites healing if you spread it on a burn or cut."

The arborists from the Rift would have been thrilled.

She monitored everyone as we walked by the plant. The message was clear. It might be helpful, but we weren't meant to touch it. We were here only to help, not to take.

I held Fell's hand as we made our way through the leaves and fronds of the various plants. He held some tall grass aside so I could pass through, letting it swing back without so much as a boot imprint to show we'd been there.

Hale caught up to us, his fingers twitching at his side.

"I am dying to try some of these." He waved his hands at the various fruits growing from some of the trees.

"I'm not even going to remind you that we've been specifically asked not to do that," I responded.

"Did you know that one over there"—he pointed to a tree

with clusters of plum pods hanging off its branches—"Is supposed to taste like caramel and chocolate? At least that's what Nien says."

In spite of myself, my mouth watered.

"I am ignoring you. I'm perfectly happy with whatever food we've packed."

We'd been supplied plenty, and since we'd started combining all the different cuisines, the options were delectable. I tried to forget the promise of chocolate lingering in my mind for a while after what Hale said.

After some time, I saw more glowing light up ahead.

"I think we're getting close to more of those healing willows," I told Fell.

Instead, as he helped me climb over a fallen tree and through some thick thistles, I saw the truth.

We'd found the crystals.

CHAPTER 29

The description we'd been given of the Wilds remaining untouched by Societals had been accurate, with one notable exception. In front of us were hundreds of clusters of crystals glowing and blooming like the Tundra wildflowers.

I knelt in front of the nearest cluster. The more I'd interacted with them, the more I was able to feel them and influence them. We understood one another, as strange as it was to acknowledge that about something I'd thought to be inanimate. But they weren't that. The crystals were aware, if not alive.

Cassia stepped up beside me, surveying our surroundings.

"The other Societies relied on danger to keep people out. We relied on respect."

"Sister, you may have failed to notice, given your sheer ferocity, but your planet's got creatures which are just as terrifying." Cassius laughed before walking past his sister to marvel at the crystals.

Cassia shook her head, braids swinging over her shoulder.

"But on your planets, you fear the creatures. Fight the creatures. Face off against them. We live in balance with them. It's our nature. The Wilds aren't avoided because we're afraid of the creatures. It's avoided to help them. I'd wager even putting the crystals here to begin with was its own serious debate. Something not taken lightly."

Cassia was right, whether she realized the weight of her words or not. At some point, somewhere along the way, the Societals had strayed from their purpose.

Based on Ama's writings, I wasn't sure it had ever really been their true purpose at all. More likely it was a lie perpetuated by those in charge. Because her diary never made mention of the oft-touted Societal priorities of conservation, balancing our own populations with the planets' existing species and resources, acting as stewards and caretakers. At least not in an altruistic way. They only wanted to avoid another catastrophe like Lone, where they'd bled the Society dry. The Choosing had been born of desperation and as a result of the many mistakes that led the Ancestors to other planets. Even what Ama had done with the crystals had been in the service of self-preservation for the Riftians. And a way to save the others from deadly fates on their own planets. Nothing more.

The Riftians began lining up, careful to avoid crushing any crystals or plants.

Behind us, the others began setting up bedrolls and the like so we'd have somewhere to rest in between clusters. Nien and Cassia hovered over them, ensuring they did as little damage as possible.

"We needed to be here to save the Society, but that doesn't mean we have to disrupt the wildlife," Cassia lectured as one of the Rovers tried to collect bits of fallen wood for a fire.

"Just a small one! How else are we supposed to heat up food?"

"Absolutely not! No fires! You can burn one all you like as soon as we reach Tundra," Nien chided.

"Ready?" Fell asked me as he hoisted my small pack off his shoulder, setting it gently beside our feet.

"I cannot wait to be able to say 'seven down,'" I responded, giving him a tired smile. He smiled back, but his eyes were sad as he leaned down and reached for a lock of my hair. The entire left side of my face was framed by white strands.

"Hope you don't prefer blondes," I joked, voice catching.

"I prefer *you*," he assured me, leaning down until our foreheads rested against each other. He tilted his head, lips meeting mine.

"You've given so much to all these people."

"Our people. All Societals," I reminded him.

"Yes, all Societals. You deserve to rest. To go back to the Rift, become the official Reader, if that's what you like."

"Spend the days on long forest walks with you while you critique my loud steps?" I teased.

It's what I wished was in store for us, but …

"We both know we'll only be half done," I reminded him.

And there was no way to know if the crystals were the easier half. The list of tasks seemed never to end, even after all we'd gone through, all we'd lost. I put a hand over the moon quartz vials in my pocket. Begtas had brought them along, slipping them to me before we'd gone through the Doorway.

There had been enough for five doses. More than I'd dared hope for, and yet I'd struggled to determine how to use them.

I'd made my choice.

While the rest of the Societals prepared, I needed to get ready as well.

"Fell, Hale, Digit, Acaius. Could you join me really quick? Begtas, you as well?"

Some of the others watched us as we walked away. I hoped the others would understand. Selfishness had me wanting to give all the doses to those closest to me, Silas included. But I also wanted to be strategic.

Fell was an obvious choice either way. I loved him, but aside from that he was skilled with weapons and stealth. If Begtas was right that the substance amplified Assimilated abilities, he'd be unstoppable with the moon quartz. Hale was an entirely selfish decision. He was a good fighter, and brave, but we had more skilled individuals. In the end, though, whether the guilt ate me alive or not, I wasn't willing to leave him defenseless.

With Digit and Acaius, I'd made carefully planned choices. I cared for them both, but that wasn't why I wanted to offer them the substance. I pulled out the small vials Begtas had given me, each containing small amounts of what appeared to be rose gold dust. I explained how it worked—that by ingesting it their Assimilated traits would grow stronger.

"Acaius, I think we all know that this whole time, we've relied on the Kites an unfair amount. You all have been the ones to fly us in and out of areas with crystals, and dangerous battles. I'll admit that my offering you this isn't a very good gift. It's me asking for another favor. If needed, I want you take it and use whatever strength it gives you to get any wounded or vulnerable individuals away from harm, if it comes to that."

He let me place the vial in his hand, but he stared at it without pocketing it.

"I'm not sure I should take this," he muttered. "If it does what you say, you might need them all. For the crystals, and for Bayard."

"No!" Begtas yelled, flinging herself between us. The fur on her legs stood up.

She lowered her voice.

"No. This substance is rare and powerful. I warned Kena against using it in this manner in the first place. She could have used it to make a weapon. Taking it this way grants great power, but it takes an equally great toll. You'll be wiped out afterward."

"You mean it could do to us what projection has been doing to Kena?" Hale waved a hand at my white hair.

It was news to me. Begtas turned to me with a sheepish smile.

"Everyone who's ever used it has experienced some changes afterward. It's hard to spot a pattern, since it's only been done a handful of times. One individual was simply bedridden for a few weeks. One lost his horns. When the quartz wore off, some of his Assimilation went with away as well."

Acaius shoved the vial away from him, eyeing it as though it were a swift viper.

"Kena. I don't know."

He ran a hand along the edge of one of his wings.

I pressed my hands over his, pushing the vial back toward him.

"Acaius. I didn't realize what I was asking." I took a deep breath. "But even though I do now, I'm asking it again. You could help people with this. You don't have to take it. Not unless it's absolutely necessary."

"And the rest of us? Kena. Why would you give me one? There's plenty of stronger options," Hale scowled at me, catching on to my plan with ease.

"Hale, you're a great figh—"

He held up a hand.

"I'm amazing. But there are plenty of people here who are better. And I don't think you should give it to me *or* them. I vote you keep it. If something happens, give it to whoever needs it most at the moment. I shouldn't get one just because I'm your friend."

I huffed at him.

"That's ridiculous! In the moment, I might not be able to get it to the person who needs it. If you take it with you now you can—"

"I'm sorry, Kena. My answer isn't going to change. You've given everything you had to this. I'm willing to do the same. Don't save me at someone else's expense. Please."

He turned and walked off. I stared after him, open-mouthed.

I turned to Fell.

He shook his head.

"I won't take it either, but not for that reason. Begtas, how long do the effects last?"

She shrugged.

"This is all based on old Clan records. It's not exact. Best guess, minutes to hours, depending on what she does with it and how fast she burns through it?"

"That's a big window," Digit breathed out.

"It is," Begtas acknowledged, "but I don't have a better guess."

"Kena. You know I don't like what's been happening to you, but I'm not going to tell you not to take a vial yourself. I think we should leave them all with you, and use them to make a weapon like Begtas suggested."

I threw my hands up at him.

"My best friend thinks I should give them to someone else, and you want me to keep them all?"

"Yes."

"Even after how upset you've been over what I'm doing to myself with the crystals? That makes no sense!"

"It makes sense that I want you to survive. I hate what this has cost you, but I'm not taking anything from you that could keep you alive. And taking one of these when you need it, like after the crystals have exhausted you, could keep you alive in a fight. Just don't use more than one at once. Listen to Begtas. I think you save them all. If you need one to stay alive, take it. If not, then after this is over Begtas and the others can craft you something from the powder."

I revealed my real plan to him.

"If we find Bayard, I could take it. I could use it to try and end him myself."

Fell put his hand over my own.

"I would caution you against that route. We could go back to the Rift after we finish with the crystals here, and have Marx use it to create a new ax. Ocala-wrapped handle and moon quartz blade, perhaps? "

"And in the meantime? We've done the briefest checks on these Societies while we focused on crystals. What about the people? What has Bayard been doing when he arrives places in our wake to find his chance of controlling Assimilation on that Society has been taken from him? For all we know, the Societals there are dead already."

My voice hitched again. I'd gotten better at tamping down my emotions, holding back my tears. My marks barely flickered. I cared, but caring hurt. It weighed so much. It was too heavy to hold all the time. I didn't dare speak what was deep in my heart to even Fell. It had to end soon. It had to. Otherwise I wasn't sure I could afford to keep caring. I lacked the energy. And if I stopped caring, if I used my projection while I was numb? What would happen then?

He held my arms and gazed into my eyes.

"You will not fail. I will not let you." As if he knew what I needed to hear, even when I hadn't voiced my concerns aloud.

"We keep going, and if you need help, we will help you. If you need rest, we will take it, and our family and friends will bear some of the burden. It will be okay."

Acaius handed his vial back as well.

"I'm not saying no. I'm just not saying yes. Ask me once we finish with the crystals here. I'll think about it and make my mind up by then."

I longed to debate him some more, but I didn't want to push him too far. I took the vial.

"Digit?" I looked hopefully at her.

She grinned, taking one of the proffered vials. I let out a laugh that was part humor and part relief.

"Why me?" She echoed Hale's question as she pocketed the moon quartz powder.

"Honestly? I'm hoping it will enhance *all* your skills. Not just shadowing and things you've picked up on Crew. With your intelligence, and skills, combined with this? My hope is we can come up with an idea for rebuilding the Hub, or some other way of connecting everyone when this is over. But if you need it to stay alive, you should use it for that."

"All right, then."

I accepted that this was the only victory I was going to get at the moment.

Fell and I joined the others to begin work on the crystals, and in my head I changed my chant.

One vial down. Three to go.

CHAPTER 30

The Riftians moved carefully over a smattering of wildflowers and on to the next line of crystal clusters. The veins behind us shimmered and glowed in the ground. The crystals on Canopy were patterned and vibrant, just like the plants, creatures, and Societals that lived there.

We'd just gotten started, and through the high grass and trees I saw long stretches of crystals in front of us. Canopy would take a while.

Fell's black hair whipped around his shoulders, and a strand of my own white and blond flew into my face as the wind picked up around us. Dirt and pebbles were thrown into the breeze, pelting my arm as the gale grew stronger.

A storm?

"What in—?"

"Change of plans!" Hok yelled over the wind. He broke the line, rushing past us and ushering several of the Societals under some nearby fronds for cover.

I looked up and felt like I was back on Lone all over again.

Nine of the dozen ships the Spear had given to the Earthers touched down, breaking trees like twigs, the sheer windy force of their landing ripping flowers and grass from the ground. The weight of the spacecraft crushed anything underneath as they landed.

Bayard had arrived.

"Guess they managed to get a few ships up and running," Digit called over to us. At least that meant there were a few still rotting on Lone. The ships themselves were almost as bad as the Earthers and Spear inside, equipped with long-range weapons.

"It's possible they're *all* up and running," Silas called. "They could have sent a few directly back to Earth. They did warn us we'd be enemy number one down there. The Earther task force members could already be well on their way, if not there already."

Another of the ships touched down, and Fell pulled me away, back to the cover of the thicker trees.

"But we've just gotten started!" I protested.

Without a word, Silas and Vanya grabbed my other arm and shoulder, hauling me out of the way as another ship landed, too close for comfort.

With a forlorn glance at the crystals they were destroying, I retreated with the others. I kept glancing back at the veins of crystals we had managed to get done. It wasn't enough. Not nearly enough.

More flashbacks of Lone hit me as we retreated into thick vegetation away from the landing zone. One of the ships slammed down directly on a thin, glowing crystal vein. It was a relief that the plants around it were ripped from their roots, because I was able to see clearly that the Assimilation-giving element remained intact, undisturbed under a transparent layer of protection.

"What do we think? We could try to skirt around them and make our way back to the Doorway?" Everleigh suggested, from where she and a group of Crew stood with cutlasses and daggers raised. She didn't look happy about it, and that alone told me that she had fully accepted the alliance. The others were behind her, nodding along. They were natural fighters, but if we wanted to, they would slink off and run away.

"No." I risked giving up just a bit of cover to stand up and step where everyone could see me. I trusted the foliage obscured us from the ships at this distance. "No more running. Bayard will see those rivulets of hardened crystal. He'll know he's losing. That leaves him nothing but the people. Canopy has already made a sacrifice; we came here last, knowing that they would defend their home. We can't leave them now. We stay and fight."

"Yeah!" Hale shouted, pumping his fist in the air. It was a blessing that the ships behind us were still on and humming, obscuring any noises we made. Whatever our response, we'd have to get it sorted out before the passengers of those ships came out.

"We make a stand here, even if it's our last one," Silas agreed, pulling out the sword he had strapped to his back. Beside him, Vanya drew her bow.

"Although," a voice piped up from the group, "we could do both."

Digit stepped up, tablet in hand.

"Most of us start fighting. The remainder go back to Tundra. More and more people have been pouring in through the Doorway in small groups. They've trickled in from their own Societies since our visits. I'd say in every Society the people are split between barricading themselves where they're at and fleeing to Tundra until it's over. And, unlike the other Societies, on Tundra everyone is already near the Doorway."

"You want to bring them here." Fell smiled at her, and her face split into a wicked grin.

"Exactly. We rally everyone left, anyone we can get. We take the Spear, and the Earthers, out—right now. One fight. One chance."

"One chance is fine, as long as no one adds 'one choice' to this speech. If you do, I'm out!" Hale added with a grin.

I held a finger up to my lips. Behind us, the ships had gotten quiet.

"They didn't just land them, they powered them down," Silas whispered. He was right; I wasn't hearing even the faint hum of machinery.

"Shouldn't they be shooting at us?" Hok asked. Sarah held a finger up to his lips and crouched down, her nails swirling with black swift viper venom.

The sound of our speech and the ships was replaced by the crunching and squishing of boots walking over grass and dirt. I peered through the leaves. Spear and Earthers were intermixed, fanning out, no doubt looking for us.

"Kena!" a voice called across the Wilds. A voice I knew.

I started to stand. Fell's hand shot around my wrist as he pulled me back down.

"Don't!"

"It's Juliard!"

His grip loosened, but he stared at me, expression pleading.

My uncle called out again.

"Kena, please. We have to settle this. You know how he'll do it. I'm your better option."

My uncle was right. I knew how Bayard would settle it. I had hardly anticipated my uncle being a superior choice, but I owed it to those around me to try.

"I'm going out. Send people to the Doorways," I instructed.

"If you're going, take the crown," Hale hissed at me. He lunged for Fell's pack and rooted around for a moment before pulling it out.

I accepted it, placing it on my head.

It wasn't going to work. I knew that. The only hope would be that I kept their attention on me long enough for the others to get around the Spear and to the Doorways. That I gave my friends time to spread out, to give them the best tactical advantage we could in the circumstances.

"No one follow me." My friends stared up at me as I began to move, in a crouch, through the vegetation and trees. I kept low, circling the Spear until I was in a new area of the Wilds. I wasn't going to give away everyone's position. I turned to look behind me.

Fell.

He'd followed me in silence. I shook my head, but he shook his right back. Decision firm. He had my back, no matter what.

I took a deep breath and stepped out from my cover and onto the hellscape Bayard's ships had created. The plant life was broken and blown flat around each of the ships, and whatever had survived the initial landing had been trampled by the Earthers and the Spear. Lines of crystals shone underneath, sparkling and untouched. Several clusters we hadn't reached were shattered, the useless pieces scattering the ground.

"You asked for me, Juliard. I'm here. What do you want?"

"Niece." Juliard moved across the field toward me. He picked up speed as he went, and when he got close I almost thought he'd hug me. He stopped short of me by a few steps, arms half-outstretched, his gaze glued to the ocala and Lone-metal crown on my brow.

"You kept it."

"I considered throwing it into the seas on Crew, but what would have been the point? I consider it a gift from Ama, not you."

I spit the name at him with venom. He flinched. He deserved it.

"What I've done, I've done for—"

"Ah, cousin. I was hoping you'd still be here to witness our arrival. After your abrupt exit from our last meeting, it's been my dearest wish to see you again."

Bayard walked up next to his father. He was back in Riftian garb, save for a cloak. He wore fitted grey pants and a tunic of stone blue. I could see the throwing knives holstered up and down his torso and spotted the tip of his folded scythe on his back.

He looked polished compared to the resistance. We'd had little time for such frivolities, and Fell's gift from Ama was likely the newest and cleanest outfit any of us had.

"Stowed makers away on your ships, did you?" I channeled Hale as I made the jab at Bayard. He frowned, looking down his nose at me.

"Why not dress up for the end of the worlds?" he shot back. He swept an arm around at the damage his army and his ships had caused.

"I like what you've done with the place. And I'm truly grateful you left me some crystals. Very clever, trying to hide Ama's secrets in the journal. I, of course, broke through your sad efforts. Even so, you managed to beat me to every planet but this one."

I had beat him to Canopy, but the point was irrelevant. He'd made it before I could get to all the crystals, and that had been my real goal.

Bayard surveyed the crystals, his expression morphing back into a scowl when he turned back to me. I let him take his time. It gave more opportunity for the others to get to the Doorway, or at least out of range of Bayard's ships.

"Once you left us on Crew, I raced to Clan. Imagine my disappointment when I arrived only to find out you'd beaten us there."

The marks on his arms flickered a beautiful blue.

"Rover or Canopy. My only two remaining options. I'd never move fast enough to beat you to both. I would *dearly* love to know where your hidden Doorways are. I should have bartered for that instead of the journal."

He snapped his fingers, and a horned Clan resident came forward, proffering Ama's journal. Bayard tossed it on the ground in front of him. It landed in the dirt, blades of disturbed grass falling on the cover. Another snap of his fingers and a Crew member who had a pattern of sword and cutlass tattoos running up and down her arms handed him a small torch. Bayard tossed it onto the book, burning my mentor's words.

We were at a tipping point, I could feel it. I clenched my fists at my sides, willing myself not to dive forward and try to save the damaged book. The marks on my hands flickered, but I kept the rest of my markings in check. Whatever he was trying to do, whatever reaction he was trying to get from me, I wasn't going to give him the satisfaction.

I stood there, enduring Bayard's theatrics for a few moments. Fell took a half-step closer to me, and it was enough to keep me from shedding a tear over the journal.

Once the book was damaged beyond use and the fire started to spread, another snap of the fingers brought buckets of water carried by two Dagan. They dumped it over the flames and saved the plants around us from burning.

"Have you made your point?" I asked Bayard. "My uncle is the one who asked me out here. I assume he has something to say."

I looked at Juliard, my self-assuredness wavering. My marks warmed as Fell moved from behind me to my side, giving me the confidence I needed to stand my ground.

"Niece, you have control over Assimilation, but we have the better army," he began.

I begged to differ, but I held my tongue.

"Would you be willing to compromise? Come to the table and discuss a solution with us. It doesn't have to be all or nothing on either side. We were willing to split the spoils with Earth, and there's no reason we can't do the same with the resistance. Earth can have a couple planets that were being scouted out for settlement; they've already got our technology."

That was news to me. I knew that Hub workers often spent lifetimes finding planets that were suitable, but it had been my impression Tundra was the only one ready to settle.

My uncle continued.

"The Spear will take Lone and three of the remaining Societies. We can discuss which ones. Everything will be split equally, and each side gets to grow and govern as they wish, promising no harm to the other."

A false utopia. I knew what he offered wasn't possible. Surely he knew it, too.

What game was he playing, and was he depending on me to play along?

In the end it didn't matter. I was done puzzling through my uncle's many layers. He'd either make the right decision in the end, or he would lose alongside his son.

"We will not give a single Society to you. Not one. Your offer isn't even worth a discussion."

Bayard looked over at his father.

"I did try to tell you she wouldn't be reasonable." He smiled as he looked back in my direction, rubbing his hands together.

He was glad Juliard's plans had failed.

"Now, we do things my way."

He nodded at the Spear and Earthers surrounding us, and they pulled in their perimeter, behind Bayard and away from Fell and me, until none of them circled behind us. Several of them ran into the ships, and they whirred to life behind Bayard.

CHAPTER 31

Fell and I stood our ground as the guns built into Bayard's ship lifted.

"I still fully intend to learn how you managed what you did, cousin. I will find a way to make you teach me how to control others. Whether I have to take the forest walker, or your friend, or this little family you've made for yourself. You will give me my answers. How about we get started now. No time like the present, right?"

Juliard's eyes widened as Bayard reached behind his back. He was a skilled fighter and the movement took less than a second. When he pulled his hand back in front of him, he wasn't holding his scythe; he was holding a contraption some of the Dagan used to spit darts at people.

He had it pressed to his mouth before I could react, and a blur flew at me.

"Kena!" Fell yelled, surging forward.

The air in front of me shimmered and I heard a series of soft thuds. I blinked, running my hands down my suit, but I wasn't hit.

Nien's camouflage fell away as he turned to face me. Down his front were five small, blue barbs.

"This seemed like the right time." He dropped at our feet.

I screamed.

"Kena! Those look like the barbs the clampers had on their tails. I think he's paralyzed!" Fell yelled into my ear.

Bayard was reloading. I bent down and tugged at Nien, hauling him away from my cousin and the ships. Fell threw himself in front of me, his daggers a blur as he knocked away the next round of barbs.

Across the field Bayard swore.

"The barbs may not have worked, but I will get to you Kena! That being said, if you want to stay alive long enough for that, I'd suggest you duck."

Bayard turned without another word and ran for the ships, waving up at them. With a frown, Juliard followed him.

My chest slammed into the dirt as Fell threw himself on top of me, flattening us both to the ground.

Bullets flew over us, peppering the ground just behind us and tearing through the trees and plants at our back. shifted, giving me just enough room to belly crawl forward. The two of us grabbed Nien and lugged him out of range of the guns. My uncle and cousin stood watching.

Bayard grinned at me, the burned skin around his eyes garish.

"I do hope your friends weren't hiding back there, hoping to give you support?" Bayard called. He didn't sound that way at all. I'd wager he hoped he'd just decimated the entire resistance. I wasn't always one to give myself credit, but I applauded myself for having the foresight to draw his attention away from their real location.

"How did I not see you for what you are?" I yelled at my cousin. The fury that Ama had lectured me about felt like it was boiling my blood. My concentration was split between focusing on Bayard and getting Nien to safety.

"For the same reason Kidan ran into the burning wreckage of the Hub, I'd say. Talent. Skill. It's something we both share. Let me make this clear to you. You've taken what I wanted and left me with no other options. My numbers dwindle, and I know yours do as well. My allies are growing impatient, and I'm more than ready to be rid of the Earthers, anyway. This must end."

I'd started shaking. I was trying so hard not to lose my temper. If I wanted this to go our way, I had to remain focused. Fell put a reassuring hand on the small of my back as we continued our slow retreat. The forest walker addressed Bayard directly.

"That's one thing we can agree on. Take your ships and go. We won't pursue you. What you want to do with yourselves is up to you. Leave the Societies."

He had to know they'd refuse the offer, but it gave me a few vital seconds to calm myself.

"These planets are ours. The Spear's. The *real* Societals. What you all have done has been a waste of time. If I must, I will blow chunks of each Society into bits. I will carve the crystals out of the ground, and I will rebuild from the ashes of whatever is left when I'm done. You've seen what I can do; you know better than to test me."

I lifted my hand, satisfied when I saw Bayard and my uncle both tense. I aimed at the handful of Spear that stood at their backs.

"Go back to your ships."

Juliard's eyes flared with bronze as a dozen individuals walked away from him and his son.

It was a calculated power play. Let them think I was able to sustain that level of control. If we'd finished the crystals, I'd never have had the energy to manage so many individuals at once. I still didn't think I could take him or Bayard on without using the moon quartz.

The light of Bayard's markings surged, and I managed a smirk.

I threw down a deal of my own.

"At dawn. When the suns of Canopy rise tomorrow, the

Spear will fall. As Fell said, you and I agree on one thing only. This must end. Juliard, I will give you until then to put yourself on the right side."

We'd reached the treeline. Fell carried Nien as we wove our way around the edge of the ships and back toward the others.

"Dawn, then, cousin!" Bayard yelled after us as we made our way through the Wilds.

Fell waited until we were some distance away to say anything.

"You know they won't hold to that. Both sides have been deceiving each other each time we've met. If we say morning, it's likely they'll begin readying everyone now. They'll come for us before nightfall."

I nodded.

"And they might destroy most of the crystals in the meantime. I only have a handful in the pack that we sent with the others," he continued.

I nodded again.

"Bayard will want to come after us now, but if my uncle sticks to how he's acted so far, he'll try to convince him to wait."

At least that's what I was hoping. Besides, Bayard liked advantages. If he thought there was even a small chance he could catch us sleeping, I bet he'd take it.

A bit further on, I jumped when Cassia materialized from the tree in front of us.

"I take it peace talks did not go well?" She frowned over her fangs, and the ear with a chunk missing twitched on the side of her head.

"They did not."

Without being asked she knelt and helped Fell carry Nien. I wished I had been able to spend more time with the twins. I had been surrounded by so many amazing people. Cassius and Cassia were just two examples. I'd been told they could both speak several languages, they were strong, and Cassia in particular thought all situations through with care. And all I was able to do was ask them to fight, over and over.

We'd become nothing but an alliance of warriors, when the Societies had promised peace.

I mulled over it as she led us to where the others were hiding. Su Jin called for a mender when she saw the state Nien was in. Together, the two Canopy residents carried him to get help.

When Silas and the other Riftians came out to greet us, I pulled them aside, along with Digit and her trusty tablet.

"If the others we sent moved quickly, how fast do you think reinforcements from Tundra could arrive?"

"With how far the Doorway is from the Wilds? And if the others in Tundra were ready to leave as soon as our messengers arrived? Tomorrow mid-morning, at the earliest," Digit answered.

It might be enough to give us a needed boost, if we managed to outlast the Spear that long.

"No one wants to run, Kena. We'll stay and fight no matter the outcome," Silas assured me.

"I demanded until dawn," I informed the two of them.

"But you don't think Bayard will stick to it," Silas guessed.

"No, and especially not if I manage to get around him and save some more of those crystals. I'm going to go back."

"Kena!" Fell gasped.

Silas regarded me, ignoring my Connected's outburst.

"Probably smart. I doubt he will. While we wait, maybe we could create an advantage for ourselves."

He didn't elaborate; he walked away, going toward the others.

"What about me?" Digit piped up, holding the tablet aloft. "I assume you needed tech support?"

She waved the tablet in my direction, and I laughed.

She put the hand not holding the tablet on her hip.

"What's so funny?" she demanded.

"I was thinking on our way back here how sorry I was that,

while surrounded by all these unique individuals, all I've been able to ask them to do is fight."

"And?"

"And you picked the Crew. You *wanted* action and excitement. You wanted adventures. You're one of the few here who was spoiling for a fight, and instead I've relegated you back to, as you put it, 'tech support.' I'm truly sorry, Digit."

She shrugged.

"I've got plenty of time for a second career as a pirate after all this. You'll see. In the meantime, I'm happy to help."

"Have we been tracking our numbers? Where everyone is and all that? I guess I'm hoping we can figure out how much help we might expect; how long it would take additional support to come directly from places like Nimue's holdout, the Mists, things like that. But with everything that's been going on, I don't know how we could have—"

Digit holds up her hand, bent fingers inches from my face.

"Say no more. Now, I won't take credit for the information. What do you think Ariadna, Samell, and the injured delegates have been up to on Tundra? They've been tracking all those things for us. It'll take me a bit, but before that dawn deadline I can have the information for you. I'll work fast."

I ran a hand through my hair, some of the strands falling in front of my face blond and others stark white.

"I hate to rush you, Digit, but as fast as you're able. We're running out of time."

"No pressure, I got it!" She ran off. I saw her grab a few from our group; maybe we had some other tech-minded individuals after all. She put her head together with Nix, Thea, and Veronica, and started gesticulating while speaking with them.

I held onto one of the white strands of hair.

Even Fell had wandered out of earshot alongside the other Riftians; it felt like a safe time to admit something out loud.

"Whatever it takes, Ama. Even if it takes everything."

I didn't want to die. I wanted to spend a whole lifetime in the

Societies, but I understood her sacrifice better than I had at first. I understood why she'd made certain decisions without asking everyone around her. Love. They loved her enough that they wouldn't have wanted her to bear the cost. And she loved them enough that she was willing to do it, with or without their permission.

By the time the Riftians and several other resistance members made their way back over to me, they had their plan, and I had mine.

"We're going to set some booby-traps!" Hale grinned, rubbing his hands together.

"If we combine the different materials and weapons we have available from everyone to create some obstacles for our opponents, it might give us both an advantage in terms of numbers, and some advance notice when they do arrive," Silas clarified.

I knew better, but I still found myself waiting for Dex to chime in and finish the speech his friend started. Instead, Vanya took over.

"There's no way around the risks. Some of these traps will be set to kill, but some will be better at incapacitating and capturing." She frowned, as though that weren't her first choice.

"We're working with what we have. If we can even slow them down, that helps."

The others went on to describe a series of defenses spread out in waves. Vanya was right. Some sounded deadly, others a nuisance.

"And while they're dangling there, it'll give us a chance to take their weapons," Cassius added as he described one of the traps.

I listened for as long as it took to get the gist of the plan and the layouts. I didn't want to risk running into the traps myself.

"All right. You all do that, and I'm going to go work on the crystals."

"Kena. They parked those ships directly on top of the crystals. That's an incredibly risky move," Sarah cautioned me.

If the Serpentina was the one warning me against a plan, I knew I was in trouble.

"I'll do what I can to stay out of sight. The crystals directly under and around the ships are a loss, but they stretch out into the Wilds. I should be able to salvage the ones further from the Spear and Earthers."

Fell stepped in front of me.

"Not alone." He offered me his hand, and I smiled in relief as I took it.

"Exactly. If you're going to do this, we're going along." Sarah flashed her nails as Charles slithered from her hair.

"And I'm—"

"You're going to stay and help set the traps, like you promised," Sarah cut Hok off, "but I'll be okay. Promise." She stood on her tiptoes and kissed the hulking Societal on the cheek. His silver marks flashed.

"I'm coming, too. You're working to save my Society, after all." Cassia added her name to the ring.

Hale stepped forward, but I stopped him before he could say anything.

"The rest of you should work on the plan. Who knows how many soldiers the Spear managed to cram into that many ships? And who knows when or if our help will get here."

"Look after yourself," he chided me before pulling me into a hug.

"You, too. I still want to have a best friend when this is all over." I tried to make my tone teasing and light, but I failed miserably.

Hale followed the others as I led Fell, Cassia, and Sarah back toward Bayard's ships.

CHAPTER 32

Juliard must have had more success than I'd anticipated. Either that, or Bayard had predicted we'd stay up all night and had determined he'd rather face a tired army than one waiting for him in the dark. It was still night, but the increased visibility hinted that the suns would rise soon enough when we heard the first round of swishing leaves and the curses that followed.

"I think our guests have stumbled upon our welcome gifts." Cassia grinned before camouflaging into the leafy background.

"Do you think you got enough done?" Sarah whispered from where she was standing guard over Fell and me. We'd been working for hours. I'd done my best to pace myself. I had no illusions about being able to rest before facing the Spear. I was tired but the work hadn't caused any more white or flickering markings. We'd fused crystals all around where the Spear had landed.

"I'd feel more comfortable if we'd gotten them all, but this is the best we could have hoped for," I responded as I finished a vein of crystal. The ground around us gleamed and glowed with stripes of Canopy-patterned colors.

Sarah nodded, not lowering her talons.

"Then let's get back to the others."

Fell wove around both of us, taking the lead and charting the quietest path. Cassia remained invisible, but she placed a hand on my arm as she breezed past me.

The yelling got louder after we passed the Spear's landing location and got closer to the Doorway. The first few Earthers or Spear had probably fallen into the hidden pits the others had created. We'd been warned the traps would be set up in such a way as to funnel the Spear and Earthers into a narrower approach, so we kept wide.

Veronica emerged from the trees once we'd passed the first of the pits.

"Wave one a success?" Sarah asked her.

"I'd say so. The Riftian weapons instructors had some pointers, and we donated some Dagan netting. We set it on a secondary spring that rolled and snapped a barbed net into place over the prisoners. Poisonous darts are hooked onto the nets, so unless the prisoners want to risk a face full of puffer poison, they'll stay put."

"Nice." Sarah grinned.

More yells echoed through the trees, along with the sound of wood hitting against wood.

"Nix and some of the others carved some makeshift alarms to let us know when they got past phase one," Veronica explained.

Hale and Nix ran up to us as we continued moving around the pits.

"They've reached wave two." Hale said with a chuckle, his hand tight over a dagger.

"And what does that entail?" Fell looked past the others in the direction of the yelling.

"This one combines Rover hunting methods used under the shifting sands, along with Clan ingenuity for facing dangerous prey in their snowy mountains. You've got Begtas, Saf, and Sorvay to thank for the ideas," Nix stated.

"Which means?" I prompted her.

"If we've put everything together right, they'll be trapped by their ankles up in a tree."

"How many trees do you even have in Rover?" I questioned, turning to Sarah.

"A few. At the oases."

"We adapted the second wave just like the first. Once they're up there, there's a secondary trip wire in place, in case the others try to get them down," Veronica assured us.

"I do so love teamwork." Hale smiled at her.

Before long, we ran into a whole group of other resistance members, crouched and hidden in the plant life. I filled them in on the status of the crystals.

"When Bayard sees that, he's bound to be incensed." A smile played on Silas's lips as he spoke. If he was anything like the others hoisting their weapons, he was spoiling for a fight. We'd been on the defensive for too long.

"Are we worried about the trapped Spear and Earthers getting out behind us if we work our way back toward the ships?" Fell asked.

His friend Marx stepped up, shaking his head.

"We used a combination of Crew knotting, and some of us from Twilight Grove were able to weave strands of ocala into a few of the nets. I doubt our enemies are escaping anytime soon."

I was impressed with how much everyone had managed to put together in such a short time. I found out that waves three and four made use of Canopy's thick and lush landscape, hiding some of Dagan's more incendiary devices in the surroundings.

"If they make it that far, the results are deadlier," Cassius warned.

Hok nodded.

"Chasing us meant they'd get closer to the Doorway. Assuming we'd like to keep that hidden, we had to be serious about defending it."

"We're at the end now. We've tried to be better than the

Spear, but we can't win if we're not willing to respond the way they are," Fell acknowledged.

While we waited for defenses round three and four to do their job, we spread out, small groups of resistance members surrounding the encroaching Spear and Earthers. I had Fell at my side, along with Silas and Vanya, as we moved back into the Wilds. It had been Fell's idea.

"If we're able to help boost your projection when you're working on the crystals, we might be able to do the same when fighting. Even if we can't, you know we'll be able to defend you."

The others had their own goals. Ours was simple.

"Bayard is bound to throw a fit when he sees what you did with the crystals, and the impact our traps are having on his soldiers. He's got to come out at some time. When he does, you'll have to face him. We can help, but you're the only one who might be able to physically force him to stop."

"Unless I manage a very well-aimed arrow," Vanya corrected.

I had no doubt Bayard would make himself known.

"Shouldn't he and Juliard have been in the center of things?" I asked as we circled back to the ships again. We hadn't seen Kaiser, either, and the absence of Spear and Earther leadership ate at me.

"I only hope they didn't send for their own reinforcements. If Bayard was being honest when he said they'd left a ship with the Earth delegates behind, and I think he was, they could have gone for more soldiers and be on their way here," Fell reasoned.

"The delegates didn't have an interest in fighting before, and I doubt they'd have one now. They're businessmen. They'll be content to spew lies about us back on Earth, poisoning whatever credibility we have left there in case this goes south," Silas guessed.

Fell held a finger up to his lips as we skirted the edge of the second-wave traps. I spotted Spear members and Earthers dangling, tangled in the trees, like we'd hoped. We passed the pits of wave one. No one had stuck around to try to free their fellow soldiers. They'd either kept moving forward or run back to their ships.

When we made it to the edges of the desolated area where the ships had landed, it became clear which option many had chosen. Lines and lines of Earthers and Spear members had fanned out through the lush vegetation. Bayard stood at the center; even from a distance I spotted his sapphire markings as they lit up the sky.

Around us, the suns had just risen over the horizon, bathing the Wilds in an orange glow.

Bayard's voice boomed.

"I hope you can hear me, Kena! I've stuck to our deal. Well, mostly. I'm nothing if not honorable. Unlike you, sneaking around with the crystals. Did you think I wouldn't notice? If you're out there, and I'm sure you are, I hope you can see this. It's the result of your actions. How does it feel, do you think, to be responsible for the destruction of a Society? We're both about to find out. This falls on your shoulders. You should have listened. Actions have consequences, and you're about to see what your actions have wrought."

Bayard lifted his hands in the air. Maybe half the Spear and Earthers around him ran for the ships. They filed into them quickly, and within minutes there was a whir of engines coming to life. They lifted off the ground, all of them moving in a slow circle in the skies around Bayard.

Bayard threw his arms out, and the ships split off, each going in a different direction, away from where my cousin stood.

They were far enough off that Bayard and those around him weren't in the line of fire when they started shooting. We were also safe where we stood, but not all the resistance members would be. Not the resistance, and not the individuals in the traps of waves one through four.

"He'll kill all his own people." I almost couldn't believe it.

"Heavy artillery!" Silas yelled over the booms that echoed around us.

"He's making good on his promise. He'll wreck the whole planet if he has to," Fell noted as we watched the ships fire at the ground.

"He's insane. He's willing to kill everyone, destroy the Societies, and leave himself the ruler of nothing but ruin," Vanya seethed, reaching for her bow. I was ready to let her take a shot at Bayard, particularly if it ended things before more lives were lost.

Behind us, we heard more thunderous noise.

"Run!" Silas grabbed hold of Vanya with one hand and me with the other as he dragged us along behind him and toward Bayard. We ran for the relative safety of the enemies in front of us to avoid the ships. We reached the edge of the clearing, and I pulled out my ax. I made contact with the raised cutlass of a Spear Crew member as a combination of Spear, Earthers, and resistance members ran around us from the edge of the clearing, fleeing the firepower of Bayard's ships. We'd tried to drive them in a small line toward the Doorways. I hoped some of them had made it and been met with reinforcements.

Bayard and I weren't so dissimilar after all. He had used his ships instead of traps, and he'd funneled us to right where he wanted us.

The Wilds became a battleground, plant life stomped beyond recognition on top of the glowing rivulets of the Assimilation-giving resource. Any crystal clusters I hadn't fused were being crushed, one by one. I glanced down in between opponents, worried and then relieved each time to find the veins I had managed to work on held firm.

My ax made contact with an Earther, throwing him to the ground. I leaned over to pull the weapon back out, and Fell leapt over me, daggers stabbing a Spear member before they could bring wings with metal-covered, sharpened tips down on me.

The ships continued their destructive work, their echoing

booms growing fainter and fainter as they flew away from the battle site, until finally the sounds ceased.

At one point Cassius flew over me, holding a Dagan under each arm as he fled the fighting.

"We've set up an aid station that way," he called, jerking his chin toward a point behind me.

Nix and Hale waded through the chaos and past me, hauling Digit along.

"Dig! You've got to at least get it looked at," Hale insisted as the petite Crew member tugged back against him.

"I can still fight!" she insisted, but I saw that one of her feet was bleeding through her boots, and I didn't stop them from forcing her to the aid station. At least long enough to get it checked out.

The exertion of battle was exhausting, the suns overhead scorching. I'd done my best to balance my projection with my ax. I'd utilized it to save my allies and friends from killing blows whenever I saw them in danger. I tried to ration the ability, using just a little at a time. I'd need my strength for Bayard.

My cousin was maddeningly elusive. Each time I spotted him and tried to fight my way toward him, he moved. After all this effort for a fight, he was avoiding me.

My head buzzed with too many emotions as the battle drew on. I heard shouts in the distance, and relief broke through the haze as I saw new winged forms swooping over us. More yelling, and chanting that grew louder at the approach of other individuals. A line of alternating Dagan, Crew, and Clan made their way out of the trees. Our help had arrived. The Clan charged our enemies in the field, the Crew following them with cutlasses and daggers, and the Dagan coming up behind to use nets and darts to take care of whatever remained. Above us, the newer Kites relieved the ones who had been fighting, prying our enemies off our winged allies.

Rovers and Riftians poured onto the trampled field around us. The Riftians wielded the variety of weapons they'd trained with, and the Rovers defended them with their rolled leather shields. Several had serpents, and they hissed and struck through openings between the shields. I spotted Rory, Kimberly, and Thomas—former Earthers I hadn't seen in ages. The Rovers threw spears at far-off targets, yelling as they chased down their weapons.

If I wasn't mistaken, many local Canopy residents had joined throughout the morning as well. There was no other way to explain the number of Spear who had fallen under seemingly invisible assailants.

I even spotted Ariadna astride her polar beast, wielding her flail and mace.

"We're winning," I said, breathing a sigh of relief as Fell backed up to me. We stood back to back. More of our friends made their way across the field to us, falling back just a bit as the newer arrivals with more energy took to the front.

"We could do it, Kena. This might be over!" Hale whooped.

No sooner had he spoken than the ground started to shake beneath our feet.

CHAPTER 33

I stumbled, and Fell dove to catch me. The dirt beneath us rolled and shuddered.

"Earthquake!" Silas yelled from somewhere in the fray.

Looking around, I saw both sides stop fighting and run. I couldn't figure out what they were running for. I wracked my brain, trying to remember if we were safer under trees or out in the open during an earthquake.

The open area Bayard's ships had created cleared. Several Riftians ran toward us, along with Hale and Nix, as the ground lurched and shook. Nix stumbled into Hale, then pitched forward. I caught her in my arms.

"Just our rotten luck to try and finish this during a natural disaster," Hale shouted as he wheeled his arms to keep his balance.

"I don't think there's anything natural about this disaster at all. I'm betting all the bombing from Bayard's ships set this off," Silas panted as he, Vanya, and Hok ran to us.

Regardless of the cause, the results were intense. People screamed around us, and the already disturbed earth in the unnatural clearing churned and heaved.

"Are we sinking?" Hale yelled as he jumped back a few steps.

"Subsidence. It can happen during these events," Silas called back. "The reason is—"

"I don't care what caused it; I care about surviving it!" Hale yelled.

The Kites had taken to the skies, carrying others away with them. Ariadna was riding Artox and hauling other resistance members onto his back. One of his six paws sank into muck and stuck there for a moment, and he roared as he pulled it back out. The riders screamed and Ariadna went tumbling off his back as he ran off.

Vanya wobbled across the shaking and rolling ground to haul her sister up.

"If we just stay calm, eventually it will stop!" Silas urged.

My concern was about the veins of fused crystals. Glowing lines of them bent and wove as the ground moved, but I didn't see any breaking or dimming.

Silas was right. After another minute or two, the shaking under our feet stilled. I looked around the decimated landscape.

Across the clearing, I spotted Hok crouched over Sarah. She wasn't moving. Hok hauled her over his shoulders, her serpent Charles slithering up his arm. He ran, carrying her, toward the aid station others were busy setting up. Ariadna was on her feet, with Vanya's help, but clutching an arm twisted in an unnatural direction.

While they made their way to the aid station, more Spear, Earthers, and resistance members were spilling out from the ravaged treeline and back onto open ground.

A natural disaster ought to have earned us a temporary reprieve, but it didn't. As more and more people made their way back to the open area, the fighting picked up once more.

There was a loud, echoing crack, and the ground began to shake again.

Across the field, a split appeared in the ground, small at first, and then a fissure formed, wide enough that only a Kite would have been able to leap across it. Deep enough to swallow a mammoth or the creatures of Dagan's Deep whole.

If this was Bayard's doing, then he really was ripping a Society apart just to beat us.

As if on cue, I heard the distant whir of his ships returning. I spun, looking again for any sign of my uncle or my cousin. It was just a bronze flash through the branches at first, but I spotted them. Juliard, and Bayard by his side, under the trees. I ran toward them before the others could stop me.

I would finish this.

"Kena!" Fell yelled at my back.

I turned my head but didn't slow down. Several Spear had run toward the other resistance members. Fell was stuck fighting them off.

I kept going.

As I got closer to the treeline, I could see well enough to pick up more detail. Bayard was grinning at me, his shirt torn at one shoulder as he held out his scythe. Juliard's eyes were wide, and he was screaming, pointing upward.

Skidding to a stop, I looked overhead to see the ships had reached the field. A voice boomed from inside one of them.

"Now?"

It sounded like Kaiser.

Bayard yelled something back up at the ships, and gunfire rained down on the field.

"No!"

Abandoning my pursuit of Bayard, I turned and ran back for the others. Fell was dodging bullets as they peppered the ground. Silas had hauled Nix up against him and rolled away from one ship's gunfire. Hale looked like he'd avoided being hit through luck alone.

I didn't know what I expected to do against guns, but I ran for my friends anyway.

Across the field I heard a yell and turned to see that Marx

had been struck in the arm. His other arm was raised, in the process of shoving Thea into Acaius's arms. Tibby and Ryshal dove through the onslaught to carry Marx and another resistance member away from the ships.

Several bodies littered the ground, but those I cared for most were all right, for now.

The fire was coming from several directions, and several ships. Still, I could swear I heard the crack of a single bullet, like thunder following lightning, as it pierced Fell's shoulder. The force of the blow threw him off-balance, and he stumbled backward, over the edge of the widening fissure the earthquake had created.

Time slowed as I watched his uninjured arm wheel through the air. I wasn't close enough to save him.

Hale was.

My best friend, ignoring the gunfire, threw himself over the edge. I saw his left hand catch Fell's, while his right slammed the blade of his ocala dagger into the dirt.

For a split-second, I thought it would hold. Then, the dagger slid over the edge and into the chasm.

My mind refused to believe what I was seeing. The gunfire had stopped, but it wouldn't have mattered. I sprinted toward the fissure.

"I'm coming! Just hold on!" I heard myself yelling as I raced toward its edge.

I was mere steps away when I heard the whistle of something flying through the air. My ankles snapped together as a rope wrapped around them, and I slammed into the ground. My chin collided with the earth. I felt grains of dirt dig into my jaw, and blood filled my mouth as I bit my tongue, but I didn't care.

Desperate, I reached behind me and struggled to free myself from the ropes as the Spear member who had thrown them, a Rover, ran toward me.

Bayard and Juliard walked out from the cover of the trees. Other Spear and Earthers followed behind them.

"Bring her to me." Bayard's voice carried across the field as he ordered the others to retrieve me.

"Leave!" I screamed at the Rover who was pulling on me.

He ran back to the trees. Kicking myself loose, I scrambled back to my feet and made it to the edge of the fissure. I had no idea how deep it actually was, but it went down far enough that darkness obscured my view.

"Fell! Hale!"

Only my own voice echoed back at me.

They were really gone.

Another Spear member caught up to me, grabbed my arm and hauled me backward. I fought him back on instinct alone, grabbing for one of my daggers and slashing at him. A few more Spear joined in, and behind them I saw Bayard, waiting for me.

What was the point? If I beat back the Spear members I was fighting, more would come.

Around the perimeter of the clearing, the ships hovered, guns at the ready. I guessed anyone who came to my aid was at risk. My cousin was going to win. A club from one of the Clan residents I fought slammed into me. I stumbled back, dangerously near the edge of the fissure. I pressed a hand to my chest as I sucked in shallow, panicked breaths.

Then I felt them. The vials.

Begtas had warned me not to take more than one, but what did I care?

My shock was beginning to wear off, replaced by rage and grief.

With one hand I grabbed my ax and swung, keeping my enemies at bay. With the other, I reached into my pocket and grabbed all four vials. I used my teeth to pull out the stoppers.

Tipping the viles back, I swallowed down all the moon quartz powder at once. The sandy substance went down dry and scratchy. My throat felt raw, but not nearly as damaged as my heart.

Within seconds of swallowing the substance, my mind

buzzed, and the hairs on my arms rose. Fire shot through my veins. With a groan, I doubled over. Every marking on my body felt like it was burning. For a moment, I thought I was going to be sick. Then, my markings flared to life and the discomfort dissipated. In its place was raw power, pulsing through me.

The Spear who had been fighting me shielded their eyes against the bright markings. It felt as if the moon quartz was amplifying everything, and not just my Assimilated traits. My grief threatened to swallow me whole, but my anger had increased as well.

All the power within me begged for an outlet, and I gave it the only one I could think of. I screamed. I stamped my boots in the dirt, and I wailed. Tears slid down my cheeks already grimy with blood and mud. My ax fell, useless, at my side. I yelled, wordless anguish at the sky.

The first Spear to recover himself lunged at me, but I grabbed his arm and pulled him close.

"Over the edge," I commanded, my voice tight.

When I released him, he turned and threw himself into the chasm.

The others in front of me froze.

"Follow him."

It didn't even take effort. They leapt after their fellow Spear member.

My markings continued to shine brighter than any sun, and Kaiser's voice boomed overhead again.

"Shoot her down!" he commanded to the surrounding ships.

CHAPTER 34

Above me the whir of the guns started up, but I wasn't afraid.

I had nothing left to lose but my life, and in that moment it mattered less than my grief and my fury. If I could hear Kaiser, I was willing to bet he could hear me.

I threw my head back, yelling up at the ships: "Stop! Power the ships down, now!"

The whirring ceased, and the ships fell from the sky, slamming into the dirt around me as they lost power. In the background, I heard screaming. I hoped the resistance members were safe behind the trees, but Bayard and his lot were waiting for me at the perimeter. Earthers stumbled out of the back of the crashed ships, some of which were on fire. Across the field, Bayard and Juliard stood still, as if they couldn't decide whether to come after me or run.

I made the decision for all of them.

"Stand down!"

I felt the words settle over the field. A voice in the back of my head was screaming Ama's warnings about rage, but I ignored it as I stood, fists clenched at my sides.

Everyone on the field went still. But I knew there could be any number of enemies hiding in the Wilds.

"Everyone out," I commanded.

Dozens at a time began making their way into the clearing. Earthers, Spear, and even resistance members. I hadn't tailored my command to exclude my friends. I wanted to release them, but I didn't want to risk the Spear getting away. They didn't deserve to go free.

"Everyone who stood against the resistance, go to the edge of the chasm." I pointed at the fissure behind me.

My enemies walked around me, Bayard and Juliard moving slowest. It was as if there were competing forces within them; they seemed to be exerting themselves as they slowly came across the field to me. Bayard wore an expression somewhere between a grimace and a smile. I couldn't tell if he was furious, or happy I'd snapped. Juliard just looked sad, his eyebrows downturned, his bronze eyes dimming and revealing the stormy grey beneath.

I waited for them to get close.

"You wanted me to show you how I control people. Are you impressed?" I asked Bayard. He glared. Juliard glanced down, drawing my attention to the markings on my arms. The shift was more subtle than Ama's, but even against the opal I could tell. The beloved shafts of green and pink had disappeared, all color leached from them. They were slowly turning a dull white, and those on my fingertips had ceased to be visible at all. I was draining myself, just as my mentor had, and I didn't care.

I would do what I should have done from the start.

Ama's words echoed in my head.

Everything costs something. Is it a price you are willing to pay?

I was.

While my father's sins were not my own, it seemed poetically just to right the wrongs he'd had such a hand in starting when he'd founded the Spear lifetimes ago. He'd started this army, and I would finish it. I locked eyes with my cousin.

"What do you think? Should I tell them all to throw themselves over the side?" I asked, gesturing toward the fissure where his army was crowded.

"Niece. Don't do this. Don't become what they're afraid you are. Don't be the villain," Juliard urged, answering for them both.

I let out a humorless laugh, but tears ran down my cheeks.

"Me? The villain? Look around you, Juliard. I didn't do this. My father did. *You* did. Your son did. The Spear did. Kaiser, Earth's task force, and every soldier they sent up here. Everyone who listened and bought into their lies about freedom through control. Life through the death of others. Building something new by destroying what we had. I'm not under your thumb anymore. You can't control me."

He reached out to me, but I flinched back. He was crying.

"I never should have tried. I thought I wanted to save you. But you're right. I used it as an excuse to carry out my own agenda. I didn't leave you to betray you. I left you to try and temper my son. I didn't do right by either of you, and look at everything it cost me. Please, Kena. Let them go. Do what's right. Be better than your father and me. Be yourself."

I wavered, watching my remaining marks paling and flickering. In spite of what I'd said earlier, Juliard kept reaching. His fingers grazed my arm, and I felt the tremor in his hands, as if the effort was immense. Perhaps it was. He and Bayard were fighting my command to remain this close to me.

"Fool," Bayard hissed at his father. "There is no need to bargain with her. She has made her choice."

He smiled at me, reaching over his shoulder as he broke free of my control. I heard a click. With not a second to spare I ducked, as Bayard's scythe swung above my head and my uncle screamed.

"No!"

The clang of metal sounded as Juliard brought up his own golden weapon to defend me against his son.

"I knew it," Bayard seethed. "Even now, you'd choose her?"

"The only thing," my uncle gritted out, "that the Spear was right about is that it shouldn't be about one big Choosing or choice. Life is choosing the right thing over and over again. And in this case, for that reason, yes, I choose her."

In my shock, I'd dropped my control over everyone else. Several of the Spear members and Earthers started running from the edge of the chasm, and I channeled my concentration back in their direction.

"To the edge!" I screamed. They froze, then ran back.

I held my arm out, needing the physical reminder of what I was doing as I watched my uncle and Bayard battle. Their fight took them closer and closer to the chasm. They were evenly matched. Bayard had the smoother movements, but Juliard had the strategy. He moved out of the way before Bayard even struck, as if he could predict what his son would do.

The two wove and ducked around each other. Bayard opened a few small cuts on his father's arms. Juliard shoved and bruised Bayard, but any time he had an opening, he failed to draw blood. I knew when my uncle missed a jab at the expense of another wound on his arm that he was going to lose.

Juliard lost his footing. Just for a moment. That was all it took. Bayard gave a wordless yell, slicing the scythe across Juliard's torso. Juliard fell, twisting and landing on his stomach. He didn't get up.

Bayard was panting. He smoothed a stray hair off his face with one hand, slamming the handle of his scythe into the earth with the other.

He stared at his father, then back at me.

"Now what, cousin? Think you can fare any better than Juliard? Would you like to try?"

Without the moon quartz, I never would have had the energy. My markings were gone all the way up to my elbows; all the hair that fell in my face was a stark white. My legs shook. It was taking everything in me to keep his army still. If I wanted to throw them all over the edge, I needed to do it soon.

I'd originally been given the moon quartz by a Clan representative. In a sense, I'd received it for threatening violence. But another way to look at it was that I had been given it because I'd tried to protect someone vulnerable, even when it could have gotten me hurt. I hadn't done it to cause harm; I had done it to save someone.

Tears filled my eyes; I dropped my hand.

I'd made my decision.

"Kneel!" I yelled at the Spear and Earthers.

"Resistance, take them!" I shouted at my allies, releasing them from my control. Several resistance members surged forward, running past Bayard to net, tie, or otherwise capture the frozen Spear and Earthers.

We would handle them later. I had one target. Only one.

"Just you and me," I told Bayard.

He just grinned.

"Terrible choice."

On the ground, Juliard groaned.

Grief threatened to erupt, but I shoved it down.

Bayard swung his scythe at me and I threw my hand out for the last time.

"Stop!"

He tripped, losing his grip on his weapon while trying to keep his balance. His eyes went wide.

I felt a chill on the skin of my arms as he fought against me. I was shaking so hard my teeth were chattering. In front of me, my fingertips were fading.

"Afraid to fight me without cheating?" Bayard hissed as he righted himself.

"Not afraid, just smart enough to know what would happen," I admitted.

There was no use denying it. He was a far better fighter. I

couldn't let him go. It cost me more to fight him than it had the rest of his army.

"Over the edge," I instructed. Sweat dripped into my eyes. My heart raced as if I'd been running the entire battle. My chest ached, and it wasn't sorrow. Something inside me was breaking. Every piece of my body hurt.

Bayard snarled at me, but he did what I'd asked. He was only a couple of steps from the edge when someone yelled at me.

"Kena, don't!"

"Fell?" The voice was faint, and it was impossible. Even so, I dropped my arm and ran toward the chasm.

Cassius and Shawd shot up over the edge of the fissure. Cassius was holding Hale, and Shawd gently dropped Fell in front of me. I threw my arms around him as he knelt on the ground with me. He was pale and bleeding, but he was alive.

"We dove down as fast as we could. They were clinging to a root hanging from the side of the chasm," Shawd explained.

Behind them all, there was a roar as Bayard broke free of my remaining hold on him and charged at us. I fumbled for my ax, realizing it was still on the ground where I'd dropped it.

I had nothing left.

The forest walker stood and spun, putting himself between Bayard and me. My cousin swung with his scythe. Fell didn't even have a weapon. He dropped and kicked Bayard's feet out from under him. The scythe went flying out of his grip, and Fell reached out with his good arm and grabbed it.

"You will not touch her," Fell pledged, his voice hard as steel.

"And you will not stop me," Bayard vowed in return. He glared up at my Connected from his knees.

Bayard lunged.

Fell swung the scythe down in an arc, and it sliced through Bayard's neck.

The leader of the Spear was gone.

CHAPTER 35

Begtas had warned me about the impact of using the moon quartz, and she was right. For two weeks after I faced off against Bayard, I was useless for anything except lying in bed.

After Bayard was felled, I'd managed to rouse myself enough to help. I ran to Juliard and helped Fell hoist him into Iduna's arms. The sour-faced Societal instructor carried him from the battlefield to the nearest mender. From what Hale told me later, during his visits my uncle had taken a liking to Iduna, and the feeling was mutual. I couldn't find it in myself to care.

The others took me back through the Doorway to Tundra for the first couple of days. The resistance leaders debated, argued, and eventually came to an agreement on the Spear prisoners. A prison was being constructed on the icy planet. Every individual would face a trial that would determine whether they were deserving of a death sentence or imprisonment. It was possible some were simply misguided; punishment and potential reform for those individuals was out of my hands as well. That's how I wanted it.

Silas and several others had returned to Lone and found two more of Bayard's ships inoperable. The final two, as we confirmed with the prisoners, had been sent back to Earth. Our reputations on our home planet were well and truly destroyed. A decision would have to be made on how to handle the Earthers, because the task force had no intention of letting their chance at control over the Societals go, with or without Bayard.

The entire thing made me tired.

After the first few days, once I was able to maintain consciousness for longer than it took to take a few bites of food that others insisted I eat, Fell took me back to the Rift. I slept through most of the journey, but he, Hale, and a couple of Kites had taken turns carrying me. Ryshal had tested out his prosthetic wing, and by all accounts it had held up splendidly.

I wasn't ready to take over Ama's home, and I wasn't sure I ever would be. Instead, Fell took me to the home I'd been given in the Rift and stayed there with me while I recovered from the moon quartz.

On the morning that marked the beginning of the third week, as the light outside filtered into my tree, I turned to find the other side of the bed empty. Emotionally, I didn't want to think about it all. But physically, I felt better. I rolled out of bed and got dressed. Instinctively, I grabbed for the bodysuit Ama had given me but then set it back down. Maybe I'd always have mixed feelings about it, after all it had been through with me. I still had some outfits I'd brought from Earth, and those felt wrong as well. After more minutes of paralyzing indecision than I wanted to admit to, I threw on a grey Hub jumpsuit that I still had.

When I emerged from the tree, I spotted Fell not far off.

"Kena! I didn't mean for you to wake up alone. I was feeding the birds over at Ama's. Did you need anything? You can get back in bed and I'll bring it to you."

I shook my head.

"No. I'm all right. Really. I think I'm done with bed for now."

If someone had asked me during the continuous work with the crystals how long I'd want to rest afterward, I might have said months. And I'd have meant it.

It turned out, that wasn't the case.

I carried a lot of bad memories, but my home in the Rift wasn't one of them. I found myself antsy to get up and do something. To go somewhere.

"I don't think I can stand staying still anymore. I need to move," I told Fell. As soon as I said it, I felt my breathing going shallow and quick. The Hub jumpsuit was too tight. I felt split between a desire to run back into my tree to slam the door, and just to run into the woods until I was out of breath.

In a few steps, Fell was in front of me, hands hovering near me.

"You're okay, Kena. I've got you."

I gave a few jerky nods of my head.

"Maybe a walk?" he suggested.

I nodded again.

Fell led us through the trees. I noted we were going on paths unfamiliar to me. Nothing that would jog any memories, pleasant or horrific. After a while we stopped under no tree in particular. I heard water running and spotted a creek in the distance.

Like the day I chose my home, I thought, smiling to myself, then frowning as I remembered the rest.

Bayard had been with us, all the Blanks who were Riftian hopefuls. He'd let us loose in the woods to pick out the tree we'd call home. I'd wandered farther than the others.

I pushed myself up and went over to the stream, kneeling when I got to the edge and looking down. I rolled up the sleeves of my Hub jumpsuit.

The water wasn't as good as a mirror, but with Riftian eyesight it didn't matter. I saw well enough. The markings on my fingertips had faded all the way up to my wrist. From there, they were stark white up past my elbows, no glow to speak of at all. My hair didn't have any blond left that I could see. And my eyes: the glow was gone. So was the opal glitter. They were back to Earther green.

No one was around but Fell, so I pulled the top half of the jumpsuit down and twisted my upper arm to see the *soul* marking I shared with him. It was still there, glowing a brilliant opal.

I felt tears streak my cheeks as I pulled the upper half of the jumpsuit back on.

"Even if it *had* gone, it could never have changed how I feel about you," he reassured me.

"I would have killed him. I would have made Bayard throw himself over the edge."

"I know."

"I wanted to throw them *all* over the edge, walk away, and never look back," I admitted, my gaze back on the water as I spoke.

"I know that, too."

Fell knelt behind me, wrapping his arms around me.

I leaned my cheek against his arm.

"I made you a killer," I sobbed.

He tensed.

"I've killed before."

It was true enough. During our fighting with the Spear, most of us had. There had been no way around it if we wanted to survive. I was certain, though, that he knew what I meant. He wasn't just another Riftian; he was the forest walker who had taken out the leader of the Spear. I was the dreaded Puppet Master the Spear and Earthers hated, who had almost sent them all to their deaths.

No matter what we did with our lives from that moment on, we were both legendary, and not for a reason I wanted.

The next day started much the same. I threw on a Hub jumpsuit, rolled up the sleeves, and made my way outside with Fell. We went to Ama's together to check on the birds, although I stayed outside. Fell went in to check on things, and when he came back out he was carrying my ax. The one I'd left in the dirt on the battlefield.

"I'm not sure whether you want it, but it's yours." He proffered it, and I took it. The jumpsuit gave me no way to secure it to myself, so I held it at my side by the handle.

"Kena! Fell!" The yelling was accompanied by loud steps somewhere in the woods.

I raised the ax as Hale burst through the foliage, his eyes going wide as he put his palms up.

"It's just us!" he squeaked.

I lowered the weapon.

Nix, Vanya, Ariadna, and Silas spilled into the clearing behind my best friend.

"Did something happen?" My hand tensed on the handle of the ax as scenarios ran through my mind so fast they blurred.

Had Juliard taken up his son's mantle as leader of the Spear? Had Bayard somehow lived and he was back? Had the prisoners from the Spear escaped? Had the Earthers attacked us?

Silas made his way over to me, his steps slow and his voice calm.

"No one is in imminent danger. We've all been working together, the resistance leaders from the different Societies, to address several things. We're going to be holding a vote on some key issues, and we wanted you and Fell to be there."

"We'll go." I cast Fell an apologetic glance as I answered for both of us.

"Are you sure?" he whispered, stepping close. "You don't have to feel obligated."

"I want to know what's going on. You'll go with me, right?"

I reached back for him, and he grabbed my hand.

"Of course."

We followed the others away from Ama's. After a quick stop by my home to grab another couple of Hub jumpsuits, we journeyed with the others back through the Mists to Tundra's Doorway.

"They've got all the Spear members contained, along with a lot of the Earthers," Hale informed me as we got close to the Mist's swirling fog.

"There's a vote tonight on what to do about the Doorways as well. A lot of people want to rebuild a new Hub, but that will take a while. Quite a few people want to keep Tundra as a bit of planet-side Hub, if you will. But not everyone agrees," Nix added.

"Don't forget to tell her about Lone," Ariadna piped up.

"Yes, that too," Vanya agreed. "It was one of the Spear's goals to settle there, not ours. Even so, now that we've seen it's habitable, there are quite a few individuals who would like to go back."

"With or without Assimilation?" I asked, clinging to a single detail to avoid being overwhelmed by everything they were throwing at me.

Silas sighed.

"That's another debate. There were some crystals salvaged on Canopy that you hadn't fused yet. Another argument that hasn't been settled. And then there are the Assimilations we've started seeing on Tundra."

Ariadna gave a vigorous nod.

"He's right. Some of the kids we rescued in particular are starting to show them. Growing thick fur, fangs like Canopy residents, and eyesight that isn't affected by the intense light on the snows or the dark nights."

"Plus, we've got more people with Assimilations from multiple places showing up. Show them, Ariadna," Hale urged.

She gave a sheepish smile before holding her hands out. She'd kept them clasped behind her before. There was a layer of white fur over the backs of her hand and fingers.

"Well," I blinked, "that must come in handy working in the gardens and wildflower fields."

"It does!" she assured me.

I'd been right to worry that stopping the Spear was only the beginning.

One thing at a time, I reminded myself. I'd tackle these issues just as I had the crystals on each Society, and I wouldn't be alone.

We'd reached the Doorway. Vanya and Nix stepped through first. Ariadna went next.

"We're all caught up now, I guess," I murmured as I prepared to step through in front of Silas. He held a hand in front of me, and I stopped.

"There's one last issue, the biggest of all. Earth has reached back out with a message, and you're not going to like it."

CHAPTER 36

He was right. I didn't like it at all. Fell and I joined the others on Tundra. They'd combined three of the larger tents to create the one we stood in, and still it barely held everyone.

"I vote we send the Queen of the Alliance down there! You saw what she did to the Spear. Have her do that with the Earthers!" some Crew captain I didn't recognize shouted.

There were a lot of new faces in the group, and I guessed them to be our reinforcements from around the Societies that had shown up on Canopy.

I was thankful when a Crew member I *did* know shouted down her fellow captain.

"Absolutely not. Have you any idea what Kena risked to save all of us? In case you failed to notice, that battle was going poorly. If she hadn't used projection against the Spear, it's likely we'd all have ended up captured or at the bottom of that chasm ourselves." Everleigh glared at her fellow Crew captain, then turned to me and gestured for me to sit in one of the few open chairs crowded around a long table.

"Precisely why we need her to do it again. It was effective! Have the Clan give her more of that lunar gem or whatever it was," a Dagan I also didn't know suggested through long, spiny teeth.

Veronica shushed them as Begtas rose from her chair.

"That supply of moon quartz is gone."

"So get her some more! We know you have it!" the Dagan argued.

Begtas pointed at me.

"Do you not see her? Do you not see her white hair, and the lack of Riftian glow in her eyes? Her flat white markings? If she takes a dose like that again it could very well kill her!"

More bickering broke out around the table.

"What do they want me to use it for? They want me to kill all the Earthers?" I leaned over and whispered to Hale, my voice shaking a bit.

"They wouldn't be sorry if you did," he muttered back.

At his other side, Silas passed over a tablet. Hale handed it to me and pointed at the screen.

"A formal communication from Earth's task force. We're all just *thrilled* that Bayard left them a way to communicate with us like this." Hale rolled his eyes.

I stared at the screen. The task force was demanding that those of us who had originated on Earth turn ourselves over for 'scientific observation.' They also wanted control of Lone, a staggering amount of gems from Clan, and access to all our technology. In addition, they expected someone to teach them how to use it. Over a dozen task force members had signed it at the bottom.

"Yep, that's dear old Dad right there." Sarah leaned over my shoulder and pointed to one scrawling signature.

"And those signatures would be from Derek and Mancio's parents," Cassius added as he joined her by my other shoulder and pointed as well. The two Earther teens had no doubt been back on Earth and comfortable while we'd been fighting an actual war.

"If we agree to the terms, then they have agreed not to

engage in open war with us," Silas told me as I passed the tablet back.

The rest of the table was still debating whether to send me down to decimate Earth.

"I'm not going to do that. Earthers aren't bad people," I said as I stood and placed my hands on the table. The arguments ceased as the others looked at me.

"Can't we try undermining the task force? Going down there and turning public opinion toward us instead?"

The very idea was daunting, but I was willing to try.

Digit stood, shaking her head and brandishing another tablet.

"The moment we got that communication, we sent down a few resistance members to scout the situation, including some of the other former Earthers. The results were ... disheartening."

She pressed a button and a picture jumped to life in front of us. I hadn't seen any holofilm since the destruction of the Hub, and I'd almost forgotten how immersive it was.

First the scene flashed to a street where an angry crowd of Earthers chased Thea down an alleyway. She threw her hands over her head as they pelted her with stones and garbage. Marx fended them off.

Digit showed a second holofilm of Kimberly, Rory, and Thomas trying to lead some sort of rally in the area we'd lived in. The Rovers were closer to their old appearances than many Societals, and the Earthers still hated them. I saw Thomas's mom make her way on stage and hug him, but most of the crowd shouted vitriol at them.

A third holofilm showed a massive crowd of Earthers screaming and waving signs that said things like *Death to the Societies*.

"I could go on. It's like that everywhere. They're largely convinced that we are dangerous, evil people. Half seem to think we'll attack them, and the rest have been convinced by the task force that we're withholding supplies, money, and solutions that would make their lives better. There are way more of them than there are of us. It would mean a whole other battle, and a different one than we fought with the Spear."

The holofilm cut off and Digit sat back in her chair.

"They hate us," I sighed.

"*Most* of them hate us. Thomas's mom and his sister are actually back on Rover now," Sarah volunteered. "That's something."

I'd seen enough death. I didn't want any more fighting. Another solution tugged at the back of my mind, but I wasn't ready to acknowledge it.

Several days later, we sat around the table again, debating the same issues. The Hub had been handled. A rebuild was underway, and people had been won over to the idea of keeping the Tundra as a central place in the meantime. The more individuals who picked up Assimilated traits here, the more popular the idea had become.

Trials had already been taking place for the Spear. They'd borrowed some Earther ideas for it. Some of the resistance members acted as intermediaries and presented evidence of how actively involved or unwillingly coerced various Spear members were. In the end, verdicts were determined by a trial of peers. Innocent residents of the Societies who hadn't fought for either side. Any Spear member released in the future would have to go through a program to integrate back into the Societies, and be monitored.

Even the governing of things had sorted itself out. With the way things were run through Tundra, everything was more connected than before. Those directly involved in helping with the crystals had realized how important their Society's decisions were to everyone else. We had committees for different things: the Hub, travel through the Doorways, the continued goal of monitoring Societal resources. It was all still there, but with more evenly distributed involvement from each group and a better set of checks and balances. I hadn't formally been asked to serve on or voted on a single committee. I hadn't tried. But all my friends had, and they'd been seeking me out for advice and input on all of them. Being the Queen of the Alliance appeared to give me an unspoken vote on everything.

I hadn't needed it to get Lone opened back up for people to move to. The majority had been in agreement that as long as the committees monitored the resources there, as they did on all the other Societies, anyone was welcome to move to Lone—with a notable exception. No Spear.

"Their message may have gotten twisted along the way, but getting back to Lone was part of their original goal. It sets a bad precedent. It makes it look like blowing up the Hub, killing the delegates, all of it, got them rewarded," Hok had argued when the debate was brought to the group.

Who knew? Over time, once some of the Spear were released and went through the reintegration program being put together by several Societals, the vote might change. It wasn't something we'd have to worry about for years. I'd made a request, which had been granted, that a memorial area be set up around Lone's Doorway in honor of Ama and all the other individuals lost to the fight with the Spear.

The only thing left to discuss was the Earthers. They'd sent more messages, including tapes of their own rallies. In them, we saw hundreds of thousands of Earthers chanting for our downfall. We hadn't even tried to bring a fight to them, but we'd already lost.

I hadn't let go of the idea I'd had days ago, and I decided to bring it to the others. I'd shared it with Fell the night before, and he'd agreed to support me.

"As long as they vote in favor. You have to promise me you won't try this one on your own," he'd stipulated.

I stood in front of the gathered Societal and resistance leaders. All the ones I knew, and the newer faces. They waited, silent, to see what the Queen of the Alliance had to say.

"If we fight the Earthers, we'll sustain heavy losses. There's too many of them. Most of them aren't bad people. They're *misguided* people."

A few of those around the table started to shout me down when I insinuated we'd lose, but my friends from the various Societies got the situation back under control.

"Go on, Kena," Silas insisted once everyone was quiet again.

"Thank you. If we can't beat them, and we can't stop them from lashing out against us, what other *choice* is left? I would argue, not a good one. We are out of good options. I think, sometimes, there's no choice we have that's the right one. At this moment, we're doing our best to rebuild. If we want to do that, we need Earth out of the picture."

"I thought you said we couldn't do that!" a Crew member yelled. Hale slapped him on the arm.

"Shut up and sit down!" my best friend hissed.

I cleared my throat.

"Many of you may not like what I'm about to suggest. In the past, Societals thought Earth rebelled against them. They thought we cut ourselves off." I included myself as a Societal, but there was no denying my history. "We now know that's not true. The Spear was responsible. Right now, Earthers think *we* are dangerous, but the task force are the ones fueling the fire, because they want things from us. Things we're not willing to give. If they hadn't found out we were up here, if they didn't know what of ours to covet, they'd settle down."

"That's true enough, but they do know. And they're not calming down. I'm with you, Kena, but we can't ignore them," Everleigh stated from her seat, as calm as I'd ever seen the Crew captain while objecting to anything.

"Yes. And that's why I'm suggesting we make them forget."

I gave my words a few moments to sink in.

"I won't make this decision by myself, and if we all agree, then I can't do it alone, either. The Riftians will need to help. We'll *all* need to help. I'm not going to call it a good solution, because it isn't one. We'll be stealing the chance of any other Earthers joining us, and I've wrestled with the weight of that. I can't think of a way around it, but I'm open to suggestions."

The others murmured and whispered among themselves.

"What about our families?" I was surprised that it was Sarah who spoke up. "Can we bring the people we care about with us, or do we need to leave them, too?"

I'd anticipated the question, if not from her.

"I would vote to extend the opportunity for the ones closest to us to join the Societies. I know what that means. It's giving them a single Choice, just like the Ancestors had when leaving Lone. Again, I can't see a way around it. If anyone else can, I'm happy to hear alternatives."

Even when I suggested it, I'd thought myself half-mad. Surely someone would speak out against the idea. Surely it would get voted down.

But it didn't.

It passed.

Digit had managed to fix the remaining two ships left on Lone by the Spear. The only thing left to consider now was the numbers. We began gathering the Riftians. Once everyone made it to Lone, we'd make our way to Earth.

After we were done, they wouldn't even remember we existed.

CHAPTER 37

Fell and the others were readying the ships and the Riftians. While no one had managed to control others through projection the way I had, several had shown an ability similar to those of Bayard and Ama. They'd be able to focus their energy on making the Earthers overlook and forget us. My Connected helped them prepare the other Riftians, and I prepared myself. I had one more thing to take care of before our trip.

"Are you sure you want to do this? You don't have to, you know." Silas had walked with me over to a tent separate from the others. Behind it, the beginnings of an icy home were being constructed.

"I'm not sure I'll be back to Tundra much after this," I admitted. "I think when this is all done, I'd like to go home." I hadn't been ready for the Rift, or anything, immediately after my battle with Bayard. Now, though, as I prepared to leave all the Societies behind, I longed for the forests.

"You intend for this to be your only visit," Silas clarified.

My "hmm" in response could have meant yes, no, or maybe. That was my intention at the moment, but things could change.

"Do you want us to go in with you?" Hale asked as we approached my uncle's temporary home.

Questioning of various Spear members by others had confirmed my suspicions about my uncle. He'd been trying to dissuade Bayard from his plans and taking actions to minimize the hurt caused to the resistance. There was no desire to imprison him, because he hadn't been an open enemy. On the other hand, he could have stayed and helped us, or done more for our cause than he had. He had prioritized saving his son over trying to save the Societies. No one wanted to accept him, either.

No one except Iduna, whose affection for him, despite her love of all things rule-based and Societal, I didn't understand.

"Maybe it's just that she's as hard to get along with as he is," Hale had suggested when I'd brought it up.

Regardless, Juliard had been banned from Lone, along with all the rest of the Spear, after he expressed a desire to settle there. He'd been smart enough, or kind enough, not to try to go back to the Rift. I didn't want him there. For the time being, he would stay on Tundra. Wherever he ended up, he'd have to be monitored by the committees.

I had arrived to present another option.

The tent flap opened, and my uncle emerged. He held up a hand to shield his eyes from the sun. Juliard had not Assimilated any Tundra traits.

"Kena?"

He lowered his hand and focused on me; Silas and Hale might as well not have even been there. I looked past him but didn't see Iduna anywhere. That was fine with me. I'd rather it be a private chat, my two friends aside.

Juliard approached me, a smile breaking out on his face as his hands rose to greet me.

I grimaced and took a step back. Beside me, Hale held his arm out, blocking my uncle. Juliard's face fell along with his arms as he abandoned the attempted hug.

He flipped his hair as he always did when upset.

"I see. Right. That was foolish of me. I'm just excited to see you."

My stomach twisted and my chest went tight. I was determined not to cry. Part of me wanted to hit him, and part of me wanted to hug him like he'd tried to do.

"I'm here to give you a choice." After all the emphasis the Societals had put on the word, it seemed only fitting to use with my uncle.

For once, instead of telling me what to do, he waited.

"You're a Societal, and a Riftian. Nothing you've done could change that. But you are also an Earther. You hid your markings before. You could do it again."

His eyes widened.

"You're kicking me out?"

"No. I'm giving you options. If you stay here, you'll always be on the fringes. The resistance mistrusts you. For good reason," I added.

"I know. I did so many things wrong. But I —"

I barreled on as though he'd said nothing.

"We're going to Earth, and we're going to use projection to make them forget they ever heard of the Societies. You can be dropped off before or after. I don't care which one. It'd be up to you whether or not you want to remember ..."—I almost said *me* but managed to stop myself—"all this."

I was getting choked up, and I had to take a moment to compose myself before I finished.

"You don't have to go, and I won't force you. The decision is yours. But either way, I'm done, Juliard. I understand why you did what you did, I really do. Lifetimes ago, my father was a murderer and a villain. You were the hero who tried to stop him. In my mind, I understand that. But in my heart, you're still the uncle who cut me off from the group I'd grown up with. You left me alone after my father died. You used me for your own agenda up here. You did try to save me at the end, but you risked my life and those of everyone else I cared about, over and over."

Despite my best efforts, I'd started crying. He had, too, tears streaming down his face reflecting a bronze glow. I sucked in a shaky breath. I could get through this. I had to.

"It's not fair. I know that. But one thing I *do* understand now is that fair isn't always what makes the decision. I need to be able to heal, and move on. After we come back from Earth, whether you stay here or there, I need to not see you again."

I'd spent the whole walk over bracing for an argument. I knew better than most how defensive and pushy he could be.

"If that's what you want," was all he said.

I shook my head as I moved closer to him.

"I don't want it, but it's what I need."

He reached his arms out again, then lowered them.

"Well, I'm glad you're taking care of yourself. I hope someday you change your decision, and you're ready to see me again. But just in case you're not?"

He held his arms up once more, hopefully.

I threw mine around him, embracing my uncle for possibly the last time.

"It is an honor being your family," he whispered.

I pulled back, wiping my hand across my face.

I turned and walked back toward the cluster of tents, refusing to look back.

In the end, solving the Earth problem was both a monumental task and somehow easier than expected. Wiping the memory of an entire planet was a massive undertaking, but the Riftians banded together to get it done.

We started with the task force members first. Once they were taken care of and that threat was out of the way, we were able to take our time on the rest. It took weeks, given the sheer size and population.

For those of us who had grown up in Verkent, getting family

out was easy. They'd spent their lives hearing about the Societies. They might not have volunteered the first time, but when given the option of an Earth never knowing about them or living among us, no one decided to stay behind.

Some of the others had more complicated scenarios. Thea and Sarah each had parents on the task force. In the end, Thea had a sister who came with us. Sarah confronted her manipulative father, who stayed. She also brought the mother she had a more complicated relationship with back to the Societies.

"She just can't be on Rover," Sarah had stipulated. I understood the issue.

It had been a relief and a continued burden to realize I could still control people just like before. While the mission was a success overall, I'd had to stop a few of the more militant task force members when they realized who had come to pay them a visit. I never pushed myself too far, and I retained the remainder of my opal markings.

On the journey back to Tundra, I was walking along the ship's narrow halls with Fell when I gasped, stumbling against one of the metallic walls.

"Kena! Are you all right? Do we need a mender?"

I pulled him into an empty room and tugged off the top of my Hub jumpsuit to reveal new markings. They wove along each clavicle and dipped down on my sternum.

"What do they say?" he asked, bending down to get a better look at them.

Even staring at them upside down I would have been able to tell, but I wasn't sure I wanted to. Ama had learned to read markings by reading people. She'd perfected the skill over lifetimes. I would never replace her, but I had decided I'd serve the Riftians as their Reader, if they wanted one.

At this moment, though, I didn't need to see them to decide.

"I think it means I'm moving forward and starting the rest of my life."

I reached forward and pulled Fell toward me. Our lips met, and then he reached for my hand.

"If you'll forgive my novice interpretation of markings, I'd like to throw in that I think there will be all sorts of great memories waiting for you there. Walks in the forest, feeding the birds, relaxing under the trees, visiting friends in every Society, and maybe even some whirlpool whiskey together as we listen to a certain tree play us the tune of a life well lived."

I liked the sound of that.

ACKNOWLEDGMENTS

First and foremost, I would like to express my sincere thanks to the readers of this series. Assimilation (The Societies Book 1), was the first book I ever completed. I love each and every one of these worlds, and I appreciate you sharing them with me.

A big thanks to Catherine for being the first person to give this series editing notes. Without you this would have ended with the first book. Lizzy, Ally, and Alyssa-thank you for providing your running commentary on each book, along with your support.

To my spouse, sister, parents, and dogs: you've all listened to me plot, comment, brainstorm, and stress about these books. I can never thank you enough.

SERIES READING ORDER

Assimilation: The Societies Book 1
Serpentina: A Societies Novella
Alliance: The Societies Book 2
Ascension: The Societies Book 3

ABOUT THE AUTHOR

Sydney Reames has long been a lover of all things reading. She's the type of individual you don't want to lose sight of in a bookstore, or she will leave with a pile of new books. She can most often be found reading, writing, and consuming coffee. When she's not doing any of those things she's often reading, or spending time with her spouse and two dogs.